MURDER AT
CROSSWAYS

Books by Alyssa Maxwell

Gilded Newport Mysteries
MURDER AT THE BREAKERS
MURDER AT MARBLE HOUSE
MURDER AT BEECHWOOD
MURDER AT ROUGH POINT
MURDER AT CHATEAU SUR MER
MURDER AT OCHRE COURT
MURDER AT CROSSWAYS

Lady and Lady's Maid Mysteries
MURDER MOST MALICIOUS
A PINCH OF POISON
A DEVIOUS DEATH
A MURDEROUS MARRIAGE

Published by Kensington Publishing Corporation

MURDER AT CROSSWAYS

ALYSSA MAXWELL

KENSINGTON BOOKS
www.kensingtonbooks.com

To Cynthia Blain for her support, encouragement, and enthusiasm for this series. Through a mutual love of Newport and mysteries, I found a friend whose optimism never fails to inspire me.

Chapter 1

A pair of footmen in livery lifted the wheelchair, one on either side, while two others opened the rear doors of the Bailey's Beach clubhouse. The foursome exchanged not so much as the slightest glance, yet operated in perfect precision like the automated works at a factory that turned wool into yarn and yarn into fabric. I, on the other hand, held my breath and questioned not for the first time the wisdom of this outing Aunt Alice had ordered for today.

The two holding the chair proceeded down the steps to the sand, while a refrain played in my mind: *Don't drop him, please, don't drop him.* Of course, I needn't have worried. They'd gotten him this far without incident. No one would dare drop Cornelius Vanderbilt II—not here at the beach, not at home on the staircase, not on the drive between the front door and the carriage.

Along with Aunt Alice and my youngest Vanderbilt cousin, teenaged Gladys, I hurried down behind them, my foot turning slightly inside its boot when I stepped onto the sand. Familiar faces dotted the beach, Astors and Cushings and Goelets and Browns—and many other families I had often reported on when I worked as a society journalist for the Newport *Observer.* Today, however, I would not be reporting. I was here merely as a niece, though if one wished to be thoroughly accurate, I was a cousin, on my father's side, about thrice removed from the present Vanderbilts, our only common ancestor being the Commodore himself. Still, with mutual fondness they had adopted me into their summer circle many years ago.

We took a hard right on the sand as the footmen carried Uncle Cornelius to the west and most desirable section of the beach, farther away from that narrow strip at the east end which no one owned, accessible from the Cliff Walk for those hardy enough to climb down from the rocks.

Stirred by the motion and the breeze, the large front wheels of the chair rotated aimlessly, while Uncle Cornelius himself bobbed slightly from side to side with each step. As we passed friends of the family, they greeted Uncle Cornelius and Aunt Alice with brief pleasantries, which my uncle acknowledged with feeble nods and tremulous attempts to smile. It did my heart good to see him being afforded the respect he deserved, while his acquaintances carefully schooled the pity from their expressions. He was by no means the only invalid on the beach today, nor was Aunt Alice alone in her faith in the healthful properties of the sea air, but to see a formidable man like Cornelius Vanderbilt brought to such a state surely left many of today's beachgoers unsettled.

We trekked several tens of yards, until we came alongside the bathhouse leased each season by the family. One of the footmen had procured a rake and had run ahead of us to smooth away any bumps and rocks in the sand that might detract from Uncle Cornelius's comfort. Yet another stood waiting with an umbrella, and as soon as the two carrying the chair set that venerable, ailing man down, a circular patch of shade was carefully positioned around him.

After a blanket had been spread over the sand, Gladys sank in front of her father's knees and reached to hold his hand. "How is that, Father? Are you comfortable? Isn't the sea lovely today?" She glanced over her shoulder to admire the deep blues and froth-edged eddies of the Atlantic, and turned back smiling. "I've brought our book. Would you like me to read to you while you enjoy the view?"

He gave a nod but no verbal answer. Gladys hadn't expected one; none of us did, for Uncle Cornelius had never fully recovered after that awful day in the summer of ninety-six when he and Neily had their dreadful row, and Uncle Cornelius had collapsed in a stroke of apoplexy. There had been smaller strokes since, leaving him incapacitated. Still, his gaze found his daughter's, brightened and brimmed with affectionate emotions, and then narrowed ever so slightly in a smile his lips could not quite form.

Gladys, still holding his hand, raised up on her knees and kissed his cheek, and as she pulled away, she whispered, "Thank you, Father."

I understood her gratitude, for it seemed to all of us that although Cornelius Vanderbilt's strength had waned, his legs no longer worked, and his mind had become trapped behind a silenced tongue, he somehow still had the power to let us know he valued us and that we were important to him. He had not forgotten how to tell Gladys how beautiful he found her.

One of the footmen produced her book and handed it to her, while the others went into the bathhouse and brought out folding wood-and-canvas chairs. Gladys settled in close to her father and began to read, while her mother sat at his other side and studied the other beachgoers.

"Good heavens," Aunt Alice suddenly said with a *harrumph*. "Is that Lucy Clews I see splashing about in the waves? In a *bathing* costume?"

Seated beside her, I raised my hand to my hat brim to further shield my eyes and glanced out over the water. Among the group of women bobbing in the waves, I recognized the dark-haired Mrs. Clews, wife of New York financier Henry Clews. "Yes, Aunt Alice, I'm afraid it is."

Aunt Alice had never gotten over her shock at the bathing ensembles women wore these days, albeit the woolen blouses, knee-length skirts, bloomers, and stockings covered every inch of skin, but for the forearms, from the neck down. Still, most people, men and women both, strolled the beach in lightweight street clothes and planned no more than a quick wade through the shallowest waters that skimmed the sand, if that. I myself had worn a linen tennis dress I'd come by secondhand from Gladys's elder sister, Gertrude. The ocean breezes kept me cool enough and I'd no desire to slog about in heavy, sodden, sandy wool.

Gladys found her bookmark and proceeded where she and Uncle Cornelius had left off in *The Life of Samuel Johnson*, by James Boswell. Poor Gladys. I knew she'd much rather be reading a novel—something by Louisa May Alcott or perhaps Jane Austen—but she was more than willing to trudge through a staid biography to please her father.

From the water came yelps of laughter as a group of women, segregated from the male swimmers, splashed one another. Some floated on life rings or wore cork life jackets. Others danced up and down with their arms held above the cresting waves. I smiled at their antics, listened to Gladys's calm reading, and enjoyed the warmth of the sun on my skirts. My thoughts wandered.

Sudden screams cut off Gladys's next sentence, and even Uncle Cornelius flinched against the wicker back of his chair. Aunt Alice leaned forward, as did I, to locate the source of the cries. Out beyond the female swimmers, one dark, shining blob floated on the currents. A fish? A bank of seaweed? A massive jellyfish? That would certainly produce screams. Then a pale arm flailed and a leg clad in a black stocking kicked, and I realized the blob could only be a woman who had lost her footing and been swept up by the tide. In an instant I was on my feet and racing to the water's edge, though what I would do when I got there, I didn't yet know.

The shrieks of laughter from the other women abruptly turned to shrieks of fright. Some of them attempted to fight the incoming waves to make their way out to their foundering friend. Their woolens made them clumsy and dragged them back. An incoming wave soaked my boots, even as I realized my own skirts and petticoats would render me equally unwieldy. Could I help, or only make matters worse? My question became moot when, all at once, several men, some in bathing costumes, others shedding their coats and shoes on their way across the sand, streamed by me and plunged into the water. Straw boaters, blown off their heads in the frenzy, floated like lilies scattered on the waves.

One man, his striped swimming clothes standing out against the surf, reached the struggling swimmer, whose head, to my horror, had gone under while her feet kicked at the air. It took him some moments to right her, and in the end he needed the help of two others, as the swells kept upsetting the balance of all involved. Finally, they dragged her in far enough that she could set her feet solidly down and maintain her upright position. I saw then that it was Mrs. Clews, who lived but a short walk across Ocean Avenue at The Rocks, a rambling timber and granite house with peaks and turrets and perhaps the best views in Newport. Had she perished, it would virtually have been in the shadow of her own home. Her friends immediately surrounded her as she coughed and sputtered, and gradually they walked her back to the shore.

Once safely on the sand, she turned toward the water as if not trusting to have her back to the waves and sank to the ground. Both hands pressed her breastbone and her head sagged between her shoulders. She continued to heave and gasp for breath as the others stroked her back and bombarded her with inquiries as to her current state. The men plodded their way back to shore, attempting to collect their boaters as they went. I've no doubt several were inadvertently exchanged, while a few remained unclaimed and traveled like tiny boats out to sea. In an unsteady, watery voice Mrs. Clews called out her thanks as they passed.

With a relieved sigh, I retraced my steps to find Aunt Alice and Gladys both still on their feet. They converged upon me for the details, which I elaborated upon as much as I could.

"Well, Emmaline, who was it?" Aunt Alice demanded. "It looked like Mrs. Clews. Was it?"

"It was indeed. But she seems all right, if a trifle shaken. It looked to me that her life jacket hadn't been secured properly, and had slipped so low as to make her tip forward head-first into the water."

"Mrs. Simmons always says life jackets are more of a hindrance than a help," Gladys offered. "And that if one is intent on going in the water, one should learn to swim unaided."

"What does Mrs. Simmons know? She's merely an elocution tutor." Aunt Alice returned to her chair. Reaching, she made an adjustment to the blanket covering her husband's knees. Gladys, meanwhile, ran up the steps into the bathhouse and disappeared inside. She returned with a picnic basket, from which she took a glass bottle and a silver goblet.

"Lemonade, Father?" At his nod, Gladys poured and held the cup to his lips.

My heart lodged firmly in my throat, and the burning behind my eyes had nothing to do with the salt-laden air. Though two years had passed since Uncle Cornelius's first episode, I couldn't resign myself to the undoing of such a formidable individual, and it caused me physical pain to see him in these reduced circumstances. Even his patience threatened to wring tears from me, for in the old days he had never suffered anyone to fuss over him. Now he submitted readily, while I wondered if, in the privacy of his mind, he railed and cursed against the injustice.

I had resumed my own seat and raised my hems a bit to allow the sun to dry my lace-up boots, when a new commotion echoed its way across the beach. At the easternmost end, no longer Bailey's Beach but a rocky area just below the Cliff Walk, a handful of children were raising a rumpus. I squinted in the sunlight to make out their shapes against the boulders.

"What now?" Aunt Alice grumbled as she, too, craned to see what the matter was. "I do wish they'd block access there from the Cliff Walk. One never can know who'll wander down onto the beach. Such a nuisance." Quieter, she confided to me, "I brought Cornelius here to benefit from the sea air, not to become overly excited by nonsense."

They had, in fact, arrived in Newport only days ago. Before that they had been at their New York City mansion on Fifth Avenue where Uncle Cornelius's physician could visit him regularly. But as the August days had grown stifling hot, Aunt Alice had decided to flee the city in favor of Newport's open spaces and fresh breezes.

"Oh, look, Mother." Gladys pointed down the beach. "It's Spouting Rock. The tide is coming in and the children have gathered to watch the spray."

Spouting Rock was a hollow basin in an outcropping. At high tide, the waves traveled beneath the rocks and then erupted in a geyser-like display. Locals and tourists alike thrilled at the phenomenon. The only ones who found it unimpressive and inconvenient were the summer cottagers who resented what they saw as an intrusion onto their private beach.

Aunt Alice shared that view. "The Spouting Rock Association should have bought that property along with the rest of the beach and walled it off. Then we wouldn't have to suffer such ill behavior."

I might have pointed out to her that as a Newporter born and raised, I, too, along with my half brother, Brady, had often begged our parents to stop there whenever circumstances brought us to this part of the island. Like the children gathered there today, we had thrilled and shouted in glee each time the water sent up its glittering spray. But that was long before the Spouting Rock Association had established Bailey's Beach and there had been no one to mind our childish antics.

"Don't the Clewses own Spouting Rock now?" Gladys asked, and then offered her father another sip of lemonade.

"No one owns it, although I wouldn't blame the Clewses one bit if someday they took a stick of dynamite to the pesky thing." With that, Aunt Alice turned her head away, as if something at the opposite end of the beach had captured her attention.

I, on the other hand, continued studying the figures in the distance. They waved their arms and continued calling out, and now two of them, boys by what I could make out, scrambled down from the rocks and ran in this direction. I came to my feet.

"I don't think they're shouting because of Spouting Rock.

Something is wrong, and I'm going to go see what it is." To Aunt Alice's verbal disapproval—"It's nothing, Emmaline, you needn't involve yourself"—I set off down the beach.

The group at the rocks turned out to be older than I'd thought, not children, exactly, but not yet adults either. There were three girls and two boys, and by their clothing I judged them to be junior house staff such as hall boys and kitchen maid assistants. They'd probably walked over from one of the nearby cottages for a brief morning distraction before returning for their afternoon duties.

Whatever pleasure they had anticipated at Spouting Rock seemed instead to have left them distraught. By now they had all climbed down to the sand and were in various states of dismay, from gasping and crying among the girls, to the boys gesticulating wildly and shouting for help. I arrived in their midst along with a number of beachgoers, many of whom openly demonstrated their displeasure at having their agreeable day so disturbed. I had no doubt these young people were about to be ordered to leave, and rather than put myself in the thick of the conflict, I strode past all of them and clambered onto the rocks. Behind me came an immediate cry.

"No, miss! Don't look. It's horrible."

The warning from the young man came too late. Near Spouting Rock, in a shallow tide pool pocked from centuries of surf, sand, and pelting stones, lay a man, his face bloated and fish-belly white, his eyes glazed and blank. The bile rose in my throat and I started to turn away. Then . . . good heavens . . . something in the face—in the shape of the nose and brow and chin—reached as if with icy fingers around my throat and drew me closer.

As I inched forward I found myself engulfed in a rush of figures scrambling by me. Apparently, the youngsters had gotten their message across and now men from the beach hurried to investigate.

"My word . . . is he dead do you think?"

"Dead as driftwood, I'd say."

"Must have fallen overboard. That storm three days ago . . ."

"But how'd he wash up this high out of the water?"

While the speculation around me grew in volume and scope, I could do nothing but stare at that face. The blood pounded in my ears. My vision darkened. A tap at my shoulder sent a jolt through me.

"Miss, you really oughtn't to be here." And then, more emphatically, "Miss Cross?"

The red and white stripes of a man's bathing costume flashed at the corner of my eye. I tore my gaze away from that blanched face and gazed up into another, nearly as familiar to me. "Robert?"

The young man looking down at me with such concern was Robert Goelet, the eighteen-year-old son of Mrs. Ogden Goelet, who owned Ochre Court. Only three weeks prior I had witnessed an appalling crime at their home, and had helped discover the culprit. Now I once again found myself caught up in violence, though whether committed this time by man or nature, I didn't yet know.

"Miss Cross, you should go." He tried to nudge me along, but I refused to budge. I was frozen in place, caught in a web of horror. I turned back to the body, to that all too familiar face—one I had known all my life, one I loved dearly—and fainted dead away.

Someone was slapping my hand, tapping my cheeks, and urgently calling my name. My eyelids fluttered but a burst of sunlight prompted me to seal them tight.

"Miss Cross, please wake up."

I recognized the voice, as well as the tone—fear. Then I remembered where I was, what I had seen, and who spoke to me so adamantly. Reaching out and catching hold of a hand, I sat up and forced my eyes open, despite the glittering sunlight and salty spray. Spouting Rock had erupted again. My clothes were damp, my skirts sticking to my legs. Sharp pains pierced my back and elbows and I realized I had been lying on the bare rock.

The physical pain didn't matter. My heart ached as though wrung out like an old sail and left to dry in the sun. I nonetheless said, "I'm all right, Robert. I'm sorry, I . . ."

I didn't finish my excuses. Instead I tightened my grip on his hand and used his strength as leverage to stand. He tried to turn me around and draw me back to the beach, and once again I resisted. "No, I have to look. I have to know."

"Know what? That some poor sot met with a watery, rocky end? Drunk, no doubt, and tumbled off his boat. Probably a scrod or lobster fisherman."

"No." I stumbled past him. "Fishermen don't dress like that." Despite the drenched state of the dead man's clothing, his garments spoke of erstwhile quality. The trousers tapered in the current style, and the coat had been tailored to a personal fit. I even spied a mother-of-pearl stud on his shirt where his necktie had slipped awry. "No," I repeated, "he was a gentleman."

At a misstep I nearly went tumbling down the outcropping into the water, if not for the hand that grabbed my elbow to steady me. The men spoke of me as if I were deaf, all of them agreeing that someone should escort me from the scene. But I reached the body and forced myself to stare back into those sightless, clouded eyes. My heart threatened to shatter into countless, irretrievable pieces.

"Brady."

Chapter 2

The Newport Police arrived about a half an hour later. By then I had left the outcropping and waited on the sand, which penetrated every fold and pleat of my damp frock. I didn't particularly notice. I'd sent a message back to Aunt Alice specifically stating that she must not allow Gladys to come anywhere near here. I suggested they pack up and bring Uncle Cornelius home.

Horror continued to course through my veins, but with it, relief, however tempered and cautious. As certain I'd been at first glance, I'd soon realized the corpse on the rocks was not my half brother, Stuart Braden Gale IV. Where Brady's hair was sandy brown and thick, this man's hair was mostly gray and thin. His skin, too, was that of a much older man, for all the face was bloated by death. But in those initial moments, I'd almost wished for death myself, rather than live with the vision of my beloved brother tossed up on the rocks like a scrap of seaweed.

I remained only half-aware of the activity on the outcropping as the coroner and the police began their inspections. Robert Goelet, young gentleman that he was, hovered nearby, though I'd insisted I would not repeat my ignominious show of weakness by fainting again. Footsteps swished in the sand behind me, but I didn't bother pulling my gaze away from the waves until a man in a dark, modest suit of clothes plopped down beside me.

"Emma, I'm told you recognized him, or thought you did. Are you all right?"

A new sense of relief cascaded through me, though for no reason other than that Detective Jesse Whyte of the Newport Police was a dear friend and could be trusted to identify the truth of the matter. I turned to peer into his blue eyes, bright against his subtly freckled complexion, and remembered that he shouldn't be here. He'd been seriously injured at Ochre Court three weeks ago, and had nearly sustained permanent damage to his hands that might have ended his career. He should be home, continuing to recuperate. But that wasn't Jesse's way. He had only ever wished to be a policeman, and inactivity was as odious to him as it was to my Uncle Cornelius.

I took comfort from his dependable presence and leaned my head on his shoulder. But only for an instant. Then I regained my equilibrium and straightened. "For the most horrific moment, I'd thought it was Brady. Dear heavens, Jesse, he looks so like Brady."

His arm went around me long enough for a warm, reassuring squeeze, and then he let me go. "How awful for you. I can't imagine what went through your mind."

"Have you seen the body yet?"

Jesse shook his head and pushed to his feet. "I'd better get up there. Why don't you go home? Is your carriage here?"

"I came with my relatives. They don't yet know what happened, although I daresay rumors are buzzing through the beach like mayflies."

"Why don't you go back to them, then. Have them bring you home, and I'll come by when I'm through here."

It was my turn to shake my head. "I should stay. I'm a journalist, aren't I? I'd forgotten that in the shock, but I have a job to do, just as you do." I reached out to him, and he drew me to my feet.

"If you're sure . . ."

Together we mounted the rocks and once there parted, Jesse to perform his duties, and I to gather as many details as I could. With none of my usual reporter's trappings with me—not even my handbag, which I'd left back at the beach—I had to rely on my powers of observation and memory. As for the latter, there weren't many details about that poor soul's countenance that hadn't been burned into my brain.

By all appearances he had drowned and been washed up onto the rocks. Yet, somehow I found the presence of mind to remember appearances could not always be trusted. To that end, I studied the sand between the rocks and the road. There had been no rain the night before to disturb the two sets of carriage wheels that veered off Ocean Avenue and appeared to have stopped side by side, nor the two sets of footsteps leading to the base of the rocks. True, anyone might have come by to view the phenomenon of Spouting Rock sending up its geyser. People did all the time. But those marks in the sand certainly threw into question whether this man's death had been accidental or not.

That night, a dream woke me. Or perhaps I should say an unwelcome vision hurled me from sleep and landed me upright in my bed. Patch, the spaniel mix I'd adopted two years earlier, lurched from his own dreams with a yelp that became a whine as he regarded me in the darkness. He rose from his place at the foot of the bed and crawled toward me until I could slip my arm around him. His nose grazed my cheek, imparting comfort at the same time he seemed to inquire why I had awakened him.

"It's impossible," I said, more to myself, of course, than to him. "But I can't shake it. C'mon, Patch, let's go see Nanny."

As I had done since I was a little girl, I donned house shoes and robe and padded down the hallway to the bedroom where Mary O'Neal, my former nanny, now my housekeeper, not to mention surrogate grandmother, slept. I didn't bother knocking, and before I'd perched on the edge of her mattress she was awake and reaching for my hand. I'd never had to nudge Nanny awake; no matter the hour, she had always seemed to know when I needed her.

"What is it, sweetie? Bad dream?" She wriggled up until she sat against her pillows. "Are you still thinking of that poor man at Spouting Rock?"

"Yes, but more than that." Patch sat at my feet, for he knew better than to jump up on Nanny's bed. She and I both reached down to pet him with our free hands. "I think I know who he might be. Oh, but Nanny, surely it's not possible."

"He's familiar to you?"

This was something I hadn't yet told her. It hadn't been Brady, so I'd seen no reason to upset Nanny with the notion that it might have been. But now, after what had occurred to me in my sleep, I had to tell someone, and I needed Nanny's advice before morning came and with it, a decision I must make.

"At first . . . at first I thought it was . . . Oh, Nanny, he looked so much like Brady. I believed it to be him until I realized this man was too old."

She put her arms around me. "No wonder my lamb had a bad dream."

"The dream wasn't about Brady." I steeled myself with a deep breath. "The dream was about Brady's father."

She immediately released me and pulled back to peer at me in the darkness. In a moment, she reached onto the bed table for her half-moon spectacles.

"I know it sounds crazy," I hastened to say. "I know it couldn't be—"

"Brady's father died years before you were born."

"Yes, I know. But . . ." I shook my head, the ghostly, bloated face once more filling my mind's eye. Even distorted, I still saw Brady—or a man who looked very much like him. "Was his body ever recovered?"

"Well, no. He died at sea."

"A yachting accident, I remember."

"There was a sudden, terrible storm and he was swept overboard, along with two others. He couldn't have survived, Emma. And even if he did, where would he have been all these years?"

She was right, my suspicions made no sense. Brady had been about two years old when his father, a sportsman here in Newport, had disappeared in the Atlantic Ocean. However wrong to speak ill of the dead, Stuart Braden Gale III had favored risks and adventures above the needs of his small family. His son, my half brother, had inherited some of those tendencies, embracing an undisciplined lifestyle until forced to learn a hard lesson several years ago.

I had no answer to Nanny's question, but a question of my own lingered. "Surely I'm wrong, but doesn't Brady deserve the right to discover for certain if this man is his father or not?"

"Why risk upsetting him for no good reason? Emma, are you that sure it could be Stuart?"

Patch licked my hand and I resumed stroking his warm head. "No. All I know is I cannot banish those features from my mind. I fainted when I first saw him, I was so certain it was Brady." We were both silent a moment, and I sensed a tentativeness in Nanny. "What is it?"

In reply, she dragged her legs over the other side of the bed and lumbered to her clothespress. She opened the bottom drawer, took out a box, and brought it back with her. "Light a lamp and bring it here, would you?"

I heard the box open as I went to the mantel. As a rule, Nanny never left lamps on her bedside table, even unlit. She considered it too dangerous to have any sort of flame near her bedding, a fear that harkened back to her own childhood. It seemed she would make an exception tonight. I found matches and lit a hurricane lantern.

"Look here," she said, holding out a photograph. "It's your mother and Brady's father, on their wedding day."

I couldn't help a quiet gasp. I'd only ever seen one photograph of my mother and Brady's father, which had also included Brady as a baby. It had been grainy and dark, their likenesses obscured. This picture was of much better quality, a brightly lit closeup of the pair sitting side by side, their hands clasped across the arms of their chairs. Mother wasn't wearing one of the wedding dresses that by then had become fashionable, but something much more practical, which she had probably worn again. Stuart Gale wore a well-tailored, dark suit of clothes, but it was the clarity of his features that drew me.

Again, but for subtleties he had inherited from our mother, Brady's face stared back at me. Something, too, in Stuart's expression spoke of my brother, especially the Brady of old—

irrepressible, incorrigible, but altogether loveable. Even in retrospect, I could see what had drawn my mother to him, probably against her better judgment.

"Well?"

Nanny's prompting seized me from my musings. "I can't be sure. The man at Spouting Rock was older. Perhaps the same age Stuart Gale would be today. I need to see him again with this photograph in hand."

"I do wish you wouldn't. Why put yourself through that? For what?" Nanny's hand came down on my shoulder, prodding me gently. "Either way, the man is no longer alive."

I let the photo drop into my lap. "But if it is Stuart Gale, doesn't Brady have a right to know? And perhaps discover what became of him all these years?" When she pursed her lips and shook her head, I persisted. "Brady isn't a child. We shouldn't make this decision for him."

Having assured myself of the only proper course, I returned to bed, but woke again well before dawn. The next couple of hours were restless ones, until I could stand it no longer and made my way to the telephone my Vanderbilt relatives had installed in the alcove beneath my staircase. I always hesitated to accept their largesse, for didn't favors, even loving ones, always come with a price? For me, that price often involved having to sit through interminable dinners orchestrated by my aunt Alice with the goal of finding me a suitable husband. Every young woman wants a husband, Aunt Alice always insisted, whether said young woman knew it or not.

I chewed my lip while Gayla, Newport's main daytime operator, put through my call to my brother's abode on Easton's Point near town. "I heard what happened yesterday at Spouting Rock," she said as she pulled wires from the switchboard in front of her and connected them to the proper circuits. "I heard you were there. That's quite a story for you, isn't it? Should sell a few newspapers, I'd think."

"I suppose you're right, Gayla," I replied indulgently. She referred to my brand-new role as editor-in-chief of the Newport *Messenger*. The unexpected opportunity had materialized after I'd been sacked from my employment as society reporter for the Newport *Observer* the previous summer, and then spent a disappointing year in New York City working for the *Herald*. I'd returned to Newport at the start of this summer wondering what on earth I would do next, only to have the challenge of a lifetime not only handed to me, but with a *pretty please*. I'd have been a fool to say no. But as for my success hinging on the misfortunes of others . . . "I'd rather not have to report on events like this," I told her truthfully.

"Still and all, you need the occasional sensational tale to be a success in the newspaper business. And from what I hear, it's not as though he was a local, thank goodness."

It seemed only I found the poor man familiar. If it turned out I was right, all of Newport would soon be abuzz with rumors and speculation. "Gayla, do I hear the line ringing?"

"Oh, yes. Hold on."

"Hello?"

I could hear the sleep in my brother's voice; I'd obviously awakened him. With a quick apology, I explained only as much as needed to convince him to throw on some clothes and meet me outside Newport Hospital. I didn't mention his father's name, not on the telephone. Not only did I wish to wait until Brady and I were face-to-face, but also if I mentioned it now, with Gayla possibly listening, word would have spread across Newport by lunchtime.

"You say he looks familiar?"

"Very familiar, Brady."

"Then why has no one else recognized him, and why do you think I will?"

"I'll explain everything when I see you. Brady, please just meet me."

"View a body before breakfast? Ugh." I could practically see him raking his fingers through his hair. "I suppose after breakfast could be worse. All right, Em, I'll be there. But I had a bit of a late night last night, so this had better be good."

He repeated the same warning when we met on the sidewalk outside the hospital. I'd telephoned ahead and spoken to a mutual friend of his and mine. We went in and Hannah Hanson, a nurse who worked at the hospital, met us in the lobby.

"What's this all about, Emma? Does it have anything to do with the body brought in yesterday? I understand you were among those that found him."

Brady's expression mirrored Hannah's questions, and they both regarded me quizzically.

"I'm sorry to be mysterious," I said. "But this isn't something I cared to discuss over the telephone. Can we talk privately?"

Hannah led us into the tiny waiting room, once a receiving parlor when this building had been a private home. No one occupied the wooden chairs lining the walls. I led the way and bade them to sit. "Yes, this is about the man found at Spouting Rock yesterday," I began. "I have questions about him, and those questions involve you, Brady."

"I don't understand." He absently rotated his derby in his hands. "I'm sorry for the poor fellow, to be sure, but—"

"Brady," I interrupted, "I don't know how to say this, except to simply say it. When I first saw him, I thought he was you."

He flinched at my brusque statement. Then a grin spread across his lips. "Well, as you can plainly see, he isn't me. I assure you, Em, I've never felt better."

"Please don't joke," Hannah scolded. She smoothed the linen apron covering her blue nurse's uniform. "Emma wouldn't have asked you to come down here if it wasn't important."

Brady looked duly chastised, though a spark of something approaching defiance remained. It was time to explain.

"How much do you remember about your father?" I asked him.

"Very little. Mostly only what Mother has told me. Why?" His puzzlement suddenly cleared, replaced by incredulity. "Surely you can't mean to imply . . . Em, my father disappeared—died—almost thirty years ago."

"Disappeared, yes. But was it certain he died?"

"Do you mean to say the man found yesterday . . ." Hannah trailed off, her azure eyes widening. Her lips formed an O.

"That's crazy." Brady leaped out of his chair and began pacing the small space. "No one disappears for that long and then suddenly turns up. Where do you suppose he's been all this time? How do you propose he got here?"

"I don't have those answers."

He slapped his derby against his thigh. "Well, even if it *is* him, why should I care? Death is one thing, but abandoning his family? I don't think I want to know that. No, I'm quite certain I don't want to live with that knowledge."

I stood up, aghast. "Don't you wish to know the truth?"

"We're not all journalists, Em. Not everyone wants to know all the dirty facts."

That stung, deeply. But I realized he'd made a valid point. I'd put my own needs, my own standards, ahead of his by blindly assuming everyone would share my appetite for the truth. "I'm sorry," I offered lamely. "I didn't mean to upset you. I see now that Nanny was right, and I was wrong."

"Wrong about what? And what are you all doing here?" Jesse Whyte came into the waiting room, looking grim. "Don't tell me. It's about the deceased from yesterday."

Hannah and I rose to our feet. I nodded and looked down at the floor. I felt horrid. Guilty and foolish. I should have taken Nanny's advice and left well enough alone.

"I didn't think anyone else knew yet," Jesse went on to say. I glanced back up at him.

"Knew what?" Had I been right in my conclusion as to the man's identity?

"That it wasn't a simple drowning. I received the coroner's preliminary report a little while ago. The death wasn't accidental, and there wasn't enough water in the lungs to suggest he'd fallen overboard from a yacht or other vessel. Emma, you were probably right about those carriage wheels and footprints."

"Not a drowning," Hannah repeated. She came to her feet.

"He was stabbed." Jesse compressed his lips, then added, "Through the heart. The water had washed away the blood on his coat, but we found enough on his vest and shirt to indicate a serious wound. It turned out to be a single thrust, the blade held sideways and plunged through the ribs up into the heart. Done with a six-inch or more blade, with frightening precision. Like that of a surgeon, or someone with intricate knowledge of anatomy."

I inhaled sharply. With a mild oath, Brady made his way back to the row of chairs and threw himself down into one. He sat with his legs outstretched before him and his head drooping between his shoulders.

Jesse studied him a moment before speaking. "No one has answered my question yet. What are you doing here?"

Brady spoke without looking up. "Emma has this outlandish notion the fellow in question could be my father." His gaze seared the tips of his polished boots.

Jesse regarded us in stunned silence. Did he think I'd taken leave of my senses? Perhaps I had. A cold wretchedness filled me. Why hadn't I kept my suspicions to myself? What good could this possibly do Brady?

Finally, Jesse said, "Well then, let's go have a look."

Chapter 3

"Is it?"

Hannah, Brady, Jesse, and I hovered together in a basement room beneath the hospital that had been fitted out to function as a coroner's examination room. White tiles lined the walls and covered the floor, while bare pipes ran along the ceiling and down one wall to a wide steel sink. Bare lightbulbs hung suspended from the ceiling, illuminating the enameled table in the center of the room and the cloth-draped body that presently occupied it. The coroner and Jesse had spoken together first. Then the man had folded down the sheet to expose the deceased man's face, and left us alone.

Brady held the photograph Nanny had given me the night before. His forehead creased as though he were in pain as he glanced from the picture to the bloated, discolored face and back again. "I don't know. I can't say with any certainty. But . . . it's possible, isn't it?" He appealed to Jesse, who was several years older than himself. "Do you remember him?"

"Not well enough, I'm afraid. It's been too long, and I was a child at the time. It's a shame your mother isn't here."

Our parents—our mother and my father—were living in Paris, where my father eked out a living as an artist. "I'm sorry, Brady," I said, not for the first time.

He shook his head and addressed his next questions to Jesse. "Have you been able to learn anything about him? Where he might have come from?"

"Not yet, but we'll be doubling our efforts now that we know his death wasn't an accident." He glanced at me, a supposition plain in his expression.

"I'll help in any way I can." It wouldn't be the first time I'd assisted Jesse in a murder investigation. With my Vanderbilt connections and my Newport upbringing, I was in the unique position of straddling two worlds, and to a certain extent I was welcome in both. Jesse had once admonished me not to interfere; now he not only accepted my insights, but applauded them, as long as I didn't overstep my bounds and create more problems than I solved. "Was anything significant found on his person? Anything to give a clue as to his identity or where he came from?"

Brady grunted and turned away.

"Only the usual things men carry. A money purse, a pocket watch, a handkerchief, and a snuff box. However, there was something found tangled about his fingers." Jesse went to a tray on the metal countertop and held up a length of blue thread. "It's as if the victim grabbed on to something for dear life, and tore this free. There must have been some amount of struggle. Although the main wound is remarkably clean, there are small cut marks on the victim's hands and wrists, suggesting he tried to ward off the fatal strike."

I went closer to examine the filament. Even having been soaked in salt water, the color had remained vibrant, the texture glossy. "The lining of the killer's cloak, perhaps?"

"An odd color for a man's cloak, even the lining," Jesse said. "And yet for a woman to have done this . . ."

"Or a man's vest, perhaps?" I suggested. "Or, your killer was indeed a woman."

Jesse laid the thread back on the counter and placed a hand on Brady's shoulder. "Perhaps we should go."

I couldn't have agreed more. Hannah and I started toward the door, followed by Jesse. We stopped when we realized Brady hadn't moved. He hadn't torn his gaze away from that lifeless face. He seemed far away, entranced.

"Brady," I murmured, hoping to dislodge him from his stupefaction.

"Give me a few minutes, please."

I went back to him and placed my hand on his forearm. The intensity emanating from him frightened me a little. "What are you going to do?"

"Do? Nothing. I just want a minute or two alone with . . . it. With him." He thrust the photograph into my hand. "Please, Em, just go."

When I hesitated, Jesse called softly to me and beckoned with an outstretched hand. Feeling culpable and helpless, I could do nothing but comply. The three of us, Jesse, Hannah, and I, left the room and closed the door behind us.

I was never to know exactly what happened in that room between Brady and the dead man. Did my brother rant, quietly, at the father who had abandoned him all those years ago? Did it even matter to him whether or not this individual was Stuart Gale? Or whether Stuart Gale actually died in that yachting accident almost thirty years ago, or had stolen off to another part of the world without a word to his loved ones?

When he joined the rest of us upstairs, his brow had smoothed, though remnants of whatever storm had played out inside him still glowered in his eyes. "Don't say anything," he said to me, and with a heavy heart I heeded the caution. He offered Hannah his arm. "Must you return to work, or can you walk outside with me a bit?"

"It's quiet today," she replied, slipping her hand through the bend in his elbow. "Let me leave a message with the desk."

She cast me a sympathetic look as they started off. I watched them go. "Oh, Jesse, what was I thinking?"

"You didn't do anything wrong."

"Didn't I? Nanny told me it was a bad idea. But I was so adamant Brady had a right to see for himself that I didn't stop to think how something like this might affect him."

"Brady's a grown man, and he's strong. Of course he's upset. That's only natural. I'm sure he doesn't blame you." We made our own way to the front door on Friendship Street. "I need to get back to the station. Can I bring you anywhere?"

"No, thank you, I have my carriage. I'm heading over to the *Messenger* for the rest of the morning."

"Are you running the story?"

"Of course I am. But only what I know, no speculations." I said this last defensively. When I took over running the newspaper for its owner, Derrick Andrews, I'd made a promise to myself to uphold the most stringent journalistic principles. Only the facts; any opinions printed in the *Messenger* would be on the Opinions page, and nowhere else.

"Don't go getting your dander up," said Jesse with a laugh. "You have a big event coming up, don't you? Tonight? To-morrow?"

"Tomorrow night at Crossways. Mr. and Mrs. Fish are holding what they're calling a Harvest Festival as a way to close out the Season. For once, though, it won't be me strolling the festivities and jotting down the details. I'm sending the *Messenger*'s society reporter."

The thought cheered me a bit. While I would much rather have dispensed with the society page altogether in favor of dedicating those columns to real news, I understood the enthusiasm with which many subscribers rifled through their newspapers until they found all the latest descriptions of fashions, soirees, weddings, and journeys abroad. I couldn't disappoint them, nor could I risk subscriptions falling off. Not if I wished to make a success of my first foray into the world of journalism management.

And not if I wished to make Derrick Andrews proud of me.

A little while later, it was with the utmost trepidation that I followed my head printing press operator, Dan Carter, into the pressroom at the very rear of the *Messenger*'s offices. I hadn't needed anyone to tell me we had trouble, nor had I needed to see the dismal expression of our office manager, Jimmy Hawkins. The moment I stepped into the front office, the utter silence told me something was very wrong. The main press lay silent, its gears and rotary motionless. No steam hissed through the pipes that fed the engine. The hush enveloped me in a sense of impending failure.

I tried my best to maintain outward calm. The two assistant press operators moved away from the main—and largest— press. We had two others, but they were small and only used for last-minute inserts or late-day extras for breaking news. With sheepish expressions, they nodded their greetings to me, perhaps fearing I'd hold them responsible for this setback. "What appears to be the problem?"

"Not quite sure yet, Miss Cross." Dan ran his hand over the upper cylinder as if comforting an ill child. "We're working on it."

"It just suddenly stopped working?"

"Well, it sort of petered out slowly. Didn't notice at first. In fact I heard it before I saw it. The engine wasn't working to capacity. You get to know these things when you work with machinery day in and day out. They're touchy things, machines, like a woman . . . oh, sorry, Miss Cross."

"That's all right, Dan. Then it's the engine?"

"Maybe. Maybe not. Could be minerals from the steam have mucked up the works. The gears and such."

"Yes, I know what the works are, Dan, thank you." Hands on hips, I moved closer to the press and surveyed its parts, as if I could possibly detect the problem. Still, it paid to appear knowledgeable when one was in charge. Especially when one was a woman surrounded by men. "What are you doing about it?"

"Going through every bit of her, cleaning everything that could be the problem, and working our way backward to the engine and the steam lines."

My spirits sank further. "That sounds time-consuming. Luckily, today's paper has already gone out. But what about tomorrow's and the Sunday edition?"

"No other way to do it, Miss Cross, except haphazardly." He spoke with the faintest condescendence, which irked me although it didn't surprise me. Dan's tone, a mixture of kindness and disbelief that I could ever hope to fully understand this business, was no different than many I'd encountered since taking up journalism. I therefore gave him my attention without showing a hint of my thoughts as he went on. "Doing it that way we might get lucky, or we might miss the problem entirely."

I sighed. "All right, then, I'll leave you to it and pray for a miracle."

"Good idea, Miss Cross. The Almighty listens to women's prayers, my gran always said."

Back in the front office, which I shared with Jimmy Hawkins, I stood by my desk and gazed out onto Spring Street. What would I do if Dan and his men couldn't get the press running in time for tomorrow's edition? And what about Sunday's paper? We depended on the sales of the Sunday edition for the bulk of our income. How could I tell Derrick we'd lost an entire week's revenue, not to mention the advertisers who would surely abandon us? How would I pay the press operators and typesetters, along with our two reporters and Jimmy besides?

"I've got more bad news," Jimmy spoke up tentatively. His flattened intonations, a product of growing up in Providence, became more pronounced. "Although, not nearly as bad as the press being down."

I regarded his wide face and broad brow and laughed softly. "Well, I guess I'm thankful for that much. What is it?" I turned back to the window.

"Two of our newsies haven't come in today. One sent a message with his younger brother that he's sick. I can only imagine that's the case with the other one as well."

"Two?" I whirled on him, causing him to pull back in his swiveling chair. "That's half our newsie force. Who's out there selling today's edition?"

"Ralphie and Tom."

"They'll never be able to cover town on their own. Couldn't you find anyone to fill in?"

He held up his hands. "Just go out and hire some random boys?"

"Yes. Or girls. I don't care which."

He eyed me askance. "Now, I understand you believe women can do pretty much anything men can do, and for some things, I'd say you were right. But you can't have little girls approaching strangers on the street and trying to sell them things."

"Tell that to the countless little girls on the streets of Lower Manhattan selling everything from flowers to fruit to fish." I didn't add that some of them also sold themselves, as I had learned during the year I'd spent living there. New York's social ills were another matter entirely and besides, my argument wasn't with Jimmy. It was with several tons of iron and steel in the back room. "Sorry, you're right. Let me make a telephone call or two and see if I can't rustle up a couple of enterprising young men. But first, is Ethan here?"

Jimmy nodded and I strolled back to our tiny newsroom, much like the one I had once shared with another reporter when I worked for the Newport *Observer.* Here, besides myself, we employed two reporters, Ethan Merriman and Jacob Stodges. The pair each had the luxury of his own desk, but shared a typewriter and a telephone. But neither of them spent much time here. Rather, they searched Newport and the rest of Aquidneck Island high and low for interesting news. Or, on slow weeks, any news at all.

Jacob was nowhere to be seen but Ethan sat tapping away at the typewriter. A bright young man two years my junior, he had spent a year at Yale before deciding he'd rather write words than study them. And, as Jimmy had admitted moments ago that a woman could do pretty much whatever a man could do, Ethan proved the opposite to be true as well. While Derrick had originally hired a female society reporter, she left suddenly and Ethan had answered the advertisement several weeks ago with such enthusiasm Derrick hadn't the heart to turn him away. And a good thing, too, as Ethan's columns were as popular as mine ever were.

I leaned in the doorway and knocked on the jamb to catch his attention. His tapping ceased abruptly and he looked up, the overhead light gleaming on his heavily oiled hair. "You'll be at Crossways tomorrow night," I said rather than asked.

"I'm looking forward to it." He sat back with a grin. "Not only is this the last big to-do of the season and the mamas' last hope of arranging marriages for their darlings before winter sets in, it's also going to be my first brush with royalty."

I shook my head, a rueful smile on my lips. He referred, of

course, to Mrs. Fish's guest of honor for the Harvest Festival, Prince Otto of Austria, nephew of the Austro-Hungarian emperor, Franz Joseph. Though Otto was born on the wrong side of the blanket, his father had acknowledged him, and after his father died, Franz Joseph had legitimated Otto and given him the courtesy title of prince. The thing of it was, his attendance at the ball was supposed to be a surprise, but somehow all of Newport knew of it. "I hope you'll have a chance to get close to him. As a Hapsburg on his father's side and a Rothschild on his mother's, he'll be surrounded by hopeful mamas all evening."

"I'm surprised you don't want to cover this one yourself." He suddenly looked worried, and perhaps wished he could call back his words.

"Very tempting." I pretended to consider, only to laugh at his openly perplexed expression. "Don't worry, Ethan. I've quite had my fill of royalty and pseudo royalty. I fully trust you with this one."

His relief was palpable, but perhaps before I could change my mind, he switched subjects. "I sure hope they get the press running again soon."

"So do I." I gestured at the typewriter. "What are you typing up?"

"Yesterday's luncheon at the Golf Club."

"Ah." How many of *those* types of events had I covered through the years? I didn't fret for an instant over missing this one at Crossways. "And how did it go?"

"Splendidly," was his animated reply. "Your cousin, Mrs. Whitney, attended the luncheon with her husband. They sure look a happy couple. Mrs. Whitney asked how you were doing with the *Messenger*. I told her 'splendidly.'"

Splendid seemed to be one of his favorite words. "Thank you for that, Ethan. My relatives mean well, but I believe

they secretly hope I'll make a mess of things here so I'll finally settle down and marry."

The next day, I found reason to regret not having wangled
an invitation to Crossways after all. Not that I would have
taken Ethan's place in reporting on the fête; I wouldn't have
had the heart to take away an opportunity he had fully
earned these past few weeks. But Jesse had telephoned to say
he'd found no clues yet as to the identity of the Spouting
Rock victim. I had termed him a gentleman based on his
clothing. If so, it was possible someone among the Four
Hundred, gathering for tonight's festivities, might have information about him, or even haphazardly comment on an
absent friend or loved one.

I arrived at the *Messenger* that morning to good news, at least
partially. Dan Carter had discovered the glitch with the press.
"Appears someone spilled an entire jar of ink into the engine.
Gummed up the works. We've been cleaning since before
sunup with alcohol and a fine-tooth comb, you might say."

"And it's working?" I could hardly contain my eagerness.

"Don't you worry, Miss Cross. We'll have that press
rolling in no time."

I didn't like to ask my next question, but I felt as the person in charge, it was my responsibility to learn exactly what
had happened. "Spilling that much ink, and on vital equip-
ment, was terribly careless. Do you know who did it, Dan?"
I held my breath, wondering what I would do about the
matter. I certainly didn't wish to fire anyone this soon into
my tenure as editor-in-chief. Perhaps a stern warning would
suffice.

"Nobody's owning up, but in my opinion, it's not the sort
of thing either of my assistants would do, nor one of the
typesetters either."

"What are you saying?"

"If I were you, Miss Cross, I'd call in the police. Maybe have that detective friend of yours take a look at our doors and windows. I took a quick peek myself and I didn't notice anything odd, but I'd stake my life that someone who doesn't work for the *Messenger* did this."

The notion unnerved me. "Was anything stolen?"

"Not that I've noticed. Yet."

This new possibility of an intruder appealed to me even less than the alternative, that of a careless accident. I couldn't imagine who would deliberately do this, not even someone from a competing newspaper. Even in a business as ruthless as journalism could be, there were codes of honor. Unless it had been someone who simply objected to a woman as editor-in-chief and wished to see me fail. If so, that widened the scope of possible culprits considerably.

At least the press would soon be up and running, and today's full edition, though late, would go out. And when I'd arrived earlier, Jimmy had informed me one of my newsies had recovered from his ailment and reported to work today. Perhaps the inked engine was an isolated incident.

Jesse wasn't at the police station when I telephoned, but I gave my report to an officer I knew, an old friend.

"Seeing as it's you, Emma, I'll try to get someone there as soon as possible, but with nothing stolen the chief won't see this as particularly urgent."

I saw his point. My gummy press wasn't going anywhere, and with no forced entry that any of us could find, the police wouldn't have much to go on. They'd probably term it an accident or a prank and tell us to make sure the doors and windows were locked at night.

Later at my desk, as the accounts receivable and payable figures began to blur, I turned my thoughts once more to the Spouting Rock victim. Now that we knew he hadn't fallen overboard, but rather was killed on land, it was likely he might have been seen in Newport recently.

I considered, also, the time frame of the death. It could only have happened between nightfall two days ago and the morning the servants found him. That would have been Wednesday night. Too many people visited Bailey's Beach and the Cliff Walk for him to have been lying on those rocks longer than that and not been seen. There had been a soiree at the Bailey's Beach clubhouse before a performance at the opera house Wednesday night. He couldn't have been killed while people were coming or going from that, or the killer would have risked being seen in the act. Ethan had covered the event. I needed to consult with him about when the party had started and ended, for that might narrow down the time of death further still.

Next I pondered where the victim might have been just prior to his death. His clothing, light of fabric and color, suggested daywear, unsuitable for an evening gathering or the opera—so he had not been part of those activities. They *were* suitable for an afternoon at the Casino watching tennis, perhaps, or a picnic, or . . . a luncheon at the golf club.

Retrieving the photograph I still carried in my handbag, I hurried into the newsroom, hoping to find Ethan. Whether the Spouting Rock victim was Stuart Gale or not, the resemblance was remarkable and the image in the old wedding photograph might spark a memory in Ethan of having seen him at the golf club luncheon. To my vast disappointment, the room lay empty and I remembered that he would be preparing to go to Crossways later.

When I arrived home that evening, Nanny had a message for me. "Ethan Merriman telephoned a little while ago in a bit of a panic. His cart threw a wheel and he has no way to get to Crossways tonight."

When I stared blankly at her, she grew concerned. "Emma, did you hear? Are you unwell?"

"No," I said wearily. I knew Ethan drove a pony cart and lived in the north end of town, beyond the hospital. "I'm just wondering what else can go wrong. First the printing press, then my newsies missing work, and now this. It's too much for coincidence, Nanny. Someone is deliberately trying to thwart me."

"Who would do such a thing? Carts are often breaking down, especially with our rocky, bumpy roads. How many times have you had to have the carriage wheels mended or replaced?"

"Yes, I suppose you're right," I concurred, but only outwardly. "I suppose it'll have to be me at Crossways tonight. Either that or we don't run a society column tomorrow." And yet, I immediately brightened, remembering that I'd now have the opportunity to discover for myself if anyone there tonight knew the Spouting Rock victim. "Nanny, come help me pick out something to wear, won't you?"

Chapter 4

Later that evening, I drove my carriage the short distance from my home, Gull Manor, to Crossways. Both properties lay along Ocean Avenue, mine on the shoreline, and Crossways on the landward side of the road, high on a rocky rise, where it looked out over its surroundings like a king on his throne. During the day I might have gone on foot, but Ocean Avenue twisted and heaved with the landscape, and made for dangerous walking at night. Upon arriving at the gates at the bottom of the main drive, I surveyed the Neo-Colonial mansion perched on its hill before me.

The secret of Mamie Fish's success, I decided, was in never doing anything right.

Or, perhaps I should say, never doing anything in the manner prescribed by her peers. The newly built Crossways had opened at the beginning of the summer after nearly two years of construction. There were many among the Four Hundred who sniggered behind their hands and called the Fishes' new home as blunt and stark as Mamie herself, and accused it of upsetting the balance of Ocean Avenue's natural environment. While most of them had hired architectural firms like Peabody and Stearns; McKim, Mead and White; and Richard Morris Hunt to design Italianate palazzos, French chateaux, or Beaux Arts mansions, Mamie Fish had stood staunchly in favor of an American showpiece. To that end she had hired Newport architect Dudley Newton to design the house, and another Newport firm, the Vernon Company, to furnish it.

The result was a house with a large, center portico supported by four massive columns and topped by a peaked and corniced roofline. The main part of the house was flanked by two identical wings delineated by cornerstones and a loggia at either end, with balconies above. Shutters adorned the windows of the lower two stories while dormer windows revealed a third floor beneath the eaves. The house was not ornate, but neither was it modest. It spoke of forthright American values such as determination, industry, and sheer stubborn strength. Rather like Mamie Fish herself.

Tonight, electric lanterns emblazoned the wide sprawl of the lawns, with colorful bunting strung along the lantern poles. Interspersed between the poles stood those guardians of the harvest, scarecrows, but these were no ordinary straw-stuffed effigies. From what I could make out of those closest to me, each had been dressed in silks and velvets, with metals across his chest and a crown on his head. A ribald tribute to Prince Otto? Only Mamie Fish would have dared such a jest.

Whatever the Four Hundred might think of the house, it was common knowledge that virtually every cottager between here and the north end of Bellevue Avenue had coveted an invitation to tonight's Harvest Festival; no wonder, with royalty attending. And, as Ethan Merriman had commented to me, tonight marked the last grand event of the summer. To my eyes, it looked as though most of the summer set had gotten their wish, judging by the countless carriages lining the drive and those still coming and going. In fact, I was forced to drive on or cause a collision as yet two more arrived.

It had been three weeks since I'd last covered a social event, and the memory of that one had me slowing my horse's pace. That event, too, had had a special theme, not autumn harvest but ancient Egypt. The fantasy element had proved the perfect concealment for a crime, and now, confronted by those regal, mocking scarecrows, I hesitated.

But surely such events would not repeat themselves. I had a job to do, a job I no longer considered mine, but necessity had brought me here and I had a responsibility to the *Messenger*'s readers.

Not being counted among the guests, I bypassed by the front entrance, which was flanked by two jack-o'-lanterns some twelve feet high, and instead drove around to the back of the house and to the servants' entrance. I was greeted with the usual suspicion, but once I'd identified myself as being from the *Messenger* I was quickly handed over to the butler. He reviewed the etiquette I'd be required to follow, nothing I hadn't heard countless times before, and brought me up the back stairs to his pantry off the dining room.

"Don't make a nuisance of yourself, but don't miss any pertinent details either," he told me, and about-faced to carry on with his duties. "Mrs. Fish wants the entire country talking about tonight's affair," he added over his shoulder before dismissing me from his notice.

Every countertop and workspace of the pantry groaned beneath burdens of trays, dishes, bowls, and glasses. Around me, serving staff came and went like the tributaries of a river. A footman bumped me from behind and set me in motion. I began my usual walk-through of the rooms, careful to remain close to the walls where I wouldn't trample on the trains of gowns or knock the elbows of guests holding small plates and glasses of champagne. I also took care to stay out of the way of the bustling footmen circulating with trays of all manner of delicacies.

All the first-floor rooms were open and being utilized. Here were no carved stone or marble embellishments such as could be found in my relatives' homes, nor gilding or Renaissance revival murals or elaborate tilework. Missing, too, was the heavy, dark paneling of houses like Chateau sur Mer and Rough Point. Rather, crisp white casings, baseboards, and chair and crown moldings defined the fireplaces, walls, and arched window recesses. Though some of the furniture had been moved out to make room for the guests, what remained spoke of Newport's premier furniture makers of over a century ago, Townsend and Goddard. The result was subdued, dignified, tasteful, orderly—in short, Colonial.

Each room had been festooned with autumn-colored bunting, thick garlands holding silk fruits and vegetables, and an abundance of late-season flowers: sunflowers and poppies, deep pink camellias, bright orange dahlias, golden chrysanthemums, and purple salvias. The guests had dressed to match, with the women wearing flowered gowns that borrowed details from traditional peasant garb, and the men sporting an unusual assortment of coordinating vests and neckties.

As I perused the house, I searched for cobalt blue—in gowns, cloaks, even hats—to attempt to link one of the guests to the Spouting Rock victim. I found nothing I believed would match the thread discovered tangled in his fingers. It had been a far-fetched hope; the killer surely would have disposed of the item by now.

A buffet of seasonal fall offerings covered the dining table. Next I came to the large, oblong entrance hall with its open, three-sided gallery above. The hall, the stairs, and the upper gallery were crowded with chattering guests, while new arrivals were admitted and relieved of their outerwear by two handsome footmen. Mr. and Mrs. Fish held court in the center of the hall, greeting their guests and keeping up a steady stream of comments and observations that had those around them chuckling. Mrs. Fish occupied an outlandish chair fashioned from farm implements.

"Howdy do, howdy do!" Mamie Fish called out to each new arrival. "Make yourselves at home, and believe me, there is no one who wishes you were there more than I do."

Mrs. Astor, the queen of polite society, would have been scandalized by Mrs. Fish's lack of elegance, but then I hadn't seen Mrs. Astor on the guest list. Many others of Newport's summer population were here, however, and none of them seemed taken aback by Mrs. Fish's uncouth declarations.

I noticed numerous guests holding glossy, embossed sheets of paper, referring to them and laughing as they scampered off in various directions. The younger people, especially, seemed captivated by this activity, while the older set looked on indulgently. I guessed Mrs. Fish had arranged a scavenger hunt of some sort. I approached her hoping to inquire what items her guests would be seeking. With an imperious gesture, she motioned to a nearby footman, who thrust a list into my hands.

Gilded pumpkins, silver gourds, jeweled cornucopias, and other familiar yet lavish symbols of autumn were apparently hidden throughout the downstairs rooms and out in the gardens, waiting to be claimed.

Music from beyond the far end of the hall drew me in that direction. On my way I passed the library, where a host of men were playing cards, smoking, and arguing—politics judging by the words that flung themselves to my ears. I kept going and entered the drawing room, nearly as large as many of Newport's ballrooms and, in fact, presently being used for that purpose. Most of the furniture had been cleared out, and what remained had been pushed to the walls. A string ensemble and harpsichord occupied one corner, currently playing a waltz.

It wasn't long before I heard the name Otto spoken numerous times, and I searched the room for the royal guest. Here was the real story worth covering, for by this time in the social season an ordinary ball hardly warranted more than a few lines in any society column. Seeing no one who fit his description, however, I continued taking meticulous notes on my observations, being sure, as the butler had charged me, not to miss any pertinent details.

A couple on the dance floor caught my attention—or rather, the young woman did, for she seemed to be leading her partner rather than the other way around. Tall and slender, she was a striking beauty and moved with the grace of a ballerina, seeming to float inches above the floor. With her raven's black hair, exotic violet-blue eyes, and heart-shaped face, she would certainly stand out in any ballroom; no doubt the young bucks had raced to fill her dance card.

I continued moving through the room, stopping to inquire here about a gown, there about the continued renovations on a mansion. I asked where families intended spending the fall and winter months, whether an upcoming wedding would be held in New York or London. I visited with my aunt Alva Vanderbilt, now Belmont. No other Vanderbilts were in attendance, as Mrs. Fish and Aunt Alice were on frosty terms at best.

Each time I interviewed someone new, I hinted at whether acquaintances or family members had recently gone missing. No one offered any insights. Though I wished to display the old photograph of my mother and Stuart Gale, I could hardly do so at a social event, or ask direct questions about the murder. What I did glean, however, were the fervent hopes of many a matron that Prince Otto would notice her daughter, become enchanted, and whisk her away to a castle in Austria. They practically tossed their daughters at me to ensure their names would be included in my article on tonight's ball. Society mothers believed, often correctly, that creating a narrative in print around their daughters' names somehow facilitated their wishes coming true. To that end, a long list of names occupied my writing tablet.

Through all my inquiries, the black-haired young woman never lacked for a dance partner, and never failed to be the center of attention with her graceful movements. During brief interludes she would drift off to the side and join a certain young man. By the perplexed expressions he exhibited while he watched her dance, one might suspect him to be a rival for her affections, but their likeness revealed him instead to be her brother—a disapproving brother at that.

The music paused, and after curtsying to her partner, the beautiful young woman once again approached the man I assumed to be her brother. Curious about them, for they were strangers to me, I moved closer. I had guessed their relationship correctly, for I overheard him say, "Do you intend to dance with every man here tonight, Sister?"

"If I have to, yes. The single ones, at least."

"Are you that hard up to find a husband?"

"Don't be crass, Auggie." Despite the words, she spoke with a pleasant smile. "And do not get in my way tonight."

"What does that mean?"

I wondered the same thing.

"When the prince arrives," she replied with a haughty tilt of her head, "I intend for him to see me happily, gleefully engaged, not standing aside like some pitiful wallflower. Now, if you'll excuse me, I do believe Charles Eldridge is coming over to offer his arm for the next set."

It would appear she had some history with the prince, and

tonight wished to impress upon him—what? That she was happy without him? Playing hard to get? That was exactly the way to catch some men, but I couldn't imagine this beautiful woman needing to employ such tactics to attract a man's attention.

She didn't move away from her brother until Mr. Eldridge reached her, a tall, elegant man with a sharply aquiline nose. She made a show of checking her dance card. Only then did she take a dainty step to join him on the dance floor. Mr. Eldridge caught her hand in his long-fingered, almost womanly one and expertly guided her through the steps. Her brother heaved a sigh and minutely shook his head.

I took that as my cue and approached him. "Good evening, I'm Miss Cross of the Newport *Messenger.*"

He started as if I'd poked him. "Yes?" He narrowed his eyes as if peering into the sun. "You're Brady Gale's sister."

"I am, indeed. I didn't know you were acquainted with my brother." I held out my hand but he didn't shake it.

"What could you possibly want with me?" He didn't sound put out, merely curious. "I'm not wearing the latest from Worth, nor am I presently engaged or planning a coming-out trip abroad."

I briefly laughed at his joke of comparing himself to a debutante. I had approached him because of his youth, because experience had taught me nice young men who escorted their sisters to balls were often naïve enough to let down their guard with journalists. In my most serious tone, I informed him, "I'm here to interview any and all of Mr. and Mrs. Fish's guests. Simply by being here, you are of great interest to our readers."

"Is that so?" He seemed rather dubious of that claim.

"Indeed. But if you don't wish to be interviewed, I'll move on and leave you to supervise your lovely sister. Speaking of Worth, is that whom she is wearing tonight?" I made a point of sending an admiring glance in the direction of the charming and no doubt costly gown, with its flowered bodice and tiny lace-covered sleeves.

"I believe she said Madame Paquin." He made no effort to hide his boredom. He didn't particularly wish to discuss his sister, but he might wish to discuss himself.

"Ah, then she spent the spring in Paris. Did you accompany her? Perhaps a word about your travels?"

At that invitation, he launched into a rather detailed description of his family's trip abroad. I soon stopped him and inquired after his name.

"August Pendleton. My sister is Miss Katherine Pendleton."

"Oh, of the Cincinnati banking Pendletons?"

"The very same," he replied with a dignified sniff. "Up until recently I served as vice president and chief financial officer. I am now the owner." He seemed not to wish to add anything to that, but instead returned to the topic of his recent experiences in Europe. I let him ramble, until I managed to circle round to his arrival in Newport and whether he had heard the news of the unfortunate occurrence at Spouting Rock.

"Rotten business, that," he said. "I understand the police haven't identified the body yet. Poor fellow. He's probably got people wondering what happened to him."

"Then you haven't heard of any missing persons among your acquaintances."

"Me? No." He began to tap his foot, and I assumed I had overstayed my welcome. With my thanks, I began to move on, when he sighed and murmured under his breath, "I wish the guest of honor would show up so I could call it a night and take Kay home."

By Kay, I assumed he referred to his sister, Katherine. Remembering what she had said about wishing to appear gleefully happy when Otto of Austria arrived, I stopped and turned back to him, my curiosity spiking. "Is your family acquainted with the prince, then?"

His lips flattened. "One might say that."

I ignored his cynical tone. "Then you must be looking forward to the prince's arrival tonight."

"Not every prince is a prince, Miss Cross."

More than a little intrigued by that revelation, I was forming my next question when his sister floated up and claimed his arm.

"Auggie, come with me, please." As before, she spoke pleasantly enough, but a hint of dismissal flashed in her eyes as her regard skimmed over me. She would have guessed at my occupation by my simple attire, along with my tablet and pencil. Did she take exception to her brother speaking with a journalist?

Brother and sister hadn't proceeded far when voices in the doorway seized not only my attention, but everyone's in the room.

"Mamie Fish, admit it. Prince Otto isn't coming tonight and never was. This was all a hoax and you've been laughing behind your hand at our expense."

Chapter 5

A woman with a snub nose set in a square face had made
the accusation—my aunt Alva Belmont. I hurried into the
entry hall as Aunt Alva swept across the floor to stand in
front of Mamie Fish. She crossed her arms in a challenging
manner and her blunt chin went up. "Well? What have you
got to say for yourself?"

"Oh, Alva, don't be ridiculous." Mrs. Fish hadn't so much
as flinched, and met Aunt Alva's challenging stare with one
of her own. "Of course he's coming. My guess is Caroline
Astor got her clutches into him and came up with some ruse
to delay him. I'm . . ." Here she showed an instant's hesitation. "I'm going to make some telephone calls and track him
down. Don't you worry." She raised her voice so all could
hear. "Otto will be here soon enough if I have to go get him
myself."

I heard Aunt Alva's *humph* even from several yards away.
She noticed me and beckoned with a crooked finger. "Are
you getting all this down?" she asked when I reached her.
She pointed at my writing tablet, into which I'd indeed been
scribbling.

"Do you really think this has all merely been a hoax?" I asked her.

Aunt Alva laughed. "No, of course I don't. Mamie might be a lot of things, but a liar isn't one of them."

"Then why—"

"Because, dear Emmaline, I enjoy shaking her laurels. She needs it, from time to time. We all do. She expects it of me, as I do of her." Still laughing, Aunt Alva signaled to a friend and started to move away.

An uneasy sensation gathered in the pit of my stomach. "Aunt Alva," I called after her, bringing her to a halt. "You don't have something to do with the prince's delay, do you?"

"Good heavens, no, child. I enjoy teasing Mamie, but I certainly don't wish to make an enemy of her." Shaking her head at my outlandish suggestion, she went off to join her friend.

Still, I wondered if Mrs. Fish appreciated Aunt Alva's joke. She didn't look as though she were enjoying anything at the moment. She looked worried and out of sorts as she traced a path to the library and waved a hand to attract the attention of someone inside.

"Stuyvie," I heard her hiss as I moved closer to listen. "Stuyvie, I need you."

Stuyvesant Fish, president of the Illinois Central Railroad, excused himself from the card table, to which he had retreated during my sojourn in the ballroom. If his wife's summons annoyed him, his expression showed no trace of it. A man with deep-set eyes and far more hair on his upper lip than the top of his head, he offered his wife a deferential smile and inquired what she needed.

"Otto's not here yet," she blurted in an urgent stage whisper.

"I know that, my dear. What shall we do about it?"

"I don't know. I'd hoped you might have an idea or two."

"I heard you tell Mrs. Belmont you'd make some telephone inquiries, did I not? I believe that would be the way to begin. Have your secretary do so immediately. Where is he staying?"

"At the Ocean House Hotel, I believe."

"There you are, then. Have Miss Powers call over to the Ocean House."

"But what if he's not there? What if he decided to stop at, say, Beechwood, and Caroline Astor gave orders that no calls are to be put through to the prince? Then what?"

"Then there is little more we can do, my dear. But the night is still early. He'll show up." He reached to pat her hand but she yanked it away.

"But Stuyvie! What if he doesn't? He's a prince—if something has happened to him, it could cause an international incident. And he only came to Newport because of our invitation. We could be held responsible."

"I hardly think so, my dear. And I'm sure he's fine, merely detained."

"Still, if he never makes an appearance, I'll be a laughing-stock. I can't have that."

Rather than becoming perturbed or angered, Stuyvesant Fish pulled back a little to bestow upon his wife a knowing grin, and in a conspiratorial tone said, "What is it you always say, my dear? They won't laugh at me if . . ."

"If I can make 'em laugh *with* me." Her hands went to her hips. "Stuyvie, what would I do without you?" They shared a laugh, and then she shooed him back into the library. "Go on, go back to your game. Only . . ."

He leaned in toward her. "Yes, my dear?"

"Make quite sure you win, Stuyvie. A nice, tidy bundle."

He went away chuckling, and Mrs. Fish turned about to catch me lingering within hearing distance. Startled, I tried to pretend I'd been observing the goings-on in the hall, but she wasn't fooled.

"You there."

I slowly turned my face toward her and gestured at myself in question.

"Yes, you. Come here." When I did, she snatched my writing tablet out of my hands. "What have you overheard? What have you written here?" She bowed over the tablet as if to make out the words, but as if terribly nearsighted, she repeated, "What have you written?"

"Nothing, ma'am. Only my observations on the festival so far." Despite my denial, I braced for her anger and for her to order me out of the house. I'd of course taken an accurate account of Aunt Alva's accusations, along with Mrs. Fish's adamant denial. What I would do with the encounter, I hadn't yet decided, but my journalist's instincts had prompted me to keep a record.

To my bewilderment, Mrs. Fish continued searching the page, her gaze traveling but never alighting on any particular sentence or phrase that I could see. "There's nothing here about a certain missing guest?"

"Um . . ." Dared I lie while she held the evidence in her hands? A realization dawned. Mamie Fish couldn't read. Good heavens. I also realized I had better play along or I would certainly find myself out the door. "As you can plainly see, ma'am, there's nothing there but details about gowns and upcoming weddings and trips to Europe. And to tell you truly, ma'am, I don't understand the fuss over a guest's late arrival. Guests are always late to my aunt Alice's events. Aunt Alva's, too."

At that she looked up. "Is that right?"

"Yes, indeed."

She thrust my notebook back at me and studied me with a shrewd gaze. Then her manner abruptly changed. "I need you to do something for me. Run up to the third floor. In the fourth room on the right from the staircase, you'll find my secretary, Miss Powers. Have her start the search for the prince. I don't care if she has to connect to every telephone in Newport."

"Uh . . . yes, ma'am." I headed for the stairs.

"Wait," she called. When I returned to her, she said, "If she hasn't found him in twenty minutes, come and find me."

"Twenty minutes? Are you sure that's enough time—"

"That's as much time as I'm willing to give it." With that, she waved me away.

Exactly twenty minutes later, I descended to the ground floor to face the unpleasant task of informing Mrs. Fish her secretary had been unable to locate Prince Otto.

Misgiving gripped me, although only momentarily. I had begun to wonder about the Spouting Rock victim. Could he be Prince Otto? But no, the prince was purported to be a young man in his twenties, low of stature but broad through the shoulders, his hair and eyes dark. The Spouting Rock victim could lay claim to none of those attributes. Besides, surely someone would have reported him missing by now, for princes didn't disappear without someone noticing. Still, my nape prickled. I had learned to suspect odd coincidences, and a dead man and a missing prince within a couple of days certainly smacked of an odd coincidence.

I found Mrs. Fish in the loggia off the drawing room. The lanterns suspended from the ceiling cast an orangey glow that smoothed years from the faces of those gathered there. The expansive windows had been thrown open to the night, and outside, where electric lights illuminated the side gardens, several of those scarecrows looked in as if wishing they, too, could join the festivities. Laughter drifted from within the foliage as some of the young people continued searching for Mrs. Fish's hidden treasures. Two sharp-eyed, elderly matrons hovered among them, serving as chaperones.

Mrs. Fish was presently speaking to Isabel Clemson, a middle-aged woman with angular, pinched features and bland brown hair and eyes. To me, she always appeared as if she were recovering from a long illness, so pale and wan was she, though I had never heard of her being indisposed. I spotted her husband at the far end of the loggia with a group of men, and every now and again his wife cast him what I would call a nervous glance. But perhaps that was merely the woman's habitual expression.

One of the old guard doyennes joined Mrs. Fish and the other women. "My daughter hasn't had a spare moment since we arrived," she announced. "Her dance card is full up, and her poor feet will be worn out by night's end." She swept Isabel Clemson with a haughty gaze and waved her fan furiously in front of her face. "Where is Thea? I haven't seen her all evening. It isn't like her to play the wallflower." The woman made a show of searching the corners of the loggia. "And with your pedigree, Isabel, the prince is sure to take notice. Then again . . ." Rather than finish her sentence, the woman flicked a glance at Mr. Clemson, started to chuckle, and compressed her lips.

A tide of heat rose in Mrs. Clemson's face. Without moving a muscle, she too darted a glance at her husband. "Thea isn't feeling well tonight. Nothing serious. She complained of being a bit under the weather."

A commonplace explanation, but then why that furious blush? Mrs. Clemson hailed from one of the early Dutch families that had settled in New York and made their fortune first in shipping, then real estate. Unlike my Vanderbilt relatives, whose money and status came much later in America's history, Isabel Clemson's social status rivaled Caroline Astor's.

So yes, the prince might indeed take notice of nineteen-year-old Thea, despite her slight overbite and tendency to squint.

Weren't the Clemsons eager to see their daughter married to European royalty? Such a marriage increased a family's standing considerably. I thought of my cousin Consuelo's marriage to the Duke of Marlborough. To put it mildly, she hadn't been at all keen on the union, but her mother had put such pressure on her daughter that, in the end, Consuelo had complied with Aunt Alva's wishes.

This passed through my mind in seconds, while I waited for Mrs. Fish to spot me. When she did, she excused herself to her guests and came over to speak with me. Again, she used that stage whisper that must have been audible to everyone in the immediate vicinity.

"Any luck?"

I shook my head. "I'm afraid not. Perhaps if you give it a bit more time . . ."

"Time's up. Here." She pressed a sealed envelope into my hand. Before she could say anything more, a handful of young people came into the loggia from outside, their chaperones trailing behind them. They were laughing and talking in animated voices. One of the elegant young ladies held a golden stone in her palm and peered at it in the lamplight.

"Look, I've found an amber pumpkin."

"And I've got a tiny ruby apple," another said, comparing the small treasure she'd discovered in the garden with the one her friend held.

A young man in their group called to Mrs. Fish. "By the way, one of your scarecrows has fallen over on the display on the far side of the garden. Lying down on the job, I'd call it. Thought you should know."

As did the others, I gazed out the open windows to where, across the garden, a display of gilded gourds, pumpkins, and silken haystacks was presided over by two of those well-dressed scarecrows. One of them, indeed, sprawled drunkenly on its side, its head half propped against the decorations.

Mrs. Fish affected an annoyed expression. "All right, everyone, who's been giving my scarecrows champagne punch?" This earned her a chorus of laughter. Then she turned back to me and spoke in a hurried whisper. "Deliver that note to Miss Powers. Tell her not to hesitate, but to follow these instructions to the letter."

I couldn't help a puzzled frown. Had Mrs. Fish written this note? Had I been mistaken in my conclusions regarding her literacy or lack thereof?

"Go, girl. Hurry!"

After racing back up three flights of stairs, I arrived breathless at Miss Powers's room and handed her the missive. She carefully opened the envelope and read the message. "Mrs. Fish gave you this? No one else on her behalf?"

"It was Mrs. Fish herself," I assured her, wondering at her accusing tone. What on earth did Mrs. Fish's note contain? I almost wished I'd peeled back one corner of the flap to attempt to read the contents.

With a nod, Miss Powers went to the telephone the Fishes had installed for her use. She picked up the receiver, but hesitated and glanced over at me. "Thank you, Miss Cross. Your part in this is over, and Mrs. Fish desires you to return downstairs for the next phase of the evening."

"The next phase?"

She didn't offer any clarification. Taking this as my cue to leave, I did just that. On my way down, I again pondered the note, both the contents and the origin. I still believed Mrs. Fish to be illiterate. Perhaps she'd gotten her husband to pen the note for her.

More grumbling about the prince's absence greeted me downstairs, along with disappointed mamas wondering if they should give up and take their daughters home. Mrs.

Fish circulated through the rooms and assured everyone they would regret leaving early, as Prince Otto had been found, had apologized for the delay, and was this very moment on his way to Crossways. This raised a chorus of relieved sighs and applause.

My suspicions about this sudden development grew when I spied Aunt Alva's attempts to stifle laughter behind her hand. Her husband, Oliver Belmont, sidled up beside her and shared in her chortling. I wished to find out what she knew, but before I could approach her, Mrs. Fish positioned me on the grand staircase opposite the front vestibule. She bade me stay put while she went scurrying around the house gathering the guests and herding them into the front hall. Many spilled over into the dining room, ballroom, and library.

Minutes ticked by, first punctuated by heavy silence, then whispers and murmurs as impatience once again mounted. People fidgeted. Some of the earlier suspicions were repeated, and I thought I detected tears gathering in the eyes of one hopeful debutante.

"It won't be long now, everyone," Mrs. Fish promised gaily. "Our guest of honor will be here any moment, and I'm counting on all of you to provide him with a good old, hearty American welcome."

"I'll believe it when I see it," murmured a man standing on the step below me. He was handsome, tall and blond, with a slight bend in the bridge of his nose that spoke of a break, an imperfection that added charm, rather than detracting from his good looks. I recognized him as Harry Forge, a self-proclaimed bachelor and a few years older than my brother. Harry had no profession that I knew of, other than his real estate investments, many of which were across the sea in Europe. I hadn't encountered him earlier, but perhaps he'd arrived late himself.

"Do you doubt Mrs. Fish's word, sir?" I challenged him cordially. He turned to assess me, taking his time about it as he looked me up and down. A corner of his mouth lifted as he took in the plain attire that marked me as a journalist, or perhaps he pegged me as a lady's maid who'd sneaked down for a glimpse at royalty.

"No, it's not Mrs. Fish's word I doubt. It's the prince's promise to show up at all tonight that I doubted right from the start."

That reply surprised me, considering he must have known that, as a journalist, I might make a note of anything he said to me. And as a lady's maid, well, servants were notorious for gossiping about their employers—and their guests. Lightly, I said, "Can the prince not be trusted to keep his word, sir?"

"When he wishes to, he does. Or when he remembers," he added with a smirk.

"Are you and the prince well acquainted, then?" I had already guessed the answer. Surely a man with Mr. Forge's looks and stature, not to mention his wealth, would be welcomed in the courts of Europe.

"You might say that. We've done our share of hunting in the past. Mostly big game in his home country. Red stag, boar, wild sheep, or what the local populace call 'mouflon.'"

I raised my eyebrows in what he undoubtedly took for admiration, but if I admired anything, it was the beauty of the species he mentioned, not a hunter's penchant for turning such creatures into trophies. "And is the prince quite a good hunter?"

"He would call it stalking, as many in Europe do. Unfortunately for him, while he is an excellent shot, his impatience more often than not foiled his intentions."

A resounding clang of the door knocker startled everyone, and a hush fell. Mr. Forge turned back around to face the hall.

"Why, whoever could that be?" Mrs. Fish's eyes sparkled with merriment, a sentiment mirrored in Aunt Alva's countenance as well as that of Alva's husband, Oliver. Mr. Fish squeezed through the crush to stand with his wife. Another clang sounded. "I suppose I had better get the door," Mrs. Fish said gleefully, and waved a footman away.

She went into the vestibule and opened the front door wide enough to peek out, but not enough for anyone in the hall to see who waited to be admitted. Conversation once more buzzed. Mothers began nudging, and then pushing, their young daughters forward, until several debutantes stood at the front of the crowd, to be among the first faces the prince would behold. My gaze found Mrs. Clemson again. She stood at the outer edge of the crush near the drawing room, and I noticed her rather heaving for breath, as if she'd hurried into the hall. Her expression was guarded, even apprehensive.

From the vestibule, Mrs. Fish's voice rang out. "Why, Your Highness, so good of you to come. Please do come in."

She backed her way from the vestibule into the hall and sank into a deep curtsey. The company followed suit, the women curtseying while the men bowed from the waist. Only I remained upright, my gaze riveted.

No, that wasn't quite true, for Katherine Pendleton also remained as straight and tall as a marble statue, her countenance as serene as it was prideful.

Mrs. Fish straightened and turned to address her guests. "Ladies and gentlemen, may I present to you Prince Otto, nephew of the Austro-Hungarian emperor, Franz Joseph."

Miss Pendleton's chin inched higher even as the assemblage bowed lower still. As I watched for the prince's entrance, my eyes went as wide as a harvest moon and my mouth dropped open—an expression soon to be mimicked by everyone present.

In walked a man in country tweeds—certainly no prince. He gripped a leash, and at the other end of the leash waddled a young chimpanzee wearing a satin tunic, a velvet cape, and holding what appeared to be a scepter. Upon stopping in the center of the hall, the little chimp let out a whimper, dropped his scepter, and scrambled up into his keeper's arms.

Chapter 6

Had I expected an angry reaction to this deception? I admit I braced for recriminations. None came, only *oohs* and *ahs* accompanied by laughter and exclamations of delight. At first the creature clung to his keeper's neck, but after a few minutes some of his shyness ebbed and he lifted his head.

"Wherever did you get him?" a male guest asked.

"We have Alva to thank for that," Mrs. Fish replied with a flourish toward my aunt. "A phone call to Harry Lehr, who has a friend in Portsmouth who keeps something of a menagerie on his property. But shush, the authorities are not to know that."

"Well, Mamie, you've gotten the best of us, haven't you?" The woman who made this pronouncement sauntered out from among the crush and approached the man in tweeds. "May I? Is he friendly, or will he take my fingers off?"

"He's as gentle as a baby, ma'am, since that is exactly what he is." He stroked the chimpanzee's head as he spoke. "His name is Maximillian. Max for short."

The woman removed her satin glove, and tentatively

brushed the fur on Max's head with a fingertip. She let out a giggle and petted him again, this time with her whole hand. "Oh, he's adorable. Mamie, we should be furious with you, but I for one can't seem to manage it."

The others apparently agreed, though I did hear several sighs of disappointment from the mamas who had hoped to connect their daughters with a prince tonight. Only one person appeared unamused by Mrs. Fish's antics. Isabel Clemson looked more relieved than anything else, and I wondered why both she and Katherine Pendleton seemed to have reason to disdain Otto of Austria. Miss Pendleton raised an eyebrow above a faint smile—or smirk, I should say. Mrs. Clemson merely aimed her gaze at the floor, breathed deeply, and turned away.

"Prince Otto really was expected tonight," Mrs. Fish declared. "And to tell you the truth, I haven't the faintest notion what happened to him."

That sparked another warning across my nape, and I pondered running back up to the secretary's room to use her telephone to let Jesse know he might have a missing aristocrat on his hands. Yet, people shirked invitations all the time. Rude, yes, but rarely sinister.

I turned my attention to the many guests, mostly women, who lined up for their chance to greet the little fellow. Before the night ended, I'd held him in my arms and marveled at how like a human infant he behaved. When more than one young lady declared her intentions of adopting a chimpanzee of her own, the trainer assured us that as Max grew his strength would increase until he became a danger to humans. By then, he would have to be caged and remain so for the rest of his life, for he will have lost his instincts for life in the wild. At those words, a deep sense of sadness descended on me.

Well after midnight, I found it necessary to stifle yawns

and avoid glancing at the clocks dispersed throughout the house. I'd continued my job of meticulously cataloging details of fashion and fashionable news, but my interest in the fête had long since waned. Despite whatever leading questions I might ask, no one admitted to a lost acquaintance, and references to Bailey's Beach and Spouting Rock failed to elicit any notable reactions. I had hit a dead end on the subject here at Crossways, and I longed to be home.

Guests began to trickle out the front door. The Clemsons, the Pendleton siblings, and many others claimed their outerwear and called for their carriages. Yet plenty of others continued to mill through the rooms. Suddenly, from the library, came a raw shriek and a cry of alarm so shrill the hair at my nape lifted. I hurried in from the front hall to discover little Max scuttling through the room, his leash trailing out behind him, leaping from one piece of furniture to another. In one of his hands, something small and colorful bobbed and flapped like a lifeless animal, until further scrutiny revealed the item to be a feathered headdress still connected to a partial hairpiece of spiraling tendrils. Near the hearth, an elderly woman, Mrs. Foster, had slapped both hands to her head in an attempt to shield her thinning hair from view. She cried out her mortification yet again, and shouted for someone to *do* something.

It was Max doing the shrieking as he scampered through the crowd. People reached for him but he eluded their every grasp. His trainer, whose name I had learned was Mr. Simmons, followed in pursuit, but could not penetrate the crush as easily as his young charge.

"Don't chase him," the tweed-clad man yelled, his hands up in a futile bid for order. "You'll only drive him farther and faster away."

Max disappeared into the loggia, and a moment later a guest called to Mr. Simmons. "He's gone outside."

Mr. Simmons hurried through the loggia and outside, and I followed close behind him. With no one now in his way, Mr. Simmons was able to almost match the little chimp's pace. I only hoped that if Max made it to the scarecrow display, he didn't decide to scale the pumpkins and bales of hay and disappear into the darkness. But as he reached the end of the garden, it was as if he'd come up against a solid wall. He halted so abruptly he somersaulted backward into the air. His motion never ceasing, he shrieked again—louder and more stridently than before—twirled about, and flew up into his master's arms.

As I reached them, I understood why.

Death has a smell one never forgets, nor ever grows accustomed to. I'd become familiar with it over the past several years, but still I recoiled now as the breeze wrapped me in a grisly essence I will only describe as nothing fresh, nothing alive, nothing hopeful or reassuring. There is only finality and a sense of one's own fragile impermanence.

Somehow, I retained the presence of mind to double back around to the house and assure everyone Max had been captured and everything was fine. Mr. Simmons remained outside, and I told the guests this was to soothe Max before returning him to the house, which was the truth. They dispersed, laughing. Someone retrieved the headdress and hairpiece from where it had fallen and discreetly returned it to its mortified, but unhurt, owner. Soon after, the remaining carriages were brought round and the last of the guests left. Mr. Simmons, looking pale and shaky, brought Max back into the house. The little fellow clung tightly round his trainer's neck, resting his furry cheek on Mr. Simmons's shoulder. After bidding him to find a seat in the drawing room, I took Mr. and Mrs. Fish aside, out of their servants' hearing, and explained to them where Prince Otto lay.

Who else could be lying in the garden but the missing prince? In the electric glow of the hanging lanterns, I'd made out fine evening clothes and the smooth features of a young man. Mr. and Mrs. Fish insisted on hurrying outside. Once there, it took them only an instant to confirm my guess.

A telephone call brought the police, but in the middle of the night there was little they could do but to remove the body and cordon off the area. The electric lighting might have brought a semblance of daylight to the gardens, but it proved inadequate for the identifying of clues. Jesse questioned the Fishes, Mr. Simmons, and me, but learned little from any of us. He stationed two officers to stand guard until morning, and sent Mr. Simmons—along with an exhausted and fussy Max—home. He sent me home as well.

Needless to say I slept little that night and rose early in the morning. While breakfasting with Nanny and my maid-of-all-work, Katie—a very light breakfast as I had no appetite—I told them of Otto's fate, how one of Mrs. Fish's regal scarecrows had been replaced by the prince's lifeless body. I remembered the young man who had come in from the gardens joking about the scarecrow having fallen over like a drunkard, and Mrs. Fish demanding to know who had given the effigy champagne punch. If only I or anyone had thought to go out and restore the scarecrow to its proper position, could we have helped the prince? Was he still alive then? We would never know.

After readying myself to leave home, I visited with my aging roan carriage horse, Barney, and then hitched my newly acquired and much younger horse, Maestro, to my buggy. Maestro, a sleek dark bay, had been a gift from Derrick Andrews earlier in the summer, and though accepting expensive gifts made me wary of a possible hidden price, he had made the gesture with such good nature that to decline it would have damaged our friendship. Besides, poor Barney, who had served both me and my great aunt Sadie gallantly for more than a decade, deserved to retire to a leisurely life of munching greens in the rear garden.

Overnight, heavy clouds had converged on the island, kicking the seas to a froth and bringing a cloying closeness to the air. I hoped the police would be able to finish collecting their evidence before the skies opened. As I came around a corner of Ocean Avenue and topped a rise, the roofline of Crossways came into view. It seemed the brooding clouds hovered only inches above the house. I reached the gates. Numerous vehicles blocked the drive, and figures in blue bustled across the lawn.

I left Maestro and my carriage at the bottom of the drive, off to one side, and proceeded on foot. No one confronted me. No one even noticed me. The bunting, lanterns, and royal scarecrows on either side of the drive had been removed, but a few on the side lawns still stood at attention and cast their mocking glares at the policemen. I spotted Jesse near the loggia at the east end of the house, but for now I didn't intrude. The front door stood open and I ventured inside.

"I see you're back. Well, come along." Mamie Fish, clad in a loose morning gown, her wavy dark hair loose and brushing her back, accosted me as soon as I stepped into the entrance hall. Here, too, last night's decorations had vanished; the servants must have worked long into the morning hours. I supposed after the discovery of Prince Otto's body, the festive ornaments had taken on a macabre quality and the Fishes had wanted them gone. "You might as well be here, I suppose. It's not as though we can keep a secret as whopping as this one."

"No, ma'am. While none of your guests were aware of what happened when they left here last night, it won't be long before newspapers all over town report the story." I allowed her to convey me into the dining room, where she sat me down and instructed one of the footmen to bring another coffee cup. "May I ask if the police have discovered anything of significance yet?"

Her lips pinched into a tight ball as she frowned. "Not that they've told me so far. Never mind that the prince expired in my garden. I suppose my husband and I will be the last to know anything." She busied herself with angrily spreading jam across a slice of nutty quick bread.

"I'm sure they wish to have all the facts before they make a report to you."

"If only Otto had deigned to show up here on time, he might still be alive." She wielded her butter knife in a vague gesture that sent a glop of bright red jam dripping onto the table linen. "Damned fool."

Mrs. Fish's harsh language and lack of sympathy shocked me, though I schooled my expression to hide the fact. "Do they at least know the cause of death?"

"Knife? Strangulation? Bullet? I don't know." She spoke with her mouth full. "Imagine dying among the scarecrows. *As* a scarecrow. If Otto were alive he'd be livid."

"What?" She didn't need to repeat herself. I'd heard her well enough, but I simply couldn't fathom anyone taking murder so lightly. The footman reentered and set a cup and saucer in front of me, and then poured from the pot sitting on the table. I ignored it.

Mrs. Fish eyed me as if seeing me for the first time. "You're experienced in these things." I nodded, and expected her to ask me to investigate as I had done in the past. "Then you can help me save face."

I blinked. "Save face?"

"Are you hard of hearing? Yes. Save face."

"Good heavens, Mrs. Fish. The prince was out there during the festival. Those young people searching for hidden treasures, they must have walked right by him and . . ." I trailed off somewhat breathless, as though a great weight had knocked the wind out of me. "Shouldn't you be more worried about the welfare of your young guests? How this will affect them once they find out?"

The thought of a body lying out in the dark, so close to the carefree revelry, thoroughly unsettled me. I'd been in the loggia as well. I had looked directly out at the prince without knowing it. A sickening sense of guilt settled over me.

"Of course. That's why I need you to help me find a way, the correct words, to soften the blow." And yet she smiled. "People will be talking about this for years and years to come."

Her lack of empathy almost made me suspect her. But then I remembered Mamie Fish never wore her emotions on her sleeve. Opinions, yes, but feelings were quite another matter. She'd never publicly succumb to fear or sadness or even the slightest show of vulnerability.

"Thank goodness our boys already returned to school," she went on after a sip of coffee, "and Marian, our daughter, left a week ago for Staten Island with her grandmother."

"You didn't wish your daughter to meet the prince," I couldn't help observing.

"She's only eighteen. That's too young to be married, in my opinion. Besides, I wouldn't want her going off permanently to some shabby little country across the ocean. She'll marry an American and stay here where she belongs."

I remembered the conversation I'd overheard during the festival. "Do the Clemsons feel the same about their daughter? She didn't attend last night either."

"Isabel said Thea wasn't feeling well. Does it matter?"

"Excuse me, Mrs. Fish—Oh, Emma. Good morning."

I'd been sitting with my back to the doorway, and turned quickly at the sound of Jesse Whyte's voice. He made no comment about my presence there, for he'd learned to expect as much. He merely came into the room, his hat in his hands.

"Mrs. Fish, I've spoken with your husband. He's still discussing matters with the men outside, but he said you'd want to know our preliminary findings. According to the coroner, the prince was stabbed." His gaze briefly shifted to me, then returned to Mrs. Fish. "Once, in the heart."

A frisson of alarm went through me, even as Mrs. Fish blurted, "Good heavens, there must be blood everywhere."

Jesse winced at her brusqueness. "Not as much as you'd think, ma'am. He appeared to have died immediately. Though, your reflecting pool is tinged pink, suggesting the killer used it to wash the evidence off his hands."

"Well, I certainly won't thank him for that." Mrs. Fish took an audible sip of her coffee.

"You must realize what this could mean, ma'am." Again, Jesse regarded me briefly. "One of your guests last night may have committed this act."

"Nonsense. Do you think I'd invite a murderer into my home? Land sakes, young man."

"Be that as it may, ma'am. It's likely one of your guests is guilty."

Mrs. Fish absorbed the information without blinking. "Well, exactly when was he killed? It's hardly likely someone did it during the festival. They'd have been seen, wouldn't they? So how long could he have been lying out there?"

"We can't yet say, ma'am. Once we've examined all the evidence we should be able to determine more."

"I certainly hope so. Someone stabbing one of my guests— of all the unmitigated gall." After finishing the last of the coffee in her cup, she lifted the silver coffeepot that sat within arm's reach.

Her composure astounded me. I wished to go outside and have a look at the crime scene. To that end, I came to my feet to face Jesse. "Any bruising on the body? Are there signs of a struggle?"

"None that we can see." His expression confirmed that he realized I was comparing this murder to that of the Spouting Rock victim. "Death appears to have come quickly, taking the prince by surprise."

"And the stab wound?" I asked him quietly.

He nodded. "Appears like the other. Clean and direct. But we'll learn more once the body's been examined by the coroner."

"A pity," Mrs. Fish commented. When Jesse and I regarded her with incredulous expressions, she clarified her meaning. "Bruises might help identify the culprit, no?"

Jesse relaxed. "That's true. But it appears whoever did this gave little or no warning. He simply struck."

"Or *she* struck," I murmured, well aware that violence was not restricted to the members of either sex.

"True enough," Mrs. Fish agreed with a shrug. "What happens now? How long before I have my house back?"

"It won't be long, ma'am." Despite Jesse's assurance, his voice rang with frustration.

"I'm going outside to see what's happening." Mrs. Fish rose and breezed past us, leaving us alone in the dining room.

"Good grief." He scanned the table. "I don't suppose there's any more of that coffee left."

I picked up my cup and held it out to him. "Here, I haven't touched mine."

He drained it in a few gulps. As he set it back on the table, I noticed how his hands trembled slightly, a lingering symptom of his near electrocution earlier in the month. I pretended I hadn't noticed.

"I suppose I should go back out, too," he said. "It's early yet, but if you ask me, it's highly likely the same person killed both the prince and our Spouting Rock victim."

"My thought exactly. The knife wound is the same?"

"It appears very similar. We'll know more after a thorough examination of the body and a direct comparison of the two wounds."

"If the deaths *are* connected, it probably means the prince and the other victim knew each other."

"Most likely, yes, although we can't make any assumptions."

I was about to say more when Mrs. Fish came striding back to the room. She stopped in the doorway and held out a hand. "Well, Miss Cross? Aren't you coming? Isn't that why you're here?"

Jesse and I followed her across the house, out through the eastern loggia, and into the crime scene.

Chapter 7

Outside, Jesse took over for the policeman speaking with Mr. Fish. "The coroner believes whoever did this knew what he was doing."

"How so?" Stuyvesant Fish asked. His wife came to stand beside him and he absently slipped an arm around her waist. Despite the circumstances, I found that simple gesture touching. So few marriages among the Four Hundred were based on true affection, much less love. But I'd always heard that Stuyvesant and Mamie Fish were genuinely happy together.

"A single thrust, directly into the desired target." Making a fist, Jesse mimicked the direction the knife had taken. "In this case, the heart. There are no other stab wounds. The killer achieved his goal with a minimum of fuss."

"It doesn't sound like a crime of passion, then," I observed. "The killer was too neat and controlled."

Jesse nodded his agreement. "My guess is that it was well planned."

The uniformed officers had already inspected the scene,

but instincts honed in recent years prompted me to make my own observations. Jesse had been right; very little blood marked the garden, other than the pink tinge in the reflecting pool. A few smears streaked the display's decorative pumpkins and haystacks where the body had fallen and rolled to the ground.

Sculpted hedges outlined this area of the gardens: privet, yew, and English boxwood, framing glorious bursts of asters, bright lemon queen sunflowers, and fiery daylilies. I moved along the winding stone footpath and searched for crushed flowers and broken hedges, but the garden appeared unmolested. As if the prince had calmly walked here to meet someone. Otherwise, if his lifeless body had been dragged or even carried here, would the killer have trod so carefully around the plants? I didn't think so. As with the Spouting Rock victim, circumstances suggested the prince had known his adversary.

I gazed across to the loggia windows, which had been open last night. As Mrs. Fish had surmised, Otto's death could not have occurred during the Harvest Festival, or someone might have seen and heard the encounter. If he was killed here, it had to have been once darkness had fallen but before many guests had arrived. It could not have been later, for one of those young scavenger hunters had reported a fallen scarecrow lying on the grass. The grass and pebbled walkways offered no distinctive footprints that could be traced to a particular individual. There was only the calculated nature of the crime and the stealth with which it had been achieved. That, I noted, spoke of sheer cunning and an utter lack of scruples.

With these initial inspections concluded, Jesse and I left our vehicles at Crossways and walked across to Bailey's Beach, and then along the sand to Spouting Rock. As we went, I related my impressions from the previous night regarding Mrs. Fish's guests. I described Katherine Pendleton's surly desire to appear carefree in front of Prince Otto; her brother's disapproval of the number of men with whom she danced; Mrs. Clemson's apparent relief when it became clear Otto would not make an appearance; and, finally, something that hadn't quite struck me as odd at the time, but which now echoed explicitly in my brain. Harry Forge had begun speaking of his hunting experience with the prince in present tense, but then had lapsed into past tense: "while he *is* an excellent shot, his impatience more often than not *foiled* his intentions."

Foiled, not foils.

"Are you sure he phrased it that way?"

"Positive. At the time, I didn't think much of it. He *could* have been referring to their past hunting trips." I paused to step carefully over a pile of rocks and shells. "Or, he could have been referring to the prince himself in the past tense. As in he already knew Otto was dead."

Jesse sighed. I knew he didn't like having to suspect members of the Four Hundred, not because he believed they were incapable of committing crimes, but because his investigation would become so much more complicated. People like the Clemsons and the Pendletons, even someone as young as August Pendleton, wielded enough power politically and socially to put undue pressure on the police and skew their activities.

But we hadn't forgotten about the other victim lying in the hospital's basement, for that was what had brought us to the beach. A prince and an unidentified stranger lay dead from nearly identical means. How were they connected?

The tide was out, meaning we could approach Spouting Rock without being drenched. The weather, though still threatening to become tempestuous, held for now as well. Jesse helped me climb the rocks, and then the two of us peered, not out over the heaving sea, but at the land that spread out in three directions around us.

"We have a direct view of The Rocks." I pointed at the Clewses' mansion in the distance, a Queen Anne villa of granite and timber and majestic peaks and turrets. "And of Bailey's Beach and the Cliff Walk."

Jesse drew off his hat, which was being threatened by the wind, and nodded. "Time of death had to be after nightfall, or, as you said, there would have been too big a risk that someone would witness the murder."

"Or, the time of death could have been earlier but somewhere else, and the body brought here after dark. Probably after the gathering at Bailey's Clubhouse."

"Perhaps he'd been part of that gathering, and was killed when everyone left."

"He wasn't dressed for the opera," I reminded him with a shake of my head. "That's where everyone was going afterward. But he *was* dressed for lunch and perhaps a round of golf. Someone at the golf club might recognize him."

Jesse turned to face me directly. "And how do you propose they do that? Do you intend to bring one of the police photographs of the deceased and stick it under the noses of people playing golf and having lunch?"

"Don't be silly. I'll bring the photo of Brady's father."

"Emma, I don't think that's a good idea. There might be a resemblance, but we certainly don't want to start a rumor about a man rising from his grave thirty years later."

"Why not? I'm still not convinced he isn't Stuart Gale."

With no answer to that, Jesse turned away to continue surveying the area. "If he wasn't killed here, why bring the body here, especially when . . ." He spoke to himself, rather than to me, but I completed his thought nonetheless when he trailed off.

"When there's an endless ocean at the murderer's disposal?"

That question had occurred to me as well. "The killer had a point to make?"

Jesse shook his head. "I don't think so, not in this case. At least, not the kind of message you're thinking of."

It didn't surprise me that he had followed the train of my thinking. He and I had been intricately involved in solving cases like this for several years now; we had grown familiar with how each other thought. I gestured at the water. "The ocean has a way of tossing things back up onto land. Perhaps the killer realized this."

"Yes, and he hadn't had the use of a boat. Which tells me he isn't someone who arrived in Newport on his own yacht. A landlubber, but someone who does have some knowledge of tides." He set his derby back on his head with a firm pat. Again, he faced me directly. "In light of this second murder, my resources will be limited with this one now. Chief Rogers, the city commissioners—they'll want answers about the prince. They're not going to care much about some unknown stranger. They'll insist we wait until someone comes looking for him."

I wanted to gripe about the unfairness of a prince's life being held in greater esteem than that of an ordinary citizen, and how an unknown stranger deserves justice as much as a prince does. But Jesse already knew those things, and though he'd fervently agree with me, his hands would still be tied. Quietly, I said, "I'll see what I can learn."

"Between the two of us, we might learn whether the victims knew each other. I'll start by having a chat with the manager of the Ocean House Hotel. Mrs. Fish tells me the prince was staying there."

"That's right. Good heavens, Jesse, the prince's family has no idea he'd dead. They need to be notified."

Jesse was nodding, his expression grim. "Yes, but I'd rather have more to tell them when that initial wire is sent."

"You can't mean to put off informing an emperor of his own nephew's death."

"This is political, Emma. Even if there was no political motive for the prince's death, the fact that he *is* dead, and died on American soil, makes this a matter of international significance. We'll have to proceed carefully. I'm quite sure my superiors will insist on it."

"Always politics," I murmured with no small amount of disgust.

"I'm sorry, but that's the way of it."

I softened my expression. "I'm not blaming you."

He gave a nod. "So, we have two men killed simply and efficiently, without signs of much of a struggle in either case. In both instances, it appears the victim might have met with his killer voluntarily. Why would the prince allow himself to be led around the side of the house before making his arrival known to the Fishes? It suggests he had something to hide, was involved in something he shouldn't have been, or was being threatened."

"Blackmail," I said. "Royalty is no stranger to such things."

"So he agreed to meet with his blackmailer, hoping to work out a solution to his difficulties, only to have a knife thrust between his ribs." Jesse's brow tightened in perplexity. "The killer would have to strike awfully quick to take the prince entirely off guard and prevent a struggle."

"If the murderer is a woman, perhaps they had arranged a tryst upon his arrival at Crossways. She could have distracted him with a kiss, and struck."

A faint blush entered his cheeks as I spoke the word *tryst*, and deepened at my suggestion of a deadly kiss. It reminded me that this was the first time we found ourselves utterly alone since earlier in the month, and a lot had happened in the meantime. In recent years Jesse had made his intentions concerning me abundantly clear, while I . . . I had been stricken with indecision due to another presence in my life, that of Derrick Andrews. If not for Derrick, I might readily have accepted Jesse's overtures. At times, I had believed I might be able to return his sentiments. He was a good man, and despite the almost ten years difference between us, right for me in so many ways but one.

Jesse had my respect, my regard, my affection, my trust, and so much more. But Derrick Andrews, son and heir of a newspaper magnate from Providence, whose family would never accept me as good enough, held my heart firmly in his grasp. I had come to fully realize and finally accept this three weeks ago, and since then had been careful not to give Jesse further reasons to hope.

We returned to Crossways and retrieved our carriages, and I continued my trip into town, to the *Messenger*. Whatever compulsion I felt to uncover the facts of either the Spouting Rock victim's or Prince Otto's deaths, my first responsibilities were to the newspaper, to the promise I'd made to Derrick.

A cold drizzle began falling as I entered town, prompting me to detour to Stevenson's livery where I could house my horse and carriage out of the rain. This meant getting wet myself as I scurried up to Spring Street, though my umbrella kept my top portion dry enough.

Upon arriving at the *Messenger*, I checked with Dan Carter that the press was in good working order. He assured me it was. Hanging on to the hope that our luck had taken a turn for the better, I went next to our tiny newsroom. It appeared Ethan Merriman hadn't yet repaired his gig, but Jacob Stodges sat at his desk, perusing a stack of notes. Rain pelted the window behind him and covered the sound of my footsteps, so that he hadn't heard me coming. I set my own notes beside his on the desk blotter. He glanced up in surprise.

"What's this?" Older than me by half a decade, Jacob Stodges had worked for the Newport *Mercury* for nearly a decade until a difference of opinion with his editor-in-chief had sent him knocking on the *Messenger*'s door. Although he had carried no references, Derrick had known of his reputation as a journalist and hired him on.

At the time, Jacob had believed he would be working for Derrick, not a woman. I often felt a strain between us, as though his disapproval of having a female in charge, especially one of my tender years, sat ready on the tip of his tongue. There was something rough-edged about him, and a wary secretiveness in his eyes that often troubled me. I supposed it came with the job, however; many journalists bore such a look as they searched out stories without tipping off their competitors. For now then, until he acted in a way that necessitated a confrontation, I chose to ignore all but the work he did for the *Messenger*, which so far had been exemplary.

"A story," I said in answer to his question. "Another murder. It happened last night at Crossways. It isn't likely any other paper will run this quite yet. And it'll need following up."

He hesitated. "You don't want the byline?"

I smiled. "I have other things to worry about."

My reply didn't appear to please him. Flat-lipped, he cast his dark-eyed gaze once more on the words I'd scribbled at home last night. He let out a low whistle, having come, I guessed, to the description of the manner of death. "He was made part of a scarecrow display? That's a rather ignominious end for a prince. Someone certainly has a dark sense of humor."

"I suppose the killer used the display to prevent the prince from being discovered too soon."

"Hmm . . ." He read on. "The manner of death sounds like the Spouting Rock victim."

"Yes, it does."

"Do you think the Fishes are involved?"

"No, and neither do the police. They barely knew the prince, and they considered his attendance at their festival quite a coup, royalty in their new home and all." Once again I thought of Mamie Fish's lack of compassion over the prince's death. They had met him during their last trip to Europe, or so she had said. Had there been more to it than a chance acquaintance? Had they, for instance, owed the prince money? It was well known that, as wealthy as the Fishes were, their fortune paled in comparison to, say, that of my Vanderbilt relatives. But no—I was assuming too much. It was possible Mrs. Fish simply didn't like to reveal her finer emotions to mere acquaintances.

"No, I don't suppose they are," he agreed as my silent speculation continued. "Mamie Fish is eccentric, but this? Can't fathom it."

Yet Mrs. Fish had predicted people would be talking about her Harvest Festival for a long time to come. Did the notoriety appeal to her? And her daughter, Marian—why had the Fishes sent her off to Staten Island ahead of the prince's arrival? Was it truly a matter of wanting her to marry an American and remain in this country?

I inwardly shook those thoughts away. As Jacob said, Mamie was eccentric. She was not criminally insane.

"Do you want the story?" I asked him.

"Of course I want it." He sounded peevish, almost angry. "I just thought you might want to claim this one for yourself. After all, tracking down murderers is what you do."

No admiration or approval accompanied this observation, but rather something akin to accusation. "What I do, Jacob, is run the *Messenger* for Mr. Andrews." I didn't add that I had already committed, privately, to finding out more about the Spouting Rock victim. If not his murderer, then his identity. I needed to determine whether he was Stuart Gale, or lay the notion to rest.

He made a sound that was halfway between an acknowledgment and a snigger.

I turned to leave, saying over my shoulder, "Let's get a preliminary article in an afternoon extra, please, before another paper beats us to the scoop."

"You surely don't have to tell me *that*, Miss Cross."

Later that afternoon, a fortuitous encounter led to new questions. Since the rain had stopped and all seemed under control at the *Messenger*, I decided to do a bit of investigating on my own. To that end, I walked up to the Newport Casino on Bellevue Avenue, and then to the New York Yacht Club station house on the harbor. At both locations I spoke to staff and some of the patrons—those willing to converse with me. My questions were occasionally met with suspicion, as the wealthy didn't typically care to allow their underlings, as they clearly considered me, to pry into their lives unless it was for good reason, such as a wedding, ball, or other social event. But reticence aside, I came away fairly certain the Spouting Rock victim hadn't shown his face at either establishment.

I collected Maestro and my carriage at the livery and next set out for the Newport Golf Club. The golf club had first entered my mind as a possibility due to the way the Spouting Rock victim had been dressed. Now, it seemed somewhat dubious that the man had played golf just prior to his death, especially since I had yet to find anyone in Newport who knew anything about him. Still, he had to have been *somewhere* before venturing to the rocks bordering Bailey's Beach.

Due to the undependable weather, no players dotted the golf course today, and the clubhouse, a wide V-shaped building, like a bird stretching its wings, presented a bleak prospect on its lonely perch overlooking Brenton Point and the ocean beyond.

Inside, however, warmth, bright lights, and delicious aromas beckoned. A luncheon was taking place in the oval dining room opposite the entryway, and upon peering through the doorway I recognized Thea Clemson sitting at a table with five or six other young women. A cheery fire blazed in the hearth, and though the many windows marching along the upper gallery let in precious little light on such a day, the white woodwork and soft green walls made a cozy backdrop for the gathering.

Despite what her mother had claimed last night, the daughter obviously hadn't stayed away from Crossways due to illness, as she looked perfectly fit today. Even from a distance, I could see the bloom in her cheeks. This renewed my curiosity as to why an eligible young lady, an heiress, would forgo her chance to meet a prince.

But with other questions to ask first, I continued past the parlors and salons to the service rooms and pantries. As I arrived in the area, waiters filed out from the kitchen with silver trays balanced high on one hand over their heads. I recognized the second of the team and approached him with the picture of Stuart Gale in hand.

"Thomas, may I have a moment, please?"

"Hello, Emma." If he was surprised to see me there, he didn't show it. "I'm sorry, but I've got to serve."

"This will be quick, I promise." I thrust the photograph under his nose. "Do you recognize this man? Has he been here recently?"

His impatience revealed itself in how he bounced on his toes in his hurry to be off. I didn't wish to cause any difficulties for him, and hoped the image, relatively clear for its age, would strike an immediate memory.

Thomas frowned in concentration. "Isn't that your mother beside him? That would make him . . . Brady's father, no? Looks just like Brady."

"Yes, that's right. The man I'm interested in looks very much like Brady's father, except he would be much older now. In his fifties."

Thomas hunched over the photograph for a better look. A fellow waiter came up beside him. "What are you gawking at? We've got guests waiting for their meals."

I asked this newcomer if he recognized Stuart Gale and was given a terse "no" before he continued on. With an apology, Thomas hurried away. Two more waiters breezed past me without a glance. It wasn't until one of them returned, his empty tray at his side, that he paused long enough to consider the image I held under his nose.

"No, I don't think . . . Hold on . . ."

"Do you recognize him?" I asked eagerly. "Only, he would be older, a good three decades older than he appears here."

"He might have been here . . ." He glanced up sharply as Thomas and another of their fellow waiters returned. His attention on the photograph waned.

"Could it have been the day before yesterday?" I prodded, remembering that Ethan had covered a luncheon here then. The timing would match up with when the victim was discovered at Spouting Rock.

"No, before that." He watched Thomas and the other young man enter the main pantry. "I really have to get back to work."

I swallowed a groan of disappointment. "Might I speak with you when you're done for the day? Your name is . . . ?"

"It's Francis. I should have time in about an hour, although there's a party coming in right about then, golfers, not that they intend to play today. They're coming to plan a tournament, and if I'm asked to help out with them, well, you know, a fellow has to make a living."

"I'll make it worth your while."

He nodded and was gone. With a sigh, I wondered what Nanny and Katie and I would have to go without the rest of that week in order to make my few minutes with Francis worth his while.

I spoke to a few more of the staff, receiving little more than a perfunctory, "Hmm, could be. Not sure. We see so many people here, and he's not a regular, is he?" Or, "If you could tell me the gentleman's name, Miss Cross, I could check the golfing registry. I'm not supposed to, mind you, but . . ."

At the sound of ladies' chatter bouncing along the corridor, I hurried back to the main part of the building. The luncheon had ended, and Miss Clemson strolled out of the dining room with a young woman at either side of her. They were laughing, appearing carefree and at ease. I loathed to intrude, and yet I did just that, especially since I didn't see Mrs. Clemson among them. Another opportunity to speak with her daughter alone might not arise.

"Excuse me, Miss Clemson? I'm Emma Cross with the Newport *Messenger*. I wonder if I might have a brief word."

She was a petite girl, not at all like her tall parents. In fact, I saw little of them in her heavy features, which, though not unattractive, didn't concur with the latest notions of fashionable beauty. Her skin was olive in complexion, her eyes were dark, and her nose hooked ever so slightly above a bit of an overbite. Yet the overall effect was endearing, and left one with an impression of quiet sincerity and genuine amiability.

"Me? Whatever would you wish to speak with me about, Miss . . . ah . . . Cross, did you say?" Her reply brought to mind August Pendleton's reaction last night when I'd made a similar request.

Her two companions giggled and ran their gazes up and down my length. One whispered in Miss Clemson's ear, something that earned the friend a quick frown, though not an ill-tempered one. More of a censorious *Now, now, be nice* sort of gesture. Miss Clemson detached herself from the others and bid them go on ahead without her. The rest of the diners, ladies in bright day dresses and high coifs topped by outrageously large, ornamented hats, streamed around us. I entertained a fledgling hope that I might be lucky enough to also encounter the beautiful Kay Pendleton, but to no avail.

"What is this about?" Thea Clemson squinted as if to bring me into focus.

"I'm following up on last night's Harvest Festival at Crossways."

"I didn't attend." She raised a hand to indicate the women making their way out the front door. "Many of them were there, however. You should speak with some of them."

"Actually . . . I'm glad to see you're recovered from your ailment last night."

"Oh?" She seemed puzzled for a moment. Then her lips compressed and an eyebrow went up. "Yes, my temporary illness. That was Mama's invention. I was perfectly fine and horribly disappointed to miss the fête." She scowled, then looked wistful. "Was it wonderful? I hear Mrs. Fish hid treasures all over the house for people to find. But Mama said Prince Otto never arrived. Such a shame for the Fishes and their guests. I'd have liked to see him again. He and I know each other."

While her disclosure revealed nothing shocking, something in the way she made it gave me pause. It also occurred to me Thea Clemson could have no idea what had happened to the prince last night, or she would not have spoken as she had. I certainly didn't want to be the one to tell her, but I did wish to hear more, especially if she could shed light on her mother's relief when a chimpanzee took Prince Otto's place. Somberly, I asked, "Are you and the prince very well acquainted?"

"Well, no. Not extremely well." She seemed to take no notice of my suddenly serious demeanor. "We met ages ago when my parents and I were visiting friends in Vienna. In those days he was a rather slight, toady-looking boy." She laughed daintily. "But while he remains compact in size, the years have improved him greatly. I so would have enjoyed meeting him again." She let loose a sigh. "I can't understand why Mama was so opposed to my going. And it was the season's last significant celebration, too. Soon we'll all board our steamers and sail away from Newport for another year."

I caught the distinct impression she wished to say more, wished to further air her dissatisfaction in having been left out of last night's amusements. "I suppose there was a very good reason for it," I prompted, wondering if that reason had anything to do with the prince's impending demise. "Did your mother say *why* she didn't wish you to attend?"

"Mama says the Fishes tend to move in fast circles, especially *Mrs.* Fish. That she's uncouth and not at all refined. But that didn't stop most of Newport from being there last night, did it? It certainly didn't stop my parents." She pouted. "Mama is always trying to protect me, I suppose."

"Protect you?" My interest was piqued, and I waited for her to say more. Perhaps, after all, their reluctance concerning the prince had nothing to do with his unhappy fate. Perhaps, like Mamie Fish, they simply didn't want their daughter to move an entire ocean away from them.

She sent a sideways glance along the now empty corridor, except for the waiters bustling back and forth as they cleared away the luncheon dishes. From outside came the high-spirited voices of the ladies boarding their carriages. "It's no great secret, is it, that my father doesn't hail from polite society, that he made his way in by the sweat of his brow. I'm not the least bit ashamed of him, but I suppose Mama is afraid his background will tarnish my reputation, or some such nonsense."

"She let you attend other parties this season, didn't she?"

"Yes, but perhaps she feared Mamie Fish might discuss Father's background openly, just for spite. I can think of no other reason for her locking me up last night. It would serve her right if I went to visit Mrs. Fish on my way home from here. Even after her late night, she must be up by now. Do you think she'd enjoy an afternoon visit, Miss Cross?" She said this with a teasing glint that told me she really had no intention of calling at Crossways. "Or," she added in a more serious tone, "I'll call at the Ocean House and let Otto know I'd be most happy to see him before we all leave Newport."

Oh dear. I could hardly let her drive away seeking out an old friend who would not be there to greet her. It struck me as odd that this sheltered young debutante knew where the prince had been staying. Where had she come by this information? Not from her parents, surely. For now, however, I let it pass in favor of a more serious concern. "Miss Clemson, there is something you should know."

She must have heard the ominous note in my voice, for she blinked and squinted at me again. "Yes?"

"I don't relish being the one to tell you, but all of Newport will have heard by the end of today. Prince Otto . . . well . . . I'm sorry to tell you he died last night. On the grounds of Crossways. The Fishes are quite distraught about it."

She gasped and pressed a manicured hand to her lips. "My goodness. Otto . . ." She backed away from me, retreating until the wall behind her brought her to a halt. Her eyes grew large and moist. "How?"

"I'd prefer not go into the details, especially since not everything is known at this point."

"It's not possible." She shook her head over and over, as if the truth simply would not or could not sink in. "I cannot believe it. Surely there has been some mistake."

I assured her there hadn't been. "Had you any contact with him since he arrived in the country?"

Trembling all over, she shook her head. "No. Of course I didn't. Why would I have?"

I wondered at the vehemence of her denial. "Did your parents?"

"No, they wouldn't have..." Suddenly, her eyes narrowed—not squinting as if she needed spectacles, but a gaze fraught with speculation. "Are you investigating, Miss Cross? Is *that* what this is about?" Her mouth fell open, then snapped closed indignantly. "I've heard about you, and I know what you do here in town, assisting the police and all. Are you trying to suggest my parents had something to do with..."

"I'm merely trying to uncover the facts, Miss Clemson."

"Well, the facts have nothing to do with me or my parents. I have nothing more to say to you. Good day, Miss Cross." She scurried away.

I was about to leave the golf club when I remembered my appointment with the waiter, Francis. It wouldn't be for a little while yet. I bemoaned today's weather with its resulting lack of golfers, as I might have positioned myself strategically between the course and the clubhouse and waited for opportunities to interview some of them. Then again, Francis had said a group of golfers were meeting here today; perhaps I might be able to inquire among them after all. I seated myself in the lobby, meanwhile, to wait until the appointed time to speak with Francis.

My thoughts returned to my conversation with Miss Clemson. I deserved her curt dismissal and regretted the direction in which the conversation had gone. After all, I had come here to try to learn something about the Spouting Rock victim, not Prince Otto's death. I was supposed to leave that to Jesse and his fellow policemen, who would receive whatever resources they needed to conduct a thorough investigation. In the past, Jesse's hands had sometimes been tied by politics and bureaucracy in the interests of protecting wealthy men from inconvenient details being brought to light. Such would not be the case this time. A member of European royalty had been brutally murdered on American soil. The authorities needed answers, quickly, to avoid an international crisis.

When one thought about it, it seemed unlikely the two deaths were related. If a member of the prince's staff had gone missing, wouldn't the police have been notified immediately? Still, two deaths within two days, by similar means.

Another thought struck me, stiffening me in my chair. Could the Spouting Rock victim's death be linked, not to Prince Otto's, but to the murders connected to Ochre Court three weeks ago? Those had involved a nefarious network of thugs and cutthroats from New York City that had found its way onto our island. I thought of what Thea Clemson had said about her father. A self-made man, his fortune earned by the sweat of his brow. I had encountered just such men three weeks ago, the type who balked at little when it came to obtaining what they wanted. Her parents had wished to protect her—from what, really?

Neily's wife, Grace Wilson, also hailed from new money. Her father, of dubious origins, had begun amassing his fortune as a blockade runner during the Civil War. Many considered him a profiteer, yet after an initial hesitation society had opened its doors to the family. Even Mrs. Astor had, after some persuasion, deigned to accept her daughter's choice to marry Orme Wilson. Only my relatives, Alice and

Cornelius Vanderbilt, had dug in and refused to accept Grace as their daughter-in-law, causing a rift in the family that left Neily cut off and Uncle Cornelius incapacitated.

Surely, Thea Clemson's inheritance, if not her personal attributes, would entice some young man and his family despite her father's perceived shortcomings. Besides, didn't her mother's early New York Dutch heritage more than make up for Mr. Clemson's new money? And as for Mrs. Fish purposely embarrassing the family—again, I doubted this very much. Blunt and sharp-spoken, yes. But deliberately cruel to a young person? I couldn't imagine it.

This tale of wishing to protect Thea simply didn't ring true, not for the reason she stated.

Then what? What had set the Harvest Festival apart from every other ball and soiree in Newport this summer? One thing, and one thing only: Prince Otto. I could only conclude Mr. and Mrs. Clemson had some reason to prevent their daughter from seeing him. Did Thea, like Katherine Pendleton, have a history with the prince, more than she had claimed? Somehow, it seemed unlikely the ingenuous Thea Clemson had ever engaged in a dalliance with anyone, much less a European prince.

The chime of a clock reminded me it was time to seek out Francis. I found him once again near the pantries, lounging against a wall. He saw me and straightened, and asked me to follow him through the service rooms to the delivery yard out back. As we walked, I slid the picture of Stuart Gale from my handbag.

Francis barely glanced at it this time. "I remember him," he said. "But not from here. I didn't want to talk about it before, not in front of the others. Not even Tom."

"He didn't play golf here?"

"No, he didn't." Francis compressed his lips and eyed my handbag in a suggestive manner. I knew what he wanted.

"Here." I reached back into the bag and pulled out a few coins. Before I handed them over, I said, simply, "Tell me."

"It was at the Narragansett."

I did a bit of a double take. "The tavern down on Long Wharf? That's a rough place."

He nodded impatiently. "Which is why I didn't want to talk about it in front of the others."

"You should take care, patronizing places like that."

"I don't patronize the place, Miss Cross. I work there when I'm not working here. But if anyone here found out—"

"I won't tell anyone," I assured him. "Although you're taking quite a chance, aren't you? Why, anyone might venture in and recognize you."

"Not someone from here. Believe me, these are two separate worlds." His jaw hardened with a defiance I didn't challenge. If he needed the extra work and was willing to risk being let go from his employment at the golf club, it was his business.

"Please tell me about him—about this man. Had you seen him previously?"

"No, only the one time. I think he'd just arrived in Newport. Came in already staggering drunk and proceeded to get drunker."

"Did you talk to him?"

"Only to ask him what he was drinking. Rum. But he talked—or rather argued—with a few of the regulars. Was making claims of having been to Europe and back."

"Interesting that you say it like that: claims. Did you have any reason to doubt him?"

"It's none of my business whether he was lying or not, but the way he was boasting, it all sounded like a load of hogwash."

"Did you notice how he was dressed? When he was found—"

"Found? What do you mean?"

Unlike with Thea, I felt no need to prevaricate with Francis. "This man was found dead at Spouting Rock the day before yesterday."

Francis backed up a step, his face becoming shuttered. I feared I'd made a mistake, that he would refuse to utter another word. "Dead, you say? How?"

"That's what the police would like to find out."

He gripped the front of his short jacket. "I hope you don't think I . . ."

"No, Francis. I'm only interested in trying to find out who this man was. Any clues would be helpful. You say he argued with some of the regulars. Did any of those arguments turn violent?"

He hesitated. "It was just words, mostly. Boasting and cussing and insults and the like. Nothing I don't hear every time I work there."

I thought about the body lying on the rocks, the dampened clothing, the blanched skin. "How did he look to you? Like a gentleman?"

He gave a snort. "Like a gentleman who'd been through the ringer, maybe."

"As though he'd been in a fight?"

"No, not a fight. Despite his fine clothes, he seemed ragged, somehow. As though he'd been on a weeklong bender."

The answer didn't surprise me. It certainly seemed in keeping with what I knew about Stuart Gale's proclivities. "Did he sound American?"

He took a moment to consider this. "Mostly, but it's hard to be sure. He sounded either like he was from some other country, but had spent a lot of time here, or like an American who'd spent a lot of time abroad. It was mostly little things that gave it away. The way he said his *R*s, the stretch of his vowels. Not completely foreign, but not completely American either."

I didn't doubt his assessment. Newport became an international city during the summer months. Anyone who spent time among society would have a good grasp of accents and dialects.

"Did you hear his name, Francis?"

Again, he shook his head. "No one seemed to call him by name that I noticed. Oh, wait a minute. There was one fellow, a boatman who comes in often—maybe you know him—Angus?"

"Angus MacPhearson?" My surprise couldn't have been greater. "Did Angus know this man?"

"He seemed to. Called him by a name. Gale. Only, the man got angry and said, 'That's not my name,' and when Angus insisted it was, he laid Angus out on the floor."

Chapter 8

However much I had wished to backtrack to town after speaking with Francis, the day had grown late and I hadn't wanted to tax Maestro with another long trek. Angus MacPhearson would still be in Newport come morning—or, rather, afternoon. I had never known the gruff boatman to show his face before noon.

Stopping, then, at the *Messenger*'s offices the next morning, I discovered Ethan Merriman in the newsroom, his pony cart having been repaired. All four of our newsboys had reported to work, and the press was up and running. It seemed our luck had turned for the better after all.

Ethan, however, sat at his desk with his head in his palm as Jacob thudded away at the typewriter. I knocked on the open door and stepped inside. "Why looking so glum, Ethan?"

"Good morning, Miss Cross. Just wishing I hadn't missed the story at Crossways, of all the rotten luck. Jacob here was telling me all about it, said you gave him the byline for the article."

"That's right. But Ethan, you're our society columnist," I

reminded him. "Jacob would have taken over the story any-way once the crime had been committed."

"Society reporters have been known to overstep their bounds," Jacob murmured without looking up or slowing the pace of his fingers on the typewriter keys.

Had he deliberately tried to bait me? I pretended not to hear the caustic comment and continued to address Ethan. "You've seemed happy in your position here. Has that changed?"

He gave a half shrug and lowered his hand to the desktop. "I suppose not. I do enjoy society events. I love reporting on who's who and what they ate and wore." Whether he willed it or not, a smile spread across his face, but then faded. "It's just that . . . is it important?"

Had I not been studying him I might have missed the slight turn of his head, the flick of his gaze in Jacob's general direction. Hmm. I suspected Jacob had been denigrating Ethan's work for the *Messenger*, putting misgivings in his head. If we had the space, I'd have moved them to separate offices, but as cramped as we were, Ethan would have to learn to ignore the censure of others.

"It *is* important, Ethan," I replied truthfully. I myself had chafed at being relegated to the society pages at the *Observer* and the *Herald*—I had wanted more—but I had never doubted the significance of those pages to the success of a newspaper or the enjoyment of its readers. "With its ex-cesses and its blindness to the plight of ordinary people, po-lite society isn't perfect. We are all well aware of that. Yet there is something about their exploits the rest of us find up-lifting, that gives us hope."

"Yes," he said, brightening. "Makes us feel there is some-thing more than everyday drudgery, even if we only experi-ence it secondhand. Like . . . looking at flowers. They don't do us much good, but they make us happy all the same, don't they?"

"That's it exactly, Ethan. And your enthusiasm shines in every column you write." I spared a cold glance for Jacob. "Don't ever doubt that."

Happier now, Ethan opened his calendar book, where the final few events of the season populated the remaining days of August. I left them and headed into the back rooms. The rumble of the press permeated the walls and sent vibrations across the floorboards. The last run of the morning edition was just about finished, and our four newsies would soon begin hawking them on the streets and delivering them to our subscribers on their bicycles. I came to the sturdy table where twine-bundled stacks of newspapers sat waiting. As Dan Carter and his assistants brought the last stacks to be bundled, he bade me good morning and handed me a paper.

"Right from the press, Miss Cross."

Indeed, the aroma of fresh ink wafted to my nose. I thanked him and brought the paper to my desk in the front office. There I scanned the front page. A vague trepidation creeped over me. I turned the page and continued scanning. Turned more pages, searching . . . but not finding what I sought.

On my feet in an instant, I crushed the paper between my hands and hurried down the narrow corridor to the newsroom. I didn't bother knocking to announce my presence, but both men had heard me coming.

"Where is it?" I blurted, glaring at Jacob. "Where is the Crossways article?"

His hands stilled on the typewriter. "What?"

I thrust the newspaper out in front of me and gave it a violent shake. "The Crossways article. It's not here. Jacob, you were supposed to have a short version in yesterday's afternoon extra and a more in-depth article in this morning's edition. Why isn't it here?"

He stared blankly back. "I . . . don't know. Are you certain?"

"Of course I'm certain." A weight sank heavily in my stomach. "I just went over every inch of every page."

"But I wrote them both up and left them for the typesetters. It was there, along with every other article for the edition. I swear it."

"Jacob, it's not here." The newspaper collapsed between my hands. "And by the time we put it in later today, every other paper in town will have run the story. Tell me the extra went out yesterday." Before he replied, I had whirled around and headed for the press room, where I asked the same question of Dan Carter.

"I didn't see an extra for yesterday," Dan said dismally.

Jacob and Ethan had followed me, and now Jacob said heatedly, "I put it in the box for John." He spoke of our head typesetter, John Davies. "John, come in here." When the man appeared in the doorway, Jacob pointed an accusing finger at him. "Did you check for extras yesterday afternoon, like you're supposed to?"

"Of course I did. There was nothing there."

My heart sank to my toes. "We were to have the lead on this. And now . . ."

Now the *Messenger* could boast no advantage in reporting the facts of the case. We could not claim our information had come firsthand, but rather would be believed to have been gathered as the other newspapers in town scrambled to gather their information about the case—by attempting to track down witnesses and waiting for the police to release what they had learned so far.

Perhaps I shouldn't have taken it personally, but I did. I

saw it as a personal failure. Once again I'd let Derrick down; I'd let the *Messenger* and our readers down.

John Davies insisted he worked directly from the articles and advertisements placed in his boxes yesterday afternoon and last night. Each box contained slats that divided the space inside according to where in the paper each article should go. If the Crossways articles had been placed in there, he claimed, he would have laid them out in type. He could not have mislaid or missed seeing Jacob's articles. And if they had been set in type, Dan Carter would not have neglected to run them through the press.

I had three men all maintaining they had done their jobs yesterday and this morning. Could one of them be lying? If so, to what end? I'd had unwell newsies, a malfunctioning press, a reporter with a broken-down cart, and now this. As I've said in the past, coincidences didn't sit well with me. I had begun to believe someone was determined to make me fail.

But I would not. I would not allow this newspaper to fail.

With no answers at hand, I turned to the business matters that needed attending. Before I left later that afternoon, I cautioned everyone to put all distractions aside and pay especially close attention to their work. Many more events like those of the past few days and we would all be without employment. Jacob regarded me sullenly, no doubt believing I held him responsible for the lost articles. If he had asked me point-blank what I believed, I don't know how I would have replied. He had never stated outright that he resented my taking over the *Messenger*, but he had made his sentiments clear enough. But allowing the *Messenger* to fail seemed foolhardy for someone who had already lost a position at another newspaper. I ruled out confronting him at this point. I had no proof, merely an unsettling hunch.

Later, heading along Spring Street, I turned my buggy west at Washington Square and continued on to Long Wharf. I brought two hopes along with me: that I would be able to find Angus MacPhearson and, if I did, that he would be sober.

Angus hailed from Easton's Point, the harborside neighborhood of Colonial houses and hardworking Newporters where Brady and I had grown up. A couple of years older than Brady, Angus had been something of a ringleader among the local boys, devising no small amount of mischief that had often landed my brother in hot water with my parents and sometimes even the law, though typically the police had merely wished to teach the boys a lesson. Since those days, Brady had found his way in life, while Angus lost his after a brief stint in the Navy.

The air teemed with dust from scores of carts, wagons, and carriages—including my own—and billowed around me to coat my eyes, skin, and clothing with grit. The road brought me past rough taverns like the Narragansett, small shops that catered to mariners, warehouses and shipyards, loading docks, railroad tracks, and all manner and size of vessels. Long Wharf bustled all day long and often at night as well. Though numerous other wharves lined Thames Street, Long Wharf, as the largest, was the heart of Newport's fiscal well-being.

I had visited Angus here before, but that had been three years ago, and it occurred to me that I didn't know if he had changed the location of his one-man business of tendering travelers back and forth between anchored vessels and the wharf. Finding him here, amid so much activity, suddenly didn't seem plausible. Perhaps it would be better to wait and seek him at home, a one-room flat at the back of a house on the Point.

But as I eased Maestro into a wide arc to turn my carriage

around, I came face-to-face with Angus. He didn't see me and walked on past, his unkempt russet hair feathering against his shoulders. Leaning over the side of my carriage, I raised my voice above the din to call out his name. He appeared confused at first and searched the busy, dusty thoroughfare. Upon spotting me, he doubled back with a grin that revealed several missing teeth, the rest of them yellowed by drink and tobacco.

"It's not every day a pretty lady comes calling for me. How are you, Emma?" Despite the friendly greeting, I detected something rather cagey in his blue gaze and wondered why that would be. Perhaps he'd just come from imbibing several ales at the Narragansett or other dockside establishment and thought I'd disapprove. The wind stirred his hair back from his face, revealing a purple bruise beside his right eye.

"I'm fine, thank you, Angus. I wonder if I might have a word with you."

His height brought him almost level with me. He wrapped a hand around the top of the carriage wheel and propped a foot on a lower spoke. "No need to be so formal. What is it?"

A train whistle shrieked. "Not here, it's too noisy. Get in."

"Me, in that nice clean carriage? That'd be a mistake and you know it. I'll walk, and you can tell me when you want to stop and talk about whatever's on your mind."

"This feels silly," I called down to him as I guided the buggy and he strode beside me. Gazing down at him, I wondered at the life he led. Ragged clothing, few accomplishments, no family of his own, and a scarcity of money earned literally by the sweat of his back as he rowed travelers and goods back and forth across Newport Harbor. Yet he never seemed to mind his circumstances. I supposed a man with little to lose, whose needs were decidedly few, also had precious few burdens thrust on his shoulders.

Our surroundings quieted considerably as the bustle of the docks faded and Washington Square came into view. I guided Maestro to an unoccupied space along the curbstone. Angus wiped his palm on his trouser leg and handed me down from the carriage.

"What's this about, Emma? Like I said, it's not every day a pretty lady calls my name. Not even a pretty lady I've known all my life."

Did I notice that wariness again, as if he hoped I wouldn't ask him about a particular matter? I believed so, but I hadn't come to beleaguer him about his lifestyle or anything else. Instead, I dug into my handbag and pulled out the picture of Brady's father. "I understand you had a bit of an altercation at the Narragansett Tavern a few nights ago."

His face reddened, clashing with his bright hair. "What of it? You wouldn't understand, Emma. Men—we fight some-times. It's nothing. Doesn't mean a thing. It's just a way to let off some steam."

"I don't care about that, Angus. What you do is your business." I held out the photograph. "Was this the man you fought with?"

He glanced at the image before his gaze darted away. "I don't remember."

"Angus, please. Look at him. Is this him? Except, this was taken years ago. He'd be almost thirty years older now."

"Maybe. It was dark. I'd had a few rounds."

"Angus." His name erupted from my lips, a sharp com-mand to cease his prevaricating.

With a deep sigh he looked again at the photograph, then took it from me. He walked a few paces away, into more di-rect sunlight, stopped, and stared down at it. He shook his head, not in indecision, but in what looked to me like regret. Apology.

I followed him and spoke over his shoulder. "Is this the man?"

He sighed in defeat. "I think so."

"Did you call him Gale? Was that why he struck you?" I reached up and gently touched the bruise beside his eye.

Angus turned suddenly to face me, forcing me a step back. "I'm sorry, Emma. I didn't mean for it to happen. But—" He handed the photograph back to me.

"Didn't mean for what to happen? The fight?"

"No. Brady. I told him. He said he didn't believe me, that I was lying. I've never seen him so mad. And ever since . . . he's been . . . well . . ."

I shook my head in mystification. "He's been what? What did you tell him?"

He held his arms out. "I told him his father had returned. I figured he'd want to know. And he said the damn—uh, that is—he said the strangest thing. And ever since, well, you know Brady."

Foreboding began at my core and radiated through my extremities. "Angus, tell me what Brady said."

"He said his father's died twice now, and that was more than any man can take."

"What did he mean by that?" Yet I already knew. Being faced with the possibility of his father not having died all those years ago, but instead having abandoned his family, had sent Brady tumbling over the edge of his newly respectable life.

"Angus," I whispered, "is Brady drinking again?"

"Well, Brady never did stop drinking, Emma. Not entirely."

I clenched my teeth in a bid for patience. "That's not what I mean. Is he indulging the way he used to?"

While I waited for Angus's answer, I thought of Hannah, who cared for Brady and believed in him. I thought of Uncle

Cornelius, who had also believed in Brady enough to give him a chance, although he had told me his faith had been more for my benefit than my brother's. And I thought of Brady himself, obviously grieving so much he had pulled away from me and everyone else who cared about him.

"I think you should go pay him a visit," Angus finally said. He avoided my gaze.

I knew then it was bad.

Chapter 9

⚜

From Long Wharf I made the short journey through the Point to Walnut Street, and the house Brady and I had grown up in, a blue clapboard Colonial that had been divided into apartments, one on each of its two main floors, and a third, much smaller one tucked beneath the eaves. Unlike the sprawling properties of Bellevue Avenue, the houses here were small and neat, close together, and abutted the narrow sidewalks. These had once been the town houses of merchants and seafarers who populated Newport in previous centuries. Many had been Quakers who had fled the intolerances of other parts of New England. They had settled here and thrived.

The neighborhood lay quiet at that time of day, with the children at school, men at work, and wives busy in their kitchens or laundry yards. Traveling along Third Street, I could taste the spicy tang of the bay waters and hear the gulls circling above the moored vessels, hoping to benefit from the scraps often tossed overboard. Our house sat just before the short trestle bridge that spanned the railroad tracks and connected the Point with Farewell Street. As a child, I would listen for the trains passing by, always hoping one might blow its whistle. As for carriages rumbling over the trestles, we grew so accustomed to the sound we barely heard it.

Until two years ago, my parents had continued to own the house despite having moved to Paris, but a shortage of ready cash had forced them to sell. Imagine my shock when I discovered the buyer to be none other than Derrick Andrews. I had reacted with anger at first, accusing him of secretly purchasing my beloved childhood home out from under me. I claimed I would have bought the property myself if I had only known my parents had put it up for sale.

But I hadn't been honest with myself. I would not have been able to raise the cash without appealing to my Vanderbilt relatives, and that was something I'd have been loath to do. At any rate, Derrick had taken over the second-floor apartment after the original tenant had moved out. The first floor was rented by an elderly woman, and the attic apartment remained Brady's as it had been for several years, except now he paid Derrick rent for the privilege of living there. Brady had insisted.

My gaze drifted back to the second floor. With a pang I regarded the closed windows and the drawn curtains that shielded the empty rooms from my view. Derrick had left Newport three weeks ago to return to Providence, leaving behind not only a vacant apartment, but a vacancy in my heart that would not be filled until his return.

Steeling myself, I pulled the lever that rang Brady's bell upstairs. He neither came down to the door nor poked his head out the window to see who had come calling. I rang again, and again received no reply. Glancing up, I saw his windows were open, the curtains swaying gently. For a better view I stepped back until I stood in the street, and could have sworn I saw movement in his parlor window.

"Brady, I see you," I called out, still not quite sure whether I had or not. "Brady?"

I achieved no results and stood, my hands on my hips, contemplating what to do. I truly didn't need my brother to let me in, for when Derrick bought the house he had neglected to retrieve the key I had kept in my possession since I lived there with my family years ago. I sighed in frustration, but knew I had no right barging in on my brother. I supposed I had to trust that when Brady was ready to speak with me, he'd seek me out.

Reluctantly, then, I returned to town and decided to stop by the police station. I found Jesse at his desk. When he saw me enter, he eagerly waved me over.

"I discovered a few things today," he said in lieu of a greeting. He came around the desk, dragged a spare chair closer, and bade me sit. "I'm glad you've come by. Tell me again about Katherine Pendleton."

His haste in bringing up the subject left me at something of a loss. He realized it, too, for he flashed a rueful grin. "Tell me about what you observed at the Harvest Festival. You said Miss Pendleton declared her intention of appearing as though she were having a perfectly fine time when the prince arrived."

"Yes. She told her brother she intended to be dancing when Prince Otto got there. Beneath her very lovely façade, however, I saw a good deal of bitterness."

"There is a reason for that." Jesse leaned back in his chair looking rather pleased with himself. "She and the prince were formerly engaged."

My mouth opened in my surprise. "Are you sure?"

He nodded, still smiling a bit. "Not only that, but he jilted her, and then didn't have the common decency to take the blame for their failed liaison."

"You don't say." It was neither a question nor a statement

of disbelief, but a further expression of my astonishment. When Uncle William and my aunt Alva shocked society with their divorce three years ago, Uncle William had allowed rumors to circulate that he had been dallying with another woman. Never mind that Aunt Alva married Oliver Belmont before another year had passed. Men simply took the blame in such matters; it was the gentlemanly thing to do, and any man worth the spittle that shined his shoes ensured his wife emerged from the scandal of a divorce with some small portion of her reputation intact.

"Do you know why he jilted her?"

"That's rather less clear at this point. But it certainly gives her a motive for murdering the prince."

"I see you've taken to heart my suggestion that the killer could be a woman."

"I don't like to think it, but under the circumstances, it's entirely possible. But if not Miss Pendleton, then perhaps her brother. He might have wanted revenge against the prince on his sister's behalf."

"Perhaps. But you said you've discovered a few things. What else?"

"Ah, yes. The prince wasn't only here to mingle with society. He's a major investor in numerous American companies, large ones, and he'd come to collect on some outstanding debts."

"Good heavens, Jesse, that expands the possible suspects to just about every member of the Four Hundred."

"Yes, well, there are a few specific members who were also at the Fishes' Harvest Festival. I don't know for certain who Otto meant to pressure into paying their debts, but I do know he was invested in Clemson Steel."

This rendered me momentarily speechless.

"You told me Isabel Clemson seemed relieved when the chimp showed up in Otto's place," he reminded me.

"Judging from her expression, I'd say yes. Her husband being in debt to the prince could certainly be counted as a motive, depending on the amount involved." I thought back to what I'd witnessed as the chimpanzee entered Crossways's entrance hall. A doubt crept into my mind. "Would she have allowed herself to appear relieved at the sight of the chimpanzee if she already knew Prince Otto lay face down outside in the garden? No, Mrs. Fish's joke genuinely seemed to take her by surprise."

"A good point," Jesse conceded.

"Of course, this doesn't discount her husband, does it," I mused aloud. "And another thing. I learned the Clemsons' excuse for their daughter not attending the festival wasn't true. I ran into Thea Clemson yesterday, and she told me outright that her so-called illness was a fiction invented by her mother. She believed her parents were protecting her from Mrs. Fish's tendency to blurt out unpalatable truths about people."

"What unpalatable truth is there about the Clemsons?" His eyebrows rose in speculation. "That her parents are in debt?"

"Actually, she claimed it was her father's impoverished origins and his climb up the social ladder."

"A climb assisted by Prince Otto's money?"

"Quite possibly."

"And perhaps Mrs. Clemson's relief was because her husband had successfully dispatched the prince."

A little chill traveled up my back. "Are you going to question them?"

"In good time. I'd like to poke around a bit more first, see if I can't find out who else was beholden to the prince's largesse."

"You might want to check into the background of his hunting partner, Harry Forge, then." I considered what Jesse had told me so far, all of this information having been gleaned in a short time. "How have you found these things out?"

His grin flashed again, but this time I detected a cynical slant to his lips. "I wired Derrick Andrews yesterday, after you and I talked at Spouting Rock. He's very knowledgeable, Derrick is, and what he doesn't know, he has his methods of discovering."

Our gazes held a moment too long for either of us to deny the knowledge that passed between us. An awkwardness settled over us as we each looked away and back and away again. Jesse fiddled with a pencil on his desk. I cleared my throat.

"Jesse, we need to discuss this."

I half expected him to question what I meant, but he said, "No, we don't."

"But we can't go on—"

"Emma, please. We *can* go on. As the friends we have always been. I understand. At least I think I do. And anyway, I may have discovered someone."

This unexpected news took me aback. "Have you?"

"Perhaps."

"Who?"

"I'd rather not say, at present. Not until, well, you see, she doesn't know herself. Not quite. I mean, we have no understanding. Neither spoken nor unspoken. So . . ."

"You can't tell *me*?"

His eyes beseeched me not to press him, to let it go, to understand that even saying that much had been supremely uncomfortable for him. Still, my mind searched for possibilities, though I found none whom I could point to and say with any authority, *yes, it must be her.*

And I felt . . . a little sad. As though I had lost something. As though in some deep part of me, I still wasn't certain.

"Excuse me, Detective Whyte?"

The voice from behind me snapped me out of my thoughts. A hand came into view, the arm clothed in the sleeve of a police uniform. Between thumb and forefinger an envelope extended toward Jesse. "This just came for you from the coroner, sir."

Jesse half stood as he reached for the note. "Thanks, Connell." He sat down and opened it. I waited patiently, staring at the scarred desktop and wondering what young woman had managed to capture Jesse's interest. Was she from Newport? Someone I knew? Someone I would approve of? Did I have any right to approve or disapprove?

Surely not, and yet I couldn't help myself. I wanted Jesse to be happy with a woman who deserved him. Anything less simply wouldn't do. With a start I realized my sentiments were those of a possessive, protective sister. At least, I hoped they were.

Suddenly, Jesse's eyebrows darted upward.

"What is it?"

He appeared to reread the message, then slapped it onto his deck. "Cocaine, of all things. Do you remember I mentioned a snuff box was found on his person? Seems there was no ordinary tobacco inside. It's off the record, though."

"Why off the record?"

Jesse quirked his mouth as he replied, "Because the Spouting Rock victim is no longer a priority, remember? All our efforts are to go toward solving the prince's murder."

"Ah, yes. How could I forget," I said dryly. I nodded toward the note, lying face up on Jesse's desk. "Is the coroner certain about the findings?"

"As certain as he can be. The man knows his business, surely."

"I've read about cocaine. It used to be considered a useful medication, especially in fighting melancholy. But nowadays even Sigmund Freud advises that doctors no longer prescribe it. Apparently, it can have adverse side effects."

Jesse nodded as I spoke, as if none of what I said came as a surprise. He said, "What makes cocaine attractive to some people is its ability to fill a person with energy. But yes, some of the effects can be harmful. Even deadly if too much is taken at once."

"Energy," I repeated. The word struck a chord in me. I contemplated its meaning. Someone filled with energy moved quickly, often flitted from task to task. "Do you remember when I told you what Harry Forge, the prince's hunting companion, said about Otto being an impatient hunter?" Jesse nodded, a frown of interest forming on his brow. "Could the use of cocaine make a man behave impatiently?"

"I suppose it could, yes."

I felt a burst of energy myself, of eagerness, in having perhaps discovered a link between Otto and the Spouting Rock victim. "You've searched the prince's rooms, I assume?"

"Of course. We conducted a thorough search. As well as turning up nothing that could help find his killer, there was no cocaine found there." Jesse stopped abruptly. "No one would have thought twice about a snuff box."

"Did you inquire about who might have visited the prince there?"

"We did talk to a couple of the desk clerks, who remembered no one with the prince. There is another clerk, though, who might know something, but it appears he left Newport for a couple of days. We'll follow up with him as soon as he's back in town."

I nodded, thinking. "What about the prince himself? Has the coroner performed an autopsy?"

Jesse's stony silence told me what I didn't wish to hear.

"Why ever not?" I demanded, then softened my tone. "You just said the police want to find the prince's murderer. Wouldn't an autopsy assist in that goal?"

"Chief Rogers doesn't think so. The manner of death was obvious—stabbing."

"Yes, but—"

"This is royalty we're dealing with. The chief and those he answers to are afraid Otto's family will consider an autopsy desecrating the body. And then everyone could lose their jobs."

"That's ridiculous."

"So is royalty, when you think about it."

My instincts urged me to turn back toward the Point when I left the police station, but I ignored the impulse. As I had already determined, when Brady wished to see me, he would let me know.

Besides, Jesse and I had decided on a plan of action. He had agreed only reluctantly and after some persuasion on my part, but he could not deny the logic in my visiting Harry Forge. Not only could I revisit the topic of the prince's shortcomings as a hunter and perhaps determine a reason, but I could also further the notion of a link between the two victims if Mr. Forge recognized the Spouting Rock victim from the wedding photograph.

I made a detour along the way and stopped at the Western Union office in Washington Square. It had occurred to me that if the Spouting Rock victim was indeed Stuart Gale, and if Stuart Gale had somehow contrived to feign his death years ago, then someone on the yacht with him at the time had to have helped him. Hoping my mother might remember who sailed with her husband that day, I sent a telegram to my parents at their Paris home, on the hilltop arrondissement of Montmartre to the north of the city. It might be days or even weeks before I heard back, however, since my parents often traveled around the country. As an artist, my father went where his work took him, and my mother accompanied him as his assistant.

That done, I next needed to learn where Mr. Forge was staying, as I didn't believe he owned a house in Newport. It would take time, but I would have to drive out to Crossways and simply ask Mrs. Fish if she knew. I assumed she did, as she had sent the man an invitation to her Harvest Festival.

Providence was with me that day. I had decided to take Bellevue Avenue out of town, and as I drove past the Casino, a familiar sight greeted me: a crest featuring a pair of entwined, scrolling *F*s, emblazoned on a fine victoria carriage. I parked my buggy and approached the footman standing at attention at the rear of the posh vehicle.

"Excuse me, I believe this is Mrs. Fish's carriage, isn't it?"

The man's gaze swept me up and down. I could discern by the slight heft of his upper lip that I had not passed muster. And no wonder, as my attire clearly identified me as no one who inhabited the cottages down the avenue.

"I attended the Fishes' Harvest Festival in a journalistic capacity, as a representative of the Newport *Messenger*." This earned me an easing of his facial muscles. "One of her guests, a Mr. Harry Forge, agreed to an interview, but I'm afraid I've forgotten his address."

Now his attitude eased into boredom. "And I may help you how?"

"You and the driver here must have delivered the Harvest Festival invitations. I thought—that is, I hope—you remember where Mr. Forge lives." I raised my intonation slightly in question and assumed my most encouraging *please help me* expression.

The man flicked a condescending glance over my shoulder. "As it is, I do happen to remember that particular invitation. The swell lives up that way." He pointed. "A street up from the Redwood Library."

"Catherine Street?"

"That's it. Green house. Has a front porch and a mansard roof." He didn't remember the number, but his description would suffice. I thanked him and went on my way.

The green house with the mansard roof was large and lovely in the New England way, with its freshly painted mix of clapboard and fishtail shingles, gleaming white gingerbread trim, and a wide bay window overlooking the street. But it was certainly not ostentatious in the way of Bellevue Avenue's cottages. This didn't surprise me. As a bachelor, Harry Forge would not be expected to entertain more than his gentlemen friends; he had no need of a large dining room, drawing room, or ballroom.

I hesitated on the sidewalk two houses down where I had parked my buggy. Perhaps I should have brought Katie with me. My maid often accompanied me in situations people would consider compromising, such as calling on a bachelor at his home. Never mind that it was the middle of the day; this would potentially raise more than a few eyebrows, especially among my Vanderbilt relatives.

Then again, I had already destroyed the better part of my reputation a year ago, when I'd dared to venture up the steps of that most hallowed of men's clubs, the Newport Reading Room, and knock at the door. A house similar to this, situated not far away on Bellevue Avenue, it was a place women went out of their way to avoid, to the extent of crossing the street to walk on the other side rather than endure the taunts of the men smoking cigars on the porch or sipping brandy before the open, front-facing windows. The Reading Room was male-only territory, a hard and fast rule, and a woman broke that rule at her own peril. To my knowledge, no woman ever had.

No one, that is, until I dared to do so on that summer's

day. I'd had good reason. A murder had occurred at Chateau sur Mer, and I had pressing questions to ask James Bennett, who had decided to avoid me by hiding out at the Reading Room. I'd gotten my answers, along with a curt dismissal from my position at the Newport *Observer*, culminating in my spending the next year pursuing my journalism career in New York. The fact that I was once more living in Newport spoke volumes about how *that* endeavor turned out.

So then, what had I to lose now in merely visiting a man in the middle of the afternoon in his home, with at least a servant or two on hand? Thus assured, I trekked along the remaining portion of sidewalk and climbed the front steps to the covered porch. I'd contemplated walking around to the service entrance, but I had a hunch that a man like Mr. Forge would appreciate my gumption and be more agreeable to speaking with me than if I played a meeker role.

I raised the knocker and let it fall not once, but twice. Decisively. Moments later a middle-aged man in a morning coat peered out at me with the usual disapproving scrutiny.

"May I help you?"

"I'm here to see Mr. Forge, please."

"Is he expecting you?"

"No." Here I prepared myself to speak a bit of a lie. "But I believe he'll wish to hear what I have to say."

The butler sniffed in that way only butlers can manage, with the ability to undo a lifetime's worth of confidence. "I'm afraid Mr. Forge is not receiving. If you would leave your card, I would be happy to convey it to him."

A voice rained down on us from an open window somewhere above the porch roof. "Never mind, Osgood. Show Miss Cross in."

Osgood looked nonplussed for all of a fraction of a moment before opening the door all the way. With little more than a grunt, he showed me into the small receiving parlor overlooking the front porch and bade me wait for Mr. Forge. I hadn't long to anticipate the meeting, as footsteps soon thudded down the stairs.

Harry Forge was still buttoning his coat as he came into the parlor. His golden hair was freshly pomaded, his chin newly made smooth. He paused just inside the threshold, made eye contact with me, and let out a laugh. This struck me as exceedingly odd, considering his friend, Prince Otto, had recently died, and under macabre circumstances.

"Why, Miss Cross. I was correct, it *is* Miss Cross, isn't it? Oh, but of course it is. Lady journalist, new owner of one of this town's fledgling little newspapers."

"I'm not the owner, merely the editor-in-chief. And it's small, to be sure, but not fledgling," I replied, coming to my feet. "The *Messenger* has been in existence for more than a decade. It's only now coming into its own as a major force of information in this city." I extended my gloved hand.

Mr. Forge laughed again as he encased my hand in a firm grasp, truly seeming to find enjoyment in my pronouncement. "Quick to the defense of one's holdings. I like that in a man—and in a woman. But come. This is hardly a room where one can be comfortable." Without another word he released me, turned on his heel, and strode off across the hall. He led me into a larger room furnished with overstuffed chairs, a sofa, and several footstools. I briefly wondered if, like at the royal courts of old, my lowly rank would require that I perch on one of the stools to better gaze up at my superior.

But no, Harry Forge gestured to a comfortable-looking overstuffed chair upholstered in rich brocade and, after ringing a bell on the wall beside the fireplace, sat in the matching one beside mine. When he spoke again, his voice rang with pleasure that bordered on delight. "What *can* I do for you, Miss Cross?"

I wondered at his joviality, as if he had no idea what had been discovered at Crossways. "Sir, are you aware of the prince's fate?"

"Oh, dear." Here he sobered. Finally. "Indeed. Terrible thing. I suppose you're reporting on it."

"The *Messenger* is, yes."

"Well, I'm glad you're not here representing the police, or I'd have to assume I fell into the category of suspect." His laugh emerged once again, this time tempered, but only slightly.

"Not at all. But I suppose it's only fair I tell you that I do, upon occasion, assist the police in gathering information. My unique situation puts me in a singular position to do so."

"Really? Then why don't all journalists work with the police?" Before I could answer, his lips formed a silent *O*. "Right. You're a Vanderbilt. Or sort of."

"Yes, well. It does help that I'm both a local here in town and well versed in who is who among the Four Hundred."

"Indeed." He crossed one leg over the other and folded his hands on his knee. "And what is it you wish to know?"

"I came because of something you said about the prince the other night. About his hunting skills." He tilted his head, his attention riveted on me. I almost had the impression he was trying to make me uncomfortable. I had far thicker skin than that, however. "You intimated that while he was an excellent shot, he was an impatient hunter."

"My own words, thrown back at me. I should remember to guard my tongue around lady reporters."

I gave him a nod to concede his point. "Can you elaborate on what you meant?"

At that moment, the door opened and the butler wheeled in a tea cart. As he started to pour, I turned to Mr. Forge. "Thank you, but none for me. I don't intend to keep you long."

"Nonsense." The butler had stopped pouring and glanced at his employer. Mr. Forge gestured for him to continue.

"Really, I . . ."

"I insist, Miss Cross."

We waited in silence until the servant handed us our cups, set a tray of crustless sandwiches on the table between us, and made a dignified exit. I took an obliging sip of tea but didn't reach for a sandwich. Mr. Forge devoured one before turning to me.

"Now, what were we saying? Oh, yes. Otto's hunting habits." He sighed, finished chewing, and washed down his last bite with a gulp of tea. "I meant that Otto often rushed to fire when he should have waited and properly framed his shot. True enough, oftentimes he hit his mark, but only because the prince was, essentially, a marksman. At other times, his haste lost him the prize."

"Was he that way in other aspects of his life?"

"I'm sorry?" He lifted the teapot from the cart and leaned to refill my cup. I tried to demur, but he wasn't having it. I decided it would behoove me to humor him if it kept him talking.

"Did you find him generally hasty?" I asked after a sip. "Reckless? Tempestuous?"

"My dear Miss Cross, however illegitimate Otto may have been, he grew up a frequent visitor to his uncle's palaces and spent much time with his father's family. Drink up." He raised his teacup in a toast and waited until I did likewise, then brought my cup obediently to my lips. "He was royal in nearly every sense of the word, and royal young men can be . . . shall we say . . . *undisciplined* at times."

"So the answer to my question is yes."

He frowned at me, though not unkindly. "All right, yes. But what does this have to do with his death?"

"Have you ever known the prince to use drugs? I mean

other than those prescribed by his physician." I ventured another sip while I waited for him to answer.

"Drugs?" He uncrossed his legs, only to cross them again in the other direction. "Are we speaking of laudanum?"

"Most assuredly not. Quite the opposite, from what I understand. Cocaine."

His eyebrows rose sharply. "No, I can't say that I ever did."

"Are you sure? You never saw him imbibe any elixirs in general?" I wondered if Mr. Forge might have imbibed himself, but I refrained from asking. I wasn't here to pry into his habits.

"Nothing that wasn't contained in a hip flask and shared round as men will do on hunting excursions, Miss Cross. Really, what are you getting at? That Otto was involved with some kind of drug-crazed ruffians who came after him? That's hardly likely."

"No, Mr. Forge. I'm attempting to detect if there is a link between Prince Otto and another man who was found murdered in a similar way—that is, stabbed through the heart—two nights earlier, near Bailey's Beach."

"Yes . . . I believe I read about that. Body found beside that geyser formation."

"Spouting Rock, yes. Do you know if the prince traveled to America with a companion?"

He shrugged, yet something in his expression revealed a less than nonchalant response to my question. "One would assume so. It would be expected of him."

"Are you familiar with the prince's traveling companions, Mr. Forge?"

"Some of them," was his succinct answer. He'd certainly lost much of his garrulousness, not to mention his humor. He again gulped his tea.

I set my own aside and opened my reticule. Drawing out

the photograph of my mother and Stuart Gale, I held it out to him. "Do you recognize this man?"

He took the photograph between his first and middle fingers. Holding it at arm's length, he studied it for some moments, during which I believed I detected the faintest color tinging his complexion.

"Mr. Forge?"

He scowled and then just as quickly sighed. "He may be . . . vaguely familiar." Reaching over, he attempted to pass the image back to me. I didn't cooperate by taking it, forcing him to continue holding it. He glanced at it again. "You must understand, there are so many individuals in the prince's retinue. I don't know them all. I might have seen this man in passing, but he never accompanied us on a hunt. That much I can assure you." He leaned toward me and practically shoved the photograph back into my hand. "Any other questions, Miss Cross?"

"Yes, one. Do you have any idea who might have diverted the prince from Crossways that night? And who might have lured him around the side of the house to the garden, where he was found?"

As I had done, he set his cup and saucer on the table between us with an air of resignation that puzzled me. Yet it only lasted a moment, for his jovial attitude returned as he regarded me. "Well, I don't like to say . . ." He paused, leaving me to wonder if he *would* say or not. As my anticipation stretched, he continued. "But when it comes to Otto, you might perhaps wish to speak with Miss Clemson."

"Thea?" I asked, rather stupidly as he could mean no one else. But his reply, or rather his demeanor, befuddled me, for he seemed to be implying much more than his words conveyed. "I've spoken to Miss Clemson, actually. She did admit to wishing she had attended the Harvest Festival. She said she has known Otto since they were children."

"Children, eh? Is that all she said on the matter?" His eyebrow quirked, further mystifying me.

Absently, I raised my teacup and sipped generously. My heart began to race even as my thoughts did. Was he hinting that it was Thea Clemson who had kept the prince away from Crossways that night? "Mr. Forge, I wish you'd simply say what you mean."

"I mean that you should speak—again—with Thea."

Chapter 10

Harry Forge seemed intent on detaining me in his home. When I stood to take my leave, he attempted to persuade me to resume my seat and have another cup of tea. I politely refused, but he somehow managed to detour me into the library, which was in quite the opposite direction of the front door, and which I tolerated only because I enjoy an extensive collection of books as much as the next person. But when I found the way back into the hall blocked by Mr. Forge's immobile figure, I realized with a start what he must be about.

I was none too happy about it and through with being polite. "Mr. Forge, if you'll excuse me, I must be on my way. I'll thank you to please step aside."

"Come now, Miss Cross. We both know why you came."

"Indeed. I came to ask you some questions, and now that I have my answers my task here is finished."

He chuckled, a deep, throaty sound that raised the hairs at my nape. "And I suppose you mean to tell me you weren't flirting with me at Crossways."

"Flir—goodness, no. Obviously, there has been a misunderstanding." My adamant desire to leave squared my shoulders, stiffened my jaw, and flared my nose. "Mr. Forge, this is neither amusing nor gentlemanly. Now, step aside or I'll be forced to call out for your man."

"Osgood? He's not likely to come to your rescue. A big coward, Osgood is." He said this as though it were all a hearty joke, and once again my nape bristled. I feared the pounding beneath my stays would become audible, and that Mr. Forge would detect the trembling in my fingertips.

"Mr. Forge, this behavior will avail you nothing. And I'll have you know, I am not incapable of defending myself if necessary." Indeed, a few years ago Derrick Andrews had shown me some combative moves all but guaranteed to discourage an attacker. I practiced them periodically and had used them effectively from time to time.

To my great frustration, Mr. Forge threw back his head and roared with laughter. Alarm rushed through me like a molten river, and I'm sure my countenance turned the very color of the crimson curtains shielding the books from an overabundance of sunlight. And yet, he did step aside, holding out his arm like a genteel courtier inviting me to precede him into the hall. I wasted no time in doing so, while glancing over my shoulder to make sure he didn't come up behind me with inappropriate intentions.

He didn't, but merely followed as I hastened my steps to the front door. There, rather than tossing open the door and escaping, I calmly turned back to him. I didn't wish to leave him with the impression that he had frightened or upset me—even if he had, a little. "Thank you for speaking with me, Mr. Forge. Good day to you, sir."

He reached past me to open the door, his forearm brushing my shoulder. I resisted the urge to flinch, and then marched out, into the fresh air and sunshine and a tremulous sense of relief.

How completely strange. I had gotten no sense of his having any interest in me at Crossways. And why should he have? I'd been there in a professional capacity, and as such had dressed simply and worn my hair in a plain, everyday style. Next to the bejeweled, silk-clad debutantes, I had paled considerably, which, of course, was the idea. Though I occasionally attended Newport balls in formal attire, I did so only when the occasion brought me to one of my relatives' homes, or in the case of a ball at Beechwood, when I went as the guest of Grace Wilson, who had gifted me with one of her beautiful Worth gowns.

My pulse continued its frantic jig as I made my way toward my buggy, and I drew deep draughts into my lungs in an attempt to regain my poise. I didn't understand why Mr. Forge's boorish behavior affected me so considerably. His were not the first unseemly advances I'd had to fend off. Normally, I did so without missing a step. Yet he had left me nonplussed and . . . shaky.

I came to a sudden halt, arrested by a sight that greeted me through the open back of my buggy. Above the seat back, a pair of shoulders hovered, clad in green, crowned by the lower half of a dark coif and the trailing ends of a few green hat feathers, the rest of which were obscured by the roof of the carriage. I hurried along.

"Mrs. Fish? What are you doing here?" Sitting in *my* carriage, I might have added, although I didn't. A quick glimpse farther down the street revealed her victoria waiting near the corner, her driver and footman at the ready.

"Oh, hello, Miss Cross." She patted the seat beside her. "Do get in." When I hesitated, she frowned. "What? Are you not happy to see me?"

* * *

"I'm . . . merely a bit confused," I stammered as I climbed up into my buggy and took up the reins. "Is there something I can do for you?"

"Indeed there is, my dear." She pointed straight ahead. "Drive."

Obediently, though with no less confusion, I released the brake and clucked Maestro to a walk. As we turned onto Bellevue, the victoria pulled out behind us but kept several carriage lengths away. Perhaps being followed caused me to flap the reins over Maestro's back, for I suddenly noticed him picking up his pace. I pulled back to encourage him to slow down.

"Now then," Mamie Fish said briskly, thumping her reticule against her skirts for emphasis. "What have you learned about the prince's death? And leave nothing out."

"Oh, uh, haven't you spoken with the police? I believe Detective Whyte is the person who would have the answers to your questions." I experienced a pang of guilt in attempting to brush Mrs. Fish and her inquisitiveness off on Jesse, yet really, I didn't think he would thank me for revealing police business to her.

"The coppers will tell me nothing, except not to worry, they'll find their man."

"I'm sure they have matters well in hand."

"Don't patronize me, my dear." She made an adjustment to her hat, realigning one of the feathers that the wind had blown against her cheek. "The police do not have matters well in hand or they'd have made an arrest by now."

"These things take time, ma'am."

She studied me a long moment, during which I kept my gaze on the road and pretended not to notice. I caught myself fidgeting with the reins again. "Your aunt Alva Belmont has told me all about you, Miss Cross. Everything. So don't go pretending you haven't any experience in this sort of thing, or that you don't have a nose for sniffing out a criminal once he sets foot on this island. Besides, this particular criminal also set foot on my property and practically ruined my Harvest Festival. Do you have the slightest idea what that could do to my reputation as a hostess? In my book, I'm entitled to know what is going on."

I briefly considered leaping from the buggy, but that would have left Maestro alone with Mrs. Fish and I had no idea whether she could manage a horse or not. So I let go a breath and accepted my fate. "So far, the police still have very little to go on, and that's the truth. However, there was another murder only two nights before your festival, and not far away, at Spouting Rock. The police are attempting to discover if there is any relation between the two."

"The police, bah. *You're* attempting to link them, aren't you? Who was the other victim?"

"The police haven't identified him yet."

She chuckled when I again mentioned the police, obviously to let me know I wasn't fooling her one bit. "Why did you visit Harry just now?"

"Mrs. Fish, really—" She folded her arms and turned a set countenance in my direction. It appeared I would not escape her inquiries until I'd satisfied her with a few answers. "Mr. Forge knew the prince. I'd hoped he might be able to connect the two men. You see, I have a picture that very much resembles the first victim. I hoped Mr. Forge would recognize him." I decided not to mention the cocaine.

"And did he?"

"No, he did not, although he did say the man might be somewhat familiar."

"Humph." Mrs. Fish faced front again. "Sounds like Harry. Never gave anyone a straight answer in his life. You shouldn't have gone there alone, you know. Harry'll take a liberty or two if he thinks he can get away with it."

"I can take care of myself," I replied truthfully. Yet why did my pulse continue to flutter and my fingers tighten around the reins until my knuckles whitened? I noticed, too, that I kept clenching my jaws until they ached.

"Well, that's fortunate for you. What did you learn from him? And where are we going now? More investigating?"

"Mrs. Fish, I hardly think it would be a good idea . . ." I left off, considering. She turned back to me with her eyebrows raised in expectation and, I judged, in preparation to argue with me. But she remained silent and waited.

I had already alienated Thea Clemson with my questions. It was quite likely she had left word with the house staff not to admit me should I come calling. But if Mamie Fish accompanied me on that call, why, the Clemsons wouldn't dare refuse to see *her*. They might be acquainted with European royalty, but here in America we had our own version of royalty, and Mamie Fish, along with Aunt Alva, Tessie Oelrichs, and Caroline Astor, ruled over society with iron fists clad in silk.

"Mrs. Fish," I said, brightening considerably, "*we* are going to visit the Clemsons. I have a few questions to ask them, and I could use your assistance."

"That's the spirit, girl. You and I—we'll make a dandy team. Tell that horse of yours to step it up."

When the footman opened the Clemsons' door to us, his pursed lips resembled nothing so much as a piece of shriveled fruit. Obviously, Thea had warned her parents about me, and they in turn had warned their servants. I had been correct to bring Mamie Fish along.

After admitting us, he strode off to see if the Clemsons were "at home," leaving us standing in the front hall, beautifully yet inhospitably tiled in Italian marble.

"Not even the decency to offer us a seat," Mrs. Fish

griped under her breath. She eyed a gilded bench along one wall whose thin velvet cushion hardly promised to soften one's wait. I didn't much mind; I felt too keyed up to sit. "What on earth *did* you say to Thea?"

"It wasn't so much what I said, as her believing I had outright accused her parents of being involved in the prince's death."

"You don't say?" Mrs. Fish looked exuberant. "I like you, Miss Cross. You and I are going to get along splendidly."

The footman returned and asked us to follow him. He led us up the marble staircase, carpeted in red to match the bench cushion, and directly across the landing into a sun-drenched room that overlooked the Cliff Walk and the sea. Mr. Clemson stood beside a wing chair in which his wife sat rigidly upright, her pointy chin high and her eyes filled with dignified outrage.

"Miss Cross. Mamie," she greeted us calmly enough, though beneath her poise she plainly seethed, evident in the two pink spots of color that glowed beneath the pallor of her cheekbones. "To what do we owe the pleasure?"

"It's hardly a pleasure to be called upon unexpectedly, Isabel, so you needn't pretend otherwise." Mrs. Fish's skirts swayed as she sauntered toward them, leaving me alone near the wide double doorway. She might feel perfectly at home in this room and with these people, but I remained acutely ill at ease given the tension crackling through the air.

After shaking Mr. Clemson's hand and leaning down to kiss Mrs. Clemson's cheek, Mrs. Fish made herself comfortable in an armchair and waved me over. "We're here on important business. Thank you for seeing us."

Eugene Clemson, still standing guard beside his wife, cleared his throat. "And what business would that be, Mamie?"

"Oh, don't be such a stiff old rod, Eugene. We're not going to bite you. Sit yourself down, do."

Beneath his muttonchop sideburns and beard, the man turned nearly purple. His lips thrust forward, I believed in preparation of ordering us from the house, but he surprised me by exchanging a glance with his wife and then taking the armchair beside Mrs. Fish's. That left me standing with no invitation to sit forthcoming, which suited me fine. On the ride over, I had familiarized Mrs. Fish with what I had learned so far concerning Thea and the prince, not to mention her mother's little white lie concerning Thea's health the night of the Harvest Festival. For now, I was happy to allow Mrs. Fish to conduct the interview while I observed, for the couple would be less likely to balk at her questions even if they happened to take offense.

Mrs. Fish angled a glance at me, and I nodded subtly. She turned back to Mrs. Clemson. "Why did Thea stay home the night of the Harvest Festival? And don't go telling me that nonsense about her being ill. We know very well she was just fine."

"Oh, well I . . . Really, Mamie, it's rather rude of you to put us on the spot this way, don't you think?" Mrs. Clemson appealed to her husband, who nodded his agreement and gave a little snort.

"Of course I'm putting you on the spot." Mrs. Fish huffed. "That's the point. Good heavens, a man is dead, and there are certain little details that don't add up. Now, why did Thea stay home?"

"Surely you're not implying Thea had anything to do with . . ." Mr. Clemson broke off while his wife glared at me. I didn't much mind that, as long as Mrs. Fish kept them talking. Although, now that I thought of it, Mrs. Fish had neglected to ask them one vital question, the very one that should have begun the conversation.

I rectified that oversight. "Is your daughter at home?"

"Thea might not have been ill the night of the festival,"

Mrs. Clemson said forcefully, "but she is certainly indisposed today. If you do not believe me, well, too bad for you, then." She clutched a lace-edged handkerchief, with which she dabbed at her eyes.

"So we can take that to mean Thea's home." Mrs. Fish raised her chin triumphantly.

"Yes, she's home." Mr. Clemson suddenly vacated his chair and strode to a corner of the room inhabited by a glass-fronted cabinet. He swung the door open and retrieved a bottle that held a richly dark liquid. Brandy or cognac, I guessed. After twisting the stopper free, he poured a liberal measure into one of the crystal snifters that graced the top of the cabinet. Without offering any of the rest of us a similar libation, he returned to his seat. I studied him a moment, taking in the leathery skin that made him look older than he must have been. The skin of a former working man, I realized, remembering what Thea had told me about his origins.

After sampling his drink, he said, "If you must know, we kept Thea home because your parties can become a bit out of hand, Mamie. Thea is a young girl, still innocent. She doesn't need her reputation tarnished because of some silly mistake performed out of excessively high spirits, brought on by one of your ridiculous antics."

Mrs. Fish whooped with laughter. "Is that so?"

Mrs. Clemson slid to the edge of her chair and leaned forward, her eye ablaze. "Yes, that is so."

"Well, I never."

Seeing the conversation sliding wildly off course, I decided on a new tack. Opening my handbag, I slid out the photograph of my mother and Stuart Gale. "Mr. and Mrs. Clemson, I'd like you to take a look at this picture. The man in it would be nearly thirty years older now, but he would still bear a striking resemblance. Is he at all familiar to you?"

I ventured closer, first holding the photograph beneath

Mr. Clemson's nose. He shook his head readily enough. "No, never seen him before in my life."

"Are you certain?"

"Certain as I can be. A man meets countless individuals in his lifetime. Surely you can't expect me to remember them all. But as far as I know, I've never met this one."

I moved to Mrs. Clemson. "Ma'am, do you recognize him?"

"I . . ." She hesitated, her lips parting and her eyes widening. Then she gave her head a little shake. "No, I don't know him. For a moment, I-I thought perhaps . . . No."

"You're sure, ma'am?"

"Of course she's sure," her husband interjected. "She just said as much, didn't she?"

Mrs. Fish waved a dismissive hand at him. "Don't get your knickers in a knot, Eugene. So then, you kept Thea home because you don't like her to have any fun."

"I never said that." Mrs. Clemson huffed.

Mrs. Fish shrugged. "And it had nothing at all to do with your not wanting her to see Prince Otto?"

Here the husband and wife exchanged wary glances. Mrs. Clemson tilted her chin. "Not at all."

"Mr. and Mrs. Clemson," I said, "I take it you've known the prince a rather long time. Since he and your daughter were children. Isn't that right?"

It was Mr. Clemson's turn to shrug. "What of it? People in our situation travel, we mingle with others in society. A great many of our children have known one another since they were very young."

"Yes, and Thea and Otto *barely* knew each other." Mrs. Clemson balled her handkerchief between her hands. "Why, we could count the number of times they've seen each other on one hand."

"Perhaps we might ask Thea herself," I suggested.

Mrs. Clemson's thin features sparked with alarm. "Certainly not."

"Why not?" Mrs. Fish demanded at the same time I pointed out, "Isn't it better for us to clear up matters here and now, rather than wait for the police to come inquiring?"

The liquid in Mr. Clemson's snifter nearly sloshed over the rim. "Is that a threat?"

"No, I was merely pointing out an eventuality," I said calmly.

Mrs. Clemson came primly to her feet. At a table against the wall she pressed a button. Mere moments later the same footman who had admitted Mrs. Fish and me entered the room. "Please let my daughter know we'd like to see her."

Thea Clemson came in several minutes later. When she spotted me she came to a halt and looked as if she might bolt. Through reddened and swollen eyes she stared daggers at me, then sent a silent appeal to each of her parents in turn. Her mother gestured none-too-happily for her to join us.

"What is this about?" the girl said as she took a seat. "Why is *she* here?"

"She's here with me, Thea," Mrs. Fish said.

"And why are *you* here?"

Both parents flinched slightly at the rudeness of their daughter's question, unaccustomed as they must have been to hearing it, but neither spoke an admonishing word.

"We're here to try to figure out what went on at Crossways during my Harvest Festival, that's what." Mrs. Fish eyed Mr. Clemson's brandy as though she desired one of her own.

"Well, as I've already told Miss Cross, I wasn't there."

"No, my question has to do with what you told me the other day at the golf club."

Her mother blew out a breath. "I knew I shouldn't have let you go to that luncheon."

I continued as if Mrs. Clemson hadn't interrupted. "You

said you knew the prince since you were children, and that you would have enjoyed seeing him at the ball."

Her mother interjected once again. "How many times do I have to tell you not to talk to strangers?"

Thea pretended not to have noticed her mother's comment. "All right, that's true, and it's not exactly a secret. What of it?"

I folded my hands at my waist. "Can you tell us how you became acquainted with the prince?"

"I can answer that," her father said. "My wife knew Otto's mother, Anna von Rothschild, when they were young, long before she and I were married. And before Otto was born, of course. They went to finishing school together. Isn't that right, my dear?"

Mrs. Clemson nodded. Mamie Fish turned to her. "Really, and where was that?"

"Oh, uh . . . a small school in Switzerland."

Mrs. Fish raised an eyebrow in interest. "Which one?"

Mrs. Clemson hesitated, her hand rising to her throat. "It was . . . Chateau de . . . Rougemont."

Mrs. Fish frowned. "Never heard of it. Is it in the town of Rougemont?"

"Just outside. Um, in the mountains. Very lovely."

"At any rate," the woman's husband put in, "we only ever saw the prince because his family often vacationed where we did, and we would see them at events."

Mrs. Fish and I exchanged a glance. We both knew there was much more to the story, but I didn't wish to come out and call Mrs. Clemson a liar. I turned back to Thea. "When did you last see the prince?"

"It was more than a year ago, and very briefly, in Paris," her mother was quick to answer. I hadn't taken my eyes off of Thea, and I watched as her color darkened to pink and then feverish red.

Mrs. Fish noticed, too. She let out a whoop and slapped her knee. "Come on, girl, tell us the truth."

"There is nothing to tell," both parents said as one. Mr. Clemson added, "That will be quite enough."

"Thea, go." Her mother pointed toward the door. Thea, however, made no attempt to rise. She sat with her head down, her lips compressed, her hands folded in her lap. I thought I detected tears gathering on the tips of her lashes.

"Miss Clemson, if there is anything you can tell us that would assist the police in catching the prince's killer," I said, "you would be helping to achieve justice for that young man."

Thea's head rose slowly. "The night he died . . ." she began so softly I strained my ears to hear.

A shudder went through her mother, as if someone had struck the woman violently. Those spots of color in her cheeks had long since faded to gray. "Thea, what are you saying? The night Otto died, *what*?"

Thea didn't look at either of her parents. Her gaze riveted on me and swimming in tears, she whispered, "I was the reason Otto was late to the Harvest Festival."

Chapter 11

Mrs. Clemson leaped to her feet with a mad flounce of her skirts. "Thea, what *can* you mean?"

"He was here, Mama."

"Thea, do not say another word," her father commanded in his baritone.

"Why not?" Thea's tears began to fall, and the words came out as a wail. "Otto's dead, and perhaps it's my fault for keeping him here, for allowing him to come here at all. Perhaps if he'd gone straight to the festival, he'd still be alive." Sobs overcame her and she wept into her hands. Her mother moved to stand before her.

"Thea, what have you done? Thea!" She grasped her daughter's hands and yanked them away from her face. When Thea peered tearfully up at her, Mrs. Clemson leaned in close. "Have you gone and destroyed your future, girl?"

Thea pulled back from her mother's hissing breath. "No. Goodness, no. We did nothing wrong, Mama. We talked, that is all."

"You expect us to believe that?"

"Isabel." Mr. Clemson called his wife's name several times before she appeared to hear him. When she turned away from her daughter, he held out his hand to her. "Please, Isabel, calm yourself. They wouldn't have been the first young people to . . ." He let the thought go unfinished, but Thea blushed furiously and buried her face in her hands once more.

Mrs. Clemson stood over her husband, shaking her head repeatedly. "No, they can't have. You don't understand, Eugene. They must *not* have."

"We didn't." Thea raised her face, her eyes nearly swollen shut from weeping, yes, but also rage, I thought. At that moment, I believed her to be experiencing a hostility toward her mother she had likely never felt before. Had never dreamed of feeling. "We talked, Mama. We discussed the future. And the fact that Otto and I . . ." A trembling sob escaped her. "We wished to marry."

Mrs. Clemson let out a cry that hurt my ears. With her hands pressed to her mouth, her eyes wide with horror, she turned and fled the room. For several long moments silence gripped those of us she left behind. As it had done earlier, my heart pounded inside me, sending my blood on a breakneck course that made the room spin around me. This might certainly explain why Prince Otto broke off his engagement to Katherine Pendleton. I wondered if Miss Pendleton had been aware of the understanding between the prince and Thea. I doubted it.

"Get out."

Through my bemusement came Mr. Clemson's furious directive. More startled than I had ever seen her, Mrs. Fish came immediately to her feet. And yet, I held my ground, which made Mrs. Fish pause and look quizzically at me.

"We aren't quite through here," I said, sounding braver than I felt.

Thea's delicate house shoe thudded against the carpet. "Can't you go away and leave us alone?"

Her father laughed once, grimly. "I suppose you suspect me of killing Otto to protect my daughter. But I tell you, I had no idea the two of them had come to an understanding of any sort. And even if I had, I would not have been opposed to it, even if he *was* born on the wrong side of the sheets. He was accepted by the emperor and that would have been good enough for me."

"Oh, Papa." Thea jumped up and went to her father. She crouched at his feet. "How kind of you to say so." They grasped hands tightly. Despite the touching scene, I couldn't help wondering if Mr. Clemson would have been quite so magnanimous had Otto been born into a less illustrious family—and a less wealthy one. As innocent as his statement seemed, he might have inadvertently admitted to needing the prince's money. And that notion raised a new question.

"Mr. Clemson," I said evenly, "was the prince invested in Clemson Steel? Did you owe him money?"

He took a moment in answering, seeming disinclined to remove his attention from his daughter's mournful countenance. Then he drew a breath between his teeth. "Your answers are yes, and no, in that order. Otto was an investor, surely, as were other members of his family. But I assure you, Miss Cross"—he spoke my name heavily laced with vitriol—"Clemson Steel is sound and in no danger of bankruptcy. I am in no one's debt. If you disbelieve me, I challenge you to check the facts for yourself."

I planned to do just that. No journalist worth his or her weight in ink would fail to verify such a detail. Yet I didn't expect to disprove the man's claim; he spoke with the confidence of someone telling the truth.

"I'm terribly sorry to have barged in on you and upset

you all," I said earnestly. "I took no pleasure in it. But two men have been murdered, and their killer must be found."

Still crouching before her father, Thea twisted around to peek up at me. "Then you don't believe any of us did it?"

"No, Thea, I don't. My questions were less about that than about finding a link between the two men."

"Could have fooled me," her father grumbled.

He had a point. I did come here wondering if any of the Clemsons had reason to resent Prince Otto, and I certainly had discovered a whale of a reason, which could be applied to either the husband or the wife. Yet Mrs. Clemson's shock at Thea's disclosure about her intended marriage had seemed authentic enough, as did Mr. Clemson's acceptance of the prince's eligibility as a potential husband.

What hadn't rung true, however, was Isabel Clemson's denial of having recognized the man in the photograph I showed them.

Mrs. Fish's carriage had not waited for her in the Clemsons' driveway. She must have given a discreet signal when we arrived for the driver and footman to return home. Thus, it seemed it would be up to me to bring her home or allow her to accompany me to my next destination, wherever that would be. I hoped she had had her fill of investigating. I also regretted the loss of my solitary carriage, for being alone would have given me an opportunity to mull over in private everything I had just learned from the Clemsons.

Mrs. Fish accepted my hand when I reached down to help her up. "Did we learn anything useful?" she asked as she settled beside me. "Because I'm not quite sure."

"I'm not quite sure yet, either." I set Maestro to a walk, steering him around the fountain and down the drive. There was nothing for it but to discuss the interview with the woman beside me, but I found myself having trouble concentrating. Inside, I had attended to every detail of our talk with the Clemsons with a clarity that surprised even me. But now, a strange sluggishness settled over me and a dull headache throbbed against my temples. I pressed a hand to my forehead.

"Are you quite all right?" Mrs. Fish examined me with a concerned eye. "You look a bit pale."

"I'm fine, just a little tired." I attempted to shake away my lethargy and turned my thoughts back to the Clemsons. "I tend to believe Mr. Clemson about his finances. I've certainly never heard any rumors about Clemson Steel. Have you?"

"I have not. But some folks are good at hiding such things. What about that little bomb Thea dropped? None of us was prepared for that."

"No, indeed." I fell quiet, and Mrs. Fish nudged me in the ribs with her elbow.

"I can tell you one thing for certain. Isabel was lying about knowing Anna von Rothschild at that finishing school she mentioned. There's no such place."

"Why would she lie about that?"

"Beats me. My guess is she met Otto through some other means she doesn't want us, or perhaps her family, to know about."

I wrinkled my nose in skepticism. "Such as what? Unless . . . perhaps her connection to the prince was through his father's family, not his mother's as she claimed. But why would she lie about that?" I contemplated this as the horse clip-clopped along Bellevue Avenue. A possibility occurred to me. "Could there be some secret between the prince's family and Isabel Clemson, something she doesn't wish known . . . ?"

"Wait one moment there. You're not thinking Isabel did it, are you? Eugene, perhaps, if he saw some threat to his daughter. But Isabel? No." She sounded adamant.

"Are you certain about that? Women aren't immune to murderous tendencies. It's rare, perhaps, but it happens." I had turned to her as I spoke. Now I faced forward again. "Trust me."

I felt her studying my profile. "Humph, that's right. I remember hearing something about a little upstart a couple of years ago. What was her name?"

My jaws clenched. I regretted my words, for I didn't wish to speak of the summer of ninety-five.

Mrs. Fish relaxed against my buggy's tattered leather squabs. "Anyway, I'd say we make a good team, you and I. Don't you think?"

I nodded, but I also suppressed a sigh. I didn't like to admit it, but she was right, at least in this case. "I wouldn't have been able to speak with the Clemsons at all if not for you. So thank you for that, ma'am."

Two open carriages rumbled side by side along Bellevue Avenue in our direction. Three young ladies and what looked like an elderly chaperone occupied one, while two young women and a gentleman sporting a boater and a long-suffering expression rode in the other carriage. Their laughter nearly drowned out the sound of the carriages' wheels as they exchanged high-spirited conversation back and forth. As they were taking up most of the lane, I guided Maestro as far to the right as I could and brought him to a stop.

"What on earth do they think they're doing?" Mrs. Fish looked none-too-pleased.

"Probably going shopping in town," I replied.

"Silly chits." She slid to the edge of the seat and leaned out. "You don't own the road, you know. Instruct your drivers to shove over." She settled back against the seat. "Young people these days." She shook her head. Once the two carriages were well past, she again turned to me. "So, you haven't said. Do you really think Isabel Clemson could have killed the prince?"

"I don't know. The thing of it is, any of your guests could have met the prince outside when he arrived. They might have prearranged a meeting, with the prince perhaps believing the individual had business to discuss. He might not have even known who he was meeting, perhaps believing it to be one person when it was really another. But there were so many guests, and so many of them were in and out of the house all night, that it's next to impossible to know where everyone was at any given moment."

Mrs. Fish took a moment to digest this, her head nodding several times. "Rather the perfect crime, then, wasn't it?"

"In some ways, yes. But at least we know now why Prince Otto was late arriving at Crossways."

"But there was that other murder, too. The one that happened by Spouting Rock. Let me see that photograph of yours."

I took one hand off the reins to hand her my bag. "It's in there."

She slid out the photograph. Leaning to the side, she held it beyond the roof of the buggy, where the sun could fall on it. "Pull over," she murmured.

I did as she said. We were near the south end of Bellevue Avenue, at the rear entrance of Belcourt, where my aunt Alva lived with her second husband of nearly three years, Oliver Belmont. While the other cottages faced out over Bellevue Avenue, Mr. Belmont had positioned his house to face Ledge Road, literally and figuratively turning his back on his neighbors.

The reason for this snub on Oliver Belmont's part made me gasp. "He's connected to the Rothschilds, isn't he?"

"Who's what?" Mrs. Fish was still intently studying the photograph.

"Aunt Alva's husband. Mr. Belmont's father was an agent for the Rothschilds' banking empire, wasn't he?"

She looked up in mild surprise. "Yes, I suppose he was. August Belmont came to this country to further their interests and ended up staying and building a fortune of his own. Why?"

I knew also that, because of their Jewish heritage, the Belmont family hadn't always been welcomed by the members of the Four Hundred, especially the old guard. But rather than being chased off, the son, Oliver, had issued the silent but resolute rebuff of turning away from his peers, not to mention the mockery of placing his service entrance in full view of their elegant front driveways.

I craned my neck to see into the property. Were Mr. Belmont and Aunt Alva at home? "It suddenly occurs to me that Mr. Belmont might have known Prince Otto, or at least be familiar with the family."

"What are you waiting for, then? Drive on in. We've already made one call unannounced. Another one won't kill us, and I daresay it won't kill your aunt Alva either."

"Would you like me to drive around to the front?" I asked in deference to her position in society.

"No need, my dear. No need." She pointed the way up the drive, to the archway that led into the courtyard. The tall gates were open, and as I drew Maestro to a stop outside them, a groom came running out to assist us. He greeted us with a puzzled expression.

"Are you ladies here to see the Mister and Missus?" He frowned in uncertainty as he took in our attire. While he might have mistaken me for some kind of servant who *should* arrive at the rear entrance, Mrs. Fish's fashionable carriage outfit left no question as to her social status.

"We are indeed, my boy. If you'll take care of the carriage, we'll see ourselves in. Don't worry, we know the way." With that, Mrs. Fish grasped the groom's hand and stepped down from the buggy. The groom handed me down next. I saw by a change in his expression that he suddenly recognized me, as I did him.

"Oh, it's Miss Cross, isn't it?"

"Yes, and you are . . . Lucas, I believe."

"Nice of you to remember, miss. Ladies, after you." Recovered from his bemusement at having to receive guests—for this was not typically a groom's job—he gestured for us to precede him into the courtyard.

We entered the slate-paved space enclosed on all four sides—the house proper along the north wall, the kitchen wing along the west, and the stables and carriage house to the south. The fourth, east-facing wall held the gated entryway we had just passed through. Rather like a medieval home, I'd always thought, embraced within safety. To further the fairy-tale imagery, the bottom story was clothed in brick, while the stories above were trimmed in Norman-style woodwork with diamond-paned windows. A massive mansard roof, ornamented by several chimneys and copper-domed dormer windows, crowned the structure. Along the second story of the living quarters, a shady loggia looked down upon us, but as far as I could see into its cool shadows, the chaise longues and comfortable easy chairs were empty.

Mrs. Fish led the way inside, into what had been, originally, the carriage house. When Mr. Belmont had Richard Morris Hunt design his bachelor digs, he had insisted on nearly the entire first floor being dedicated to his beloved horses. He had spared no expense for them, either, as the large open room we entered had been tiled in a mosaic pattern in beautiful rose marble. There were no horses or carriages in sight today, however. When my aunt Alva moved in as the lady of the house, she had insisted on a few changes, and now this room, spacious and sparsely furnished, served as a banquet hall for their sumptuous parties.

A wide doorway at the far end led into the main portion of the downstairs, and we passed into the Grand Hall, decorated in dramatic Renaissance style with blood-red damask lining the walls. Here Mrs. Fish came to a halt and called out.

"Ollie, Alva, are you at home?"

Quiet footsteps directly behind me made me gasp and whirl about. Only a few feet away stood a dark-skinned man, tall and lean, wearing exotic silk livery. His eyes were the shape and color of almonds and held a quiet wisdom, while his smooth features concealed his age, which might have been thirty or fifty for all I could tell. "Ah, Miss Cross. Good afternoon."

"Good afternoon, Azor." I gestured to my companion. "Do you know Mrs. Fish?"

"Indeed, ma'am." He offered her a deferential bow.

"We're sorry to arrive unannounced," I went on, conscious of having broken several strict rules by barging in this way. "But we do have a very good reason. Are Mr. and Mrs. Belmont at home and receiving?"

"Follow me, if you please."

He led us up the grand staircase to the upper hall, where we waited as he went to the open doorway of the dining room. I couldn't help peeking in, as the design never ceased to fascinate me. Round in shape, the creamy white room featured floor-to-ceiling mirrored doors all around, which reflected the electric lighting installed by Thomas Edison himself along a recess in the ceiling. Today, three of those doors had been opened to the outside, but not as doors typically open. These slid upward to reveal floor-to-ceiling windows, which in turn had been opened to let in the temperate summer breeze. It was a feat of engineering that even The Breakers and Marble House couldn't boast. But then, as for the latter, Aunt Alva lived here at Belcourt now in the summer, and Marble House stood empty, its treasures buried under linen sheets.

As I gazed into the dining room, I spied Aunt Alva, Oliver Belmont, and another gentleman sitting around the table. I recognized that last individual immediately from the elegance of his long limbs and the sharpness of his aquiline nose. Without a word, Azor caught their attention and gave another of his smooth bows. Only then did he speak. "Mrs. Fish and Miss Cross to see you."

"Emma is here? And Mamie, too?" Aunt Alva came immediately to her feet and swept to the doorway. "Emma, Mamie, do come in. You're just in time for a bit of lunch. Whatever are you two doing prowling about Newport together?"

I felt a moment's hesitation, as Mrs. Fish and I hadn't taken the time to agree upon what we would and would not reveal during our visit. It was one thing to question Mr. Belmont about Prince Otto and his retinue, quite another to discuss who might be considered suspects in his death or reveal what we had learned from the Clemsons. I had no desire to fuel rumors about anyone. Could I trust the garrulous Mamie Fish to be discreet? It appeared I needn't have worried.

"What's for lunch?" that woman asked, and marched her way to an empty chair at the table.

"We're very sorry to interrupt your meal," I said, but Aunt Alva waved my apologies away. She kissed my cheeks and drew me to the table. The gentlemen had stood, but Aunt Alva urged us all into our respective seats.

"We're not being formal today. I'll just ring for another couple of place settings." She pressed a button beside the door. "Emma, I believe you know our houseguest, Mr. Eldridge."

Though we had never formally met, I was indeed familiar with Charles Eldridge. What was more, he had attended the Harvest Festival and had danced with Katherine Pendleton, which had earned him a share of August Pendleton's disregard. Did Mr. Eldridge, I wondered, genuinely care for Miss Pendleton? And how would he feel if he learned her interest in dancing with him that night had been merely for the sake of proving she no longer carried a torch for Prince Otto?

A pair of footmen soon arrived with plates and silverware, and Mrs. Fish and I helped ourselves to the various dishes laid out along the center of the table. The food restored me, and whatever odd malady had struck me in the carriage passed. After a few minutes of trading the typical pleasantries about the weather and the remaining events that would round off the summer season, Aunt Alva got to the point.

"So, tell me, what has forged this unholy alliance between you two?" She barely paused before her expression became animated. "Of course. Prince Otto's death. We all know Emma can't resist a puzzling crime. But you, Mamie?"

"Aunt Alva, since Prince Otto was found at Crossways, naturally Mrs. Fish—"

"You don't need to speak on my behalf, my dear." Mrs. Fish set down her fork. "Someone had the gall to toss a shadow over Stuyvie's and my first summer in our new cottage, and I intend to find out who it was. No one bedevils me and gets away with it."

My fingers tightened around my own fork and I compressed my lips to prevent myself from reminding Mrs. Fish that a man's death was far more important than her reputation as a hostess.

"But what has brought you here today?" Several years his wife's junior, Oliver Belmont was a pleasant if unremarkable-looking man with a clean-shaven face. Their marriage had

spawned a tempest of gossip and controversy, but also grad-
ual changes in how the Four Hundred viewed matrimony.
Mr. Belmont had been a close friend of both Aunt Alva
and her then husband, William Vanderbilt, and had often
accompanied them on voyages abroad on their yacht, the
Alva.

It was during one of those trips that Uncle William supposedly had been unfaithful to Aunt Alva, resulting in their
divorce. But opinions concerning his ungentlemanly behavior quickly changed when, less than a year later, Aunt Alva
and Mr. Belmont married. Then it became all too clear that
perhaps Aunt Alva hadn't been the injured party after all.
For a time, society shunned her, especially other members of
the Vanderbilt family. But little by little over the past couple
of years, she had regained her footing and her popularity as a
hostess, and now only the staunchest members of the Four
Hundred, such as Mrs. Astor, continued to snub her and her
husband.

I was glad Mr. Belmont asked his question, for it gave me
the opportunity I needed. "I am not so much looking to
solve the crime of Prince Otto's death—"

"Maybe *you're* not, but I certainly am," Mrs. Fish interrupted.

"As I am hoping to identify another man," I continued,
"who was found dead near Spouting Rock two days before
the Harvest Festival."

"And how do you think we can help you with that?"
asked Aunt Alva.

"I thought perhaps you and Mr. Belmont knew the prince,
or at least his family. He *was* a Rothschild on his mother's
side."

"Yes, that's very true," Mr. Belmont said, "but my family's
close connection with the Rothschilds ended in my father's

time. Besides, despite the prince's father and uncle acknowledging him, his mother's family did quite the opposite. They ostracized her and had very little to do with Otto."

My shoulders sagged. "Oh. I'd so hoped you might be able to help in this."

"Don't just give up, dearie." Mrs. Fish shook her head as if deeply disappointed in me. "Show them that photograph of yours."

Chapter 12

꧁꧂

Aunt Alva and her husband stood by the windows and pored over the photograph of my mother and Stuart Gale. Occasionally they passed the photo back and forth and made thoughtful little murmurs. Finally Aunt Alva turned back around.

"This is your brother, isn't it?" she asked me.

"No," I said. "That's not Brady."

Aunt Alva gave a harrumph. "Well, he's very familiar."

"Of course he's familiar," Mrs. Fish agreed. "That picture is of Stuart Gale from years ago. Quite a man about town, as I recall. As charming as he was boastful. Not to mention reckless." She shot me a glance. "Got himself killed, didn't he? Or so we all thought."

"Ah, yes." Mr. Belmont let the hand holding the photograph fall to his side. He squinted as if looking into the past. "I remember him. He styled himself Stuart Gale the Third, but no one ever knew if there had been a Stuart Junior." He chuckled. "He was rather like Miss Cross here."

I reacted to the comparison with a start. I didn't believe

I had much in common with a boastful, reckless man. Mr. Belmont apparently noticed my chagrin.

"What I mean is, he seemed equally at home among society *and* Newport residents. Like you, Miss Cross, he belonged to both worlds, so to speak. I raced with him, a time or two."

I nodded. "Yacht races?"

Mr. Belmont nodded. "Horses, too, but yes, yachting. Sometimes on the same vessel, sometimes on opposing ones. He didn't own a yacht of his own."

"No, he wouldn't have been able to afford one," I said. "Do you remember the race that took his life?"

Mr. Belmont exchanged a frown with his wife and shook his head. "I'm afraid I couldn't tell you a thing about it. There have been so many over the years."

"Yes," I said, "but three men went into the water during that race. Surely it must stand out in your mind."

"It's not an unusual occurrence," Mr. Belmont said apologetically. "Why, just two years ago, there was that race Mrs. Astor organized beyond Beechwood. A man went overboard that day, too."

I remembered all too well. Mrs. Astor had arranged the race for the enjoyment of her guests at her season-opening lawn party, and I was there to cover the event for the *Observer.* Foul play had been suspected, and later, the possibility that the death had been faked. The memories of that time had the power to send chills through me, and as I attempted to subdue them, I felt half tempted to let this matter go, as well.

But I could not, and so I persisted. "Stuart Gale might have raced with foreigners that day. With Europeans."

Aunt Alva shrugged. "There are almost always Europeans about, Emma. Unfortunately, races were more informal back then. We didn't have a New York Yacht Club station in Newport where records could be kept. Have you tried writing to your mother? If anyone will remember, it's she."

"I sent a wire earlier today, actually, but I don't know when I might hear back." Or *if*, I silently acknowledged.

"But why all these questions?" Aunt Alva returned to her seat at the table. "Why are you so interested in what happened to someone all those years ago? I understand he was your half brother's father, but still."

"Because the man who was found dead at Spouting Rock looked so remarkably like Stuart Gale, only older, that I'm left to wonder if he really did die all those years ago."

"That's a rather fanciful notion, isn't it?" Aunt Alva sounded as though I'd taken leave of my senses. "People don't just disappear for thirty years and suddenly pop up again."

"Not usually, no," I conceded. "But it could have happened, especially if that person disappeared in order to escape a particularly vexing situation."

"Such as what?" The question came from Charles Eldridge, who thus far had remained fairly quiet, yet who, I believed, had been listening intently. Perhaps he hadn't wished to interfere in what was, essentially, a family matter.

"Such as debts, probably," I replied. Brady's father hadn't been the most responsible individual when it came to finances, and he had left my mother burdened by debt. With my aunt Sadie's help, and, later, my father's, Mother had managed to pay them.

"That being the case," Mr. Belmont said as he, too, resumed his seat at the table, "your real questions are whether this man"—he tapped the photograph—"had been seen recently, and whether he came to Newport with the prince."

"Those are my questions exactly," I said eagerly.

"I'm afraid I don't recognize him from recent times, and while I *had* been acquainted with Otto, I didn't know him well enough to be familiar with members of his retinue." Mr.

Belmont pushed the photograph across the table toward Mr. Eldridge. "Charles, any thoughts?"

The other man bent his head over the image. "I'm afraid not."

Once again, the wind abandoned my sails.

Mrs. Fish changed the subject. "Mr. Eldridge, tell us, have you seen Katherine Pendleton since the Harvest Festival?"

He looked up from his plate, looking startled. "Miss Pendleton?"

Mrs. Fish grinned. "Don't play coy with us, Charlie. We all saw you dancing with the young lady. She's quite a beauty, that one, and she'll bring some lucky fellow a tidy dowry. You could do a lot worse." She turned to me, still grinning. "You did make note of their dancing, didn't you?"

The tips of Mr. Eldridge's ears glowed, yet he didn't appear offended, merely embarrassed at becoming the center of attention. "I took notes about many of the couples who graced the dance floor," I said demurely.

Mr. Eldridge cleared his throat. A small smile curled his lips. "Miss Pendleton is a lovely young woman and I enjoyed dancing with her very much. In fact . . ." He blinked, seeming to fight a grin that threatened to rival Mrs. Fish's. He glanced down at his hand, the fingers long and white and unblemished, the hands of a man of leisure. "I look forward to dancing with her again in the near future."

"She was once engaged to the prince, wasn't she?" Mrs. Fish made this announcement so casually she might have been discussing the weather, yet the rest of us verily squirmed at her bluntness.

"Mamie," murmured Aunt Alva in admonishment. "Be nice."

"What? It's true." She appealed to me. "You knew it, didn't you?"

So much for discretion. "I did come by that information

recently," I admitted. I had no intention of divulging what Miss Pendleton had told her brother about wishing to appear happy and carefree when the prince arrived at Crossways, and that she used Mr. Eldridge to that purpose.

"If I were you, Charles," Mrs. Fish went on, undeterred, "I'd set my cap firmly for Katherine Pendleton and not waste any time. I'm surprised she's still available. The prince was a fool to let a prize like that slip through his fingers. Although . . ." Her eyes twinkled, and I realized she might be about to speak of Thea Clemson.

I acted quickly, and came to my feet. "We've really kept you long enough. Thank you for your help, Aunt Alva, Mr. Belmont."

"Such as it was," the gentleman said. Everyone else stood, and Mrs. Fish and I took our leave.

After bringing Mrs. Fish to Crossways, I spent the next hour at The Breakers, visiting with Uncle Cornelius. The butler, Mr. Mason, directed me to the upper loggia, where I found Uncle Cornelius sitting up in a lounge chair with a light blanket tossed over his legs. Perhaps Aunt Alice had been right about the sea air. His color was good, and he seemed not only alert, but also to possess a bit of his old spark. His secretary sat beside him, and the two men appeared to be going over reports from the New York Central. Despite Cornelius Vanderbilt's incapacity, he insisted on being kept up to the moment on all matters pertaining to the business.

The secretary stood and excused himself at my approach, and went inside carrying a bundle of folders. Uncle Cornelius smiled when he saw me, and lifted a shaky hand to beckon me over. I took the seat his secretary had vacated.

Uncle Cornelius reached for my hand and held it against his chest. "Emma. Good."

Those words translated, I knew, to "Emma, so good of you to come," or "Emma, it's good to see you today," or any number of like sentiments. I swallowed the small lump that grew in my throat.

"I hope I didn't interrupt business matters," I said. "I didn't mean to chase off Mr. Wiles."

He shook his head. "No. Glad." One eyebrow quirked in a familiar, quizzical way. He wished to hear my news of the past days.

Judging murder to be too disquieting a topic—especially if Aunt Alice should happen upon us—I chatted instead about my work at the *Messenger* and went so far as to mention the mishaps. His forehead crinkled with concern, but it was the kind of concern that engaged his mind, rather than unsettling him. Uncle Cornelius had once told me that, had I been a man, he would have employed me at the New York Central. Whereas Aunt Alice had reacted to my taking over the running of the *Messenger* with mild horror, Uncle Cornelius had nodded sagely and met my gaze with a steady one of approval. Now his fingers tightened briefly around my own in a show of support.

After leaving him, I returned home and called in to the *Messenger* to let Jimmy Hawkins know I'd be working the rest of the day from my desk at Gull Manor. He assured me all was well, and I hung up grateful for the office manager who had followed Derrick from Providence to Newport, and then remained when I took over running the paper. I'd feared he might wish to return to Providence and his former position at the *Sun*, owned by the Andrews family. Surely he earned more money there. His remaining in Newport showed the strength of his loyalty to Derrick in wishing to help ensure the success of the *Messenger*, especially when its failure would please Derrick's parents no end. They wanted no reason for their son to return to Newport—or to me.

In the morning, I finished up the work I had begun the night before. There had been several articles to edit, inquiries to write up for potential advertisers, and some letters to be answered from the *Messenger*'s small pool of investors.

Nanny, Katie, and I enjoyed an early lunch together, and then I readied myself for the ride to town. A surprise greeted me on my front drive, not far from where Maestro and my buggy sat waiting for me.

"Where to next?" Mrs. Fish waved gaily to me from the seat of a small, single-horse tilbury carriage. To my astonishment, she had apparently driven herself to Gull Manor. There wasn't a footman in sight. "Who else is on that list of yours?"

My mouth opened but no words came out, just a few sputtered sounds.

"Is something wrong? Have you lost your tongue?" Though she frowned at me from beneath her hat brim, I nonetheless recognized her amusement.

I recovered my voice. "I'm surprised to see you, Mrs. Fish. I'm afraid I need to go to work this afternoon. I do have responsibilities."

"You mean you're giving up?" She had mentioned giving up yesterday, in the same disappointed tone. "Going to let a killer go free?"

"Of course not," I replied, affronted by the very notion. "But as I said, I have other responsibilities that must be seen to first."

"Oh, bah." She flicked a gloved hand. "I'll hire someone to take over for you."

The very idea sent the flat of my hand out, as if I could halt such a plan as a police officer might halt traffic on a busy road. "That won't be necessary, thank you. Besides, the police are investigating Prince Otto's death. As I've said, I'm far more interested in identifying the Spouting Rock victim."

"Yes, yes, Stuart Gale." She acted as though she were dealing with a very young child. "But if the two are connected, as you seem to believe, investigating the one will lead to answers about the other."

"Mrs. Fish . . ." I trailed off, doubting very much that I could win this argument or be rid of the determined woman's "assistance." She had acquired a taste for the hunt and would not be deterred. "All right, then. Whom do you suggest we question next?" I asked her with feigned patience.

"The Pendletons. Either one of them had reason to resent Otto."

I nodded, unable to refute the fact. "Not to mention that, as a banking family, they might have been in the prince's debt. Am I to drive, or you?"

"I rather like being in control of my own buggy." Her eyes twinkled, and I wondered if she had a penchant for speed, and whether I would find myself holding on for dear life. But again, seeing her determination, I doubted I could change her mind.

"I'll just need to go in and ask my maid-of-all-work to unhitch my horse and bring him back to the barn. Will you come in?"

"No, I'll wait here. You go on, but don't be long."

Her answer came as a relief. I didn't relish having members of the Four Hundred inside my comfortable but admittedly shabby home. It suited me fine, but then, I tended not to notice the bare spots, the worn fabrics, or the cracks in the paint. Not only that, but my dining room still lay in shambles after a fire not long ago. No one had been hurt and the structural damage had been minimal, but I was in the process of having woodwork and furnishings replaced. And the sharp scent of smoke had yet to fully dissipate.

Nanny and Katie expressed their relief as well—especially Katie, who had once worked at The Breakers but had been dismissed without a reference for being in the family way. Not that that had been her fault. But surely Katie had no reason to feel comfortable among members of the Four Hundred. Nanny, on the other hand, considered most of them decadent and pompous, utterly at odds with her New England prudence.

Mrs. Fish and I set out and soon arrived at the house the Pendleton siblings were leasing on Ruggles Avenue, on the ocean side of Bellevue Avenue. I hadn't known where they were staying, so once again I had reason to be glad of Mrs. Fish's accompaniment.

Katherine and August Pendleton's father had died a year and a half earlier, and their mother, who hadn't been well ever since, rarely left their Cincinnati home. That left August to escort Katherine in society, which made his behavior at the Harvest Festival all the more puzzling. Why bring his sister to Newport for the summer only to scowl at every man who showed even a passing interest in her?

Perhaps Mrs. Fish and I would find out today. If, that was, we would be received. Once again, we had come calling without prior notice.

"This way, if you please," the middle-aged housekeeper said upon admitting us to the house. She instructed us to wait in a sunny alcove off the front hall, but Mrs. Fish wouldn't hear of it. Instead, she followed the housekeeper, an individual obviously not used to being defied in such a way, into a library off the drawing room. I trotted along behind them.

We came upon Katherine Pendleton, dressed in a summery afternoon gown, sitting at a desk that dominated the room. A pen in hand, she appeared to be poring over an assortment of papers and ledgers. "Has that brother of mine decided to show his face?" she asked without looking up. "If so, it's about time."

"I'm afraid not, Miss Pendleton," the housekeeper replied. Her thin lips pursed in disapproval. "But you do have guests."

Miss Pendleton glanced up and regarded us in surprise. "To what do I owe the . . ." Her gaze settled on me, and she took on a wary look. "What on earth is this?"

"I'm sorry, Miss Pendleton." The housekeeper clutched her hands at her waist. "I asked them to wait in the hall. . . ."

Miss Pendleton waved her away. "Yes, yes. It's all right, Mrs. Jennings. You may go."

The woman scurried away, closing the door behind her.

"You didn't answer my question," Miss Pendleton said coolly. "What on earth *is* this? Why is *she* here?" She meant me, of course.

"What on earth is *that*?" Mrs. Fish countered, and pointed to the jumble of paperwork cluttering the desktop. "Don't tell me you've gone into business for yourself?"

"Don't be ridiculous."

From where I stood, I could make out what looked like columns of numbers and charts depicting percentages or the like. Mrs. Fish's question didn't strike me as ridiculous at all. I craned my neck to see more and even inched forward.

Miss Pendleton noticed my movement. She scooped the disarray into one neat pile, opened a drawer, and stuffed it all inside. For good measure, she produced a key from a pocket in her dress and locked the drawer. "Now then, I suppose I'd be rude if I didn't invite you to sit down. Let's go into the drawing room. May I offer you refreshment?"

Mrs. Fish shook her head. "No, Katherine, that's quite all right. We won't keep you long."

Miss Pendleton led the way into the next room, and without casting me even the briefest glance, bade Mrs. Fish to make herself comfortable on a sofa while Miss Pendleton chose an easy chair opposite her. I stood a moment longer wondering what to do, when Mrs. Fish came to my rescue.

"Miss Cross, do sit here." She patted the cushion beside her. "Katherine, as you know, Miss Cross is a journalist."

"Yes, I am well aware of that." She spoke with derision, no mistake. The night of the Harvest Festival, she had practically dragged her brother away from me as if she feared I might extract some secret information from him. What had she feared he might reveal? "I cannot imagine why you've brought her here."

Mrs. Fish pulled the pin from her hat and removed the concoction of silk, ribbon, and feathers from her carefully arranged hair. "I have good reason. You see, I hired her to do a bit of whitewashing concerning my Harvest Festival. A death on my property is not the thing I wish to be remembered for. Miss Cross will see to it that we leave a much better impression in people's minds."

Mrs. Fish's falsehood took me by surprise, but I schooled my features not to show it. I hadn't expected her to lie so neatly, and believably, too, considering her tendency to view the world with a narrow focus that always held her own needs and desires at its center. Anyone who knew her well would never question that statement.

"And how can I be of help with that?" Miss Pendleton folded her hands in her lap primly and tilted her chin.

"Did you enjoy our little fête? I noticed you dancing with quite an assortment of gentlemen." Mrs. Fish leaned forward eagerly. At the same time, she nudged me and motioned to my handbag. Taking the hint, I reached inside and drew out my notepad and pencil.

"I had a delightful time," Miss Pendleton said, though without much enthusiasm. She shrugged. "The decorations were quite unique. I've never attended a harvest festival that didn't involve real straw, hay, and the like. I much appreciated your silks and, of course, those hidden jewels for the scavenger hunt."

"What did you find?" Mrs. Fish asked, her eyebrows raised in interest. Meanwhile, I took notes on every word Miss Pendleton uttered; at least, I pretended to. My mind had drifted, in actuality, to those papers she had whisked out of our sight. Katherine sought to hide something from us, but why lock the desk drawer? Did she fear Mrs. Fish or I might be so bold as to sneak back into the room and discover her secret?

I confess I longed to do exactly that. The two women had gone on talking, and I realized I'd merely made squiggles on my notepad. I returned my attention to them.

Mrs. Fish made a show of searching the room with her gaze. "Is your brother home? I'd love to have his opinion of the evening."

"No." Miss Pendleton pouted and then let out a long-suffering sigh. "He is not. I tell you, Mrs. Fish, I don't know what's gotten into him lately. Maybe it's what happened at Crossways. He left the house yesterday and hasn't returned, and he's left me terribly at loose ends."

"Oh, you know how men are, especially the young ones." Mrs. Fish laughed. "But I say, it's awfully good of him to act as your escort for the summer. I suppose he wants to marry you off as soon as possible."

I braced for Miss Pendleton to take offense at those words, but instead she gave a quick eye roll and skewed her lips. "One would think so."

Once again I pictured August Pendleton's scowls regarding his sister's dance partners. What brother didn't wish to see his gently born sister comfortably settled?

Mrs. Fish perched at the edge of the sofa and leaned closer still to Miss Pendleton. "Is your brother intent on keeping you all to himself?"

"Auggie is . . . overprotective." The derision in her voice led me to conclude that all was not peace and harmony between brother and sister.

"Ah, I see." Mrs. Fish paused and assumed a tragic air. "You almost married Otto, didn't you? I suppose he hurt you very much, did he?"

Miss Pendleton's complexion turned a harsh shade of pink. "That was a long time ago."

"Was it? It doesn't seem all that long ago. Oh, but poor Otto. Poor, poor Otto." It was Mrs. Fish's turn to let out a sigh. "You must be broken up about his death. Or . . . are you? After all, you probably consider him quite the cad. What *did* he do that ended the engagement?"

Miss Pendleton's chin came up. "I truly fail to see how any of this ancient history can help Miss Cross write an article extolling your virtues as a hostess, Mrs. Fish. Otto and I broke off our engagement by mutual agreement. We decided we simply didn't suit." Miss Pendleton tensed as if about to gain her feet. "Really, if that's all, I have things to do."

Her explanation contradicted what Jesse had learned about the matter, and what I myself had witnessed in Miss Pendleton's behavior at the Harvest Festival, but I couldn't blame her for wishing to save face now.

Did her brother's scowls signify a wish never to see her hurt in like manner again?

Perhaps, but I wasn't convinced. Katherine Pendleton seemed strong and capable of taking care of herself. Surely her brother realized that. No, I was nearly certain there must be some other reason for August Pendleton's disapproval of his sister's dance partners, and now it struck me that perhaps the reason had to do with whatever Miss Pendleton had locked away in her desk.

She obviously didn't care for journalists, or for some reason didn't care for me in particular. But then, a journalist's job was to bring hidden truths to light, and she seemed disinclined to allow that. Since she was unlikely to converse with me, I had to somehow induce Mrs. Fish to ask a pertinent question.

My opportunity came when the two women began discussing other guests at the Harvest Festival. I quickly drew a thick, dark arrow pointing toward the library, and beneath it a scribbled representation of a desk. Leaning toward Mrs. Fish, I angled my notepad so that she could see it, but Miss Pendleton could not. "Is this the name you just mentioned, Mrs. Fish?"

She stared at the page with a perplexed frown, which led me to believe my ruse had failed. Then her expression cleared and she nodded. "That's right," she said in an offhand manner, and turned back to Miss Pendleton. "So, what *were* you doing when we arrived? You simply don't strike me as the studious type and I'm intensely curious."

I suppressed a grin of admiration for Mrs. Fish's skill at putting people on the spot without her motives being obvious.

Miss Pendleton shifted in her chair, compressed her lips, and for an instant looked worried. "Nothing important, really. Just . . . uh . . . planning out my fall activities. Auggie and I will be on Long Island for a month, and then we're due to visit friends in Virginia for a bit, and then it's back to Cincinnati for Christmas."

"Ah, keeping busy. That's good. Young people should keep busy, I always say. Otherwise, they get into trouble. Well, we've taken up enough of your time, my dear. Do give Auggie my best. Miss Cross, come along now." Mrs. Fish got to her feet, set her hat decisively back on her head, and drove her hatpin home with practiced skill. She paused, and addressed me as if a sudden thought had come to her. "Have you got that photograph on you still?"

Of course I did. I took it from my purse and handed it to her. She held it out to Miss Pendleton. "Is this man familiar to you? He's a . . ." Her hesitation was barely perceptible before she continued. "Friend of the prince, and we're trying to track him down to tell him what happened to poor Otto.

Except, this is an old photograph of him. He's quite a bit older now."

Miss Pendleton stood and took the photo. She studied it closely, and that livid color from a few minutes ago spread once more through her face. "I . . . no. I'm sorry. I don't know him."

"Are you sure? You seemed to recognize him just now." Mrs. Fish went to stand beside Miss Pendleton so that she, too, could peruse the picture. "You knew the prince a number of years. Certainly you must remember some of the people who surrounded him."

"Y-yes, now that you mention it, he does seem somewhat familiar. But the prince and I ended our acquaintance nearly two years ago. I wouldn't know where to find this man."

"Can you at least tell us his name?"

"Mr. Stern, I believe. Herr Stern, in German. Or something to that effect. I wouldn't have a clue as to his given name."

"Stern. Hmm." Mrs. Fish took the photograph from her and handed it back to me. Then she and I left. Outside, as we settled into Mrs. Fish's carriage, she turned to me. "Lies. All of it. I don't think she spoke a single word of truth."

Chapter 13

"I fear you're right, ma'am. But we did learn one thing," I said to Mrs. Fish as she guided her horse onto Ruggles Avenue. I had to admit, she maneuvered the carriage with more skill than I would have given her credit for. Then again, Mamie Fish was no ordinary society matron. Even my great-aunt Sadie, who by choice had never married and who had believed in a woman's right to assert herself, would have enjoyed Mrs. Fish's company.

"Both Katherine Pendleton and Isabel Clemson have a history with the prince," I said, "and both recognized the man in the photograph. I know Mrs. Clemson denied it, but she hesitated a moment too long and I saw the recognition in her eyes. I would wager both women know exactly who this man is, and for some reason don't wish to admit it. That in itself is telling. We can certainly conclude that the man found at Spouting Rock was connected to the prince." But whether that man was Stuart Gale or merely someone who resembled him, remained a mystery.

"At least we got a name from Katherine. Stern. That

should make tracing him a bit easier, wouldn't you say?" Mrs. Fish turned onto Bellevue Avenue, heading toward town. Perhaps she intended bringing me to the *Messenger*. If so, I would have to arrange for transportation home later. An inconvenience, but one I decided not to mention. "Someone here in Newport *must* have seen him before he died," Mrs. Fish went on. "Especially if he came with Otto. Such an odd thing. One wonders if Otto realized his friend had gone missing, or if they parted upon arriving in New-port, each to pursue his own activities. Otto was staying at the Ocean House. Has anyone inquired there if Otto had been accompanied by this man?"

"The police did, and apparently no one they've spoken to so far had seen him with the prince." The midday sun baked the road ahead of us; carriages, including our own, sent up swirls of fine brown dust. I raised a hand to shield my face. My carriage dress would need a vigorous shaking out later.

"Perhaps Otto killed his friend and then he killed him-self," Mrs. Fish said half to me, half to herself.

"Don't be absurd." The dust made me cough, and then I realized what I'd said, and to whom. I braced for her scathing retort, but met with laughter instead. Mrs. Fish pos-itively whooped.

"Good heavens, I like you, Miss Cross. I truly do." Con-tinuing to laugh, Mrs. Fish held the reins with one hand and used the other to dab away a tear of mirth. "No one speaks to me that way. But it was high time somebody did. Yes, in-deedy. May I call you Emma?"

"Of course, if you like."

"Good." She did not invite me to call her Mamie, and I would not have wished to. In fact, I believe I would have cringed a bit each time I spoke it. Despite my parents' un-conventional ways, they had raised me to respect my elders and to refrain from undue familiarity. It would have been akin to referring to my aunt Alice simply as Alice, and to my ears that sounded horridly improper. "Now," Mrs. Fish went on briskly, "what makes you so certain Otto didn't kill himself?"

"He couldn't have. The angle of the blade ruled out that possibility."

"Hmm. All right, then, any ideas where to go next?"

"Actually . . ." Something she had said a moment ago had given me an idea. "It's not true that no one in Newport had seen this Herr Stern. Someone did."

"Who? We'll go and talk to that person this very moment. Just point me in the right direction."

"It's not exactly the kind of place you and I should go, Mrs. Fish."

"Why ever not?"

"Because it's a tavern. On Long Wharf."

She compressed her lips but didn't quite hide her grin. "If you promise not to tell Stuyvie, I won't tell Alice Vanderbilt." With a flick of the reins, she encouraged the horse to pick up the pace.

"Mrs. Fish, please think about this. I know only too well the consequences of treading where one shouldn't. I'm sure you heard all about my foray up the porch steps of the Reading Room last summer."

"I most certainly did, my dear. Did my heart good to hear about a young woman with such pluck."

"Yes, well, that pluck set my life on a detour for an entire year." I paused to regard her. "What if your daughter had shown that kind of pluck? What would you have to say about it then?"

My question struck home; Mrs. Fish sobered considerably. "My Marian wouldn't dare. But that's different. She's . . ."

She struggled to complete her sentence, and I marveled at having been able to strike Mamie Fish dumb, even for a moment. How many others could boast such a feat? But I decided not to let her struggle for too long. I said, "She's a young society debutante with a glittering future as the wife of some important man."

"That's right. And . . ." Once again, she became tongue-tied. The horse slowed, a result of the reins going slack in Mrs. Fish's hands. I came to her rescue.

"It's all right, ma'am. I understand. You and I hail from very different worlds, and I would never dream of encouraging your daughter to follow in my path. Unless, that is, she very much wished to." I couldn't help adding those last words, for otherwise I would have been a liar at worst, a hypocrite at best. "At any rate, I have little to lose nowadays. If you're quite sure, we'll go to the Narragansett Tavern."

Mrs. Fish relaxed beside me and the horse once again stepped lively. At my insistence, we stopped first at the *Messenger*. I dropped off the articles I'd edited, along with the other business I'd attended to at home, and I checked that operations were running smoothly, which they seemed to be.

Even at that time of day, men stumbled in and out of the Narragansett Tavern. As always, Long Wharf bustled with activity, and when the sailors, fishermen, and longshoremen finished their toils, no matter the time of day or night, they inevitably wandered into one of Newport's many dockside taverns.

This particular tavern stood between a warehouse and a sailmaker's shop. Mrs. Fish watched the men in ragged, salt-faded clothes with a leery eye. I instructed her to stop the carriage just outside the Narragansett, and then signaled to a youth who came striding out of the sail shop carrying a bundle over his shoulder.

"You there," I called to him. "Have you a few minutes to spare? I'll pay you to watch our carriage." Ordinarily, I never worried about where I parked my buggy. As an island,

Newport was mostly spared thefts of that sort, but I didn't drive a fine tilbury that might prove too much of a temptation for a workman in his cups.

The boy, a scrawny youth of about fourteen, hefted his load off his shoulder and lowered it to the ground at his feet. "How much, ma'am?"

His accent declared him to be from the South, perhaps a cabin boy from one of the visiting ships. Before I could answer him, Mrs. Fish dug into her handbag and drew out a half dollar. "Is this enough, young man? You can have it when we come back."

The boy's hazel eyes popped wide. "Yes'm, that's enough." He glanced around as if searching for something, or perhaps someone. "Just don't be too long. Don't want to get hollered at or worse when I git back."

Outside the tavern door, we both halted and took deep breaths. I grinned at Mrs. Fish; she grinned back and nodded. Upon that signal, I pushed the door open and strode inside. Immediately the odors of stale beer, sweat, tobacco, and some kind of fish stew assaulted our noses. Mrs. Fish's expression contorted into one of distaste, and I half expected her to do an about-face and march right back outside. To my surprise, she squared her shoulders and held her ground, though I noticed she drew the shallowest of breaths. We glanced about the large, dusky room. There were only a handful of men present, some tucking into bowls of stew with enthusiasm, others slumped over tankards of beer. In the far corner, three men took turns tossing darts at a cork target on the wall.

"Brady!" I exclaimed upon spotting my brother sitting hunched at a table near the bar. He was not alone, as Mrs. Fish was quick to point out.

"Auggie Pendleton!"

* * *

Two more sheepish men I could not imagine. The two of them jumped up in surprise, knocking against their table and sloshing beer over the rims of their tankards. Perhaps they might have bolted, had they been more steady on their feet. They hovered, wobbled a bit, and after a moment sank back into their chairs. Brady's voice carried across the room on a groan.

Mamie and I exchanged a look. *Drunk*, she mouthed with a disgusted shake of her head. She and I crossed to their table.

"Auggie Pendleton," Mrs. Fish said sharply upon our arrival, "I'll have you know your sister is exceedingly unhappy with you. Apparently, she requires your presence at home for whatever she was working on when Miss Cross and I arrived there earlier."

Mr. Pendleton gave his head a shake, as if to dislodge water from his ears. "What?"

"You heard me, Auggie. Katherine is most peeved with you."

"Oh, bother Kay." He curled his lip and wrinkled his nose. "She's no fun at all."

"And what are you doing here, Brady?" I spoke sternly, but I placed a hand on my brother's shoulder to soften my inquiry.

"Did Angus tell you where to find me?" His words slurred together.

"No, it's an unhappy coincidence I've found you here like this." I gestured at Auggie Pendleton. "This is no place for either of you."

"I'm a grown man, Em," Brady said petulantly. His blood-shot eyes avoided mine. "So's Auggie. We go where we please."

"This isn't like you. Not anymore." No, ever since a bottle of bourbon had nearly destroyed his life three summers ago, my brother had stopped drinking to excess, taken responsibility for his actions, and become respectable. Now . . .

he looked like the Brady of old. The one I used to bail out of jail after nights of drink and recklessness, who believed he could take shortcuts to success, who was, in short, his father's son.

"Don't talk to me about who I am, Em. You don't know. You have a picture in your mind of what I should be. Well, I'm not that man. Never was. Never will be." He raised his beer to his lips. Some spilled over the side of the tankard and dribbled onto his coat. The pit of my stomach felt hollow and cold.

"And what's your excuse, Auggie?" Mrs. Fish crossed her arms and tapped her foot, and I realized it didn't matter to her one bit why Brady was here. He wasn't her concern. His presence was merely incidental to the reason that had brought us to the Narragansett. "What on earth are you doing in a place like this?"

Mr. Pendleton dropped his forehead into his palm and spoke with a whine. "I suppose you're going to tell Kay I was here. I'll never hear the end of it."

Mamie dragged a chair from the next table over, but before she sat, she pulled a handkerchief out of her bag, unfolded it, and draped it over the seat. "Why don't you tell me what you're hiding from?"

"I'd think that would be obvious. Kay."

"You're hiding from your sister?" Mrs. Fish leaned closer to him. She began to prop her elbow on the table, then obviously thought better of it and placed both hands firmly in her lap. "Why?"

"She's bossy."

I pulled over a chair for myself. "How so? What was she doing when we saw her at home a little while ago?"

"The books," he whispered, then slapped a hand over his mouth. A giggle escaped through his fingers. Brady snorted and swallowed a mouthful of beer.

Mamie sent me a puzzled glance. "What books, Auggie?"

"Er . . . um. Excuse me." He pressed both palms on the tabletop and pushed unsteadily to his feet. "I've got to . . . uh . . ." He stumbled away toward the back of the tavern. I assumed he was going out to relieve himself. Brady's hand came down on my wrist.

"What are *you* doing here, if not to check up on me?" His gaze lit on Mrs. Fish, and he squinted as if to bring her into focus. "What's *she* doing here? Isn't that . . ." He paused and muffled a burp against his coat sleeve.

"Don't be daft," Mrs. Fish said with a toss of her head. "I only look like her. *She'd* never set foot in a place like this."

Brady nodded. "Don't suppose she would."

"Brady." I gripped his shoulder to recapture his attention. "We're here to find information about the man found at Spouting Rock. He—"

"You mean my dear father?"

"Brady, please listen. Angus said he turned up here one day before he died. We were hoping the bartender might remember him."

"So go ask him."

His peevish tone grated on my patience, and I replied with equal testiness. "I intend to. I didn't expect to run into you here, or Mr. Pendleton. Look at the two of you, neither doing the other any favors. Let me take you home when Mrs.—" I'd started to say Fish, but quickly amended it. "When my friend and I leave."

He sniggered into his collar. "You're deeply disappointed in me, aren't you, Em?"

I sighed and didn't answer. Suddenly it dawned on me that August Pendleton had been gone quite a while, longer than the average call of nature. I came to my feet.

"Where are you going?" Mrs. Fish asked with a look of alarm.

"Outside to see what's keeping August. I'll be right back. Unless you wish to come with me."

"No, thank you." She wrinkled her nose. "I'll go question the barkeep. Hand me that photograph, won't you?"

Lucky for me, Brady's attention had wandered back to his beer as I slipped the photograph into Mrs. Fish's hand. I didn't need to make matters worse by flashing the image of his father under his nose. I gestured at him and murmured to Mrs. Fish, "Please take care not to let him see it. It'll only upset him more."

Rather than follow the path August had taken, I exited through the front door. The boy we'd asked to watch the carriage stood faithfully beside the horse, although I could see by the way he hopped from one foot to the other that his patience was running thin. Of course, Mrs. Fish hadn't given him the half dollar yet, which had been good thinking on her part. "I need you to do something else," I said to him. "Would you run around to the back of the tavern and look for a well-dressed young man with thick black hair. Tell him the lady he was speaking with asks that he go back inside. Then come back and let me know when he does. Can you do that for me?"

"Sure, miss." He foot tapped the bundle on the ground beside him. "Will ya watch my sails?"

I assured him I'd guard them with my life, and off he went. Minutes passed, and it dawned on me that he, too, took an inordinately long time at the simple task I'd set him. Had Auggie refused to return to the tavern? But then wouldn't the boy have run back to tell me that? Perhaps Auggie hadn't gone outside for the purpose he stated, but had planned to run off instead to avoid Mrs. Fish's and my questions—and perhaps he'd paid the boy to keep his whereabouts a secret. After weighing my options, I steeled myself for a walk around the old timber building faced in weather-silvered clapboard.

Knowing I couldn't very well stride around the last corner unannounced, at least not without causing a stir and perhaps meeting unwelcome sights, I shielded my eyes and called out. "Excuse me, but I'm looking for August Pendleton. Mr. Pendleton, are you back there? Please answer me."

I heard several muttered expletives, the shuffling of feet in the rocky dirt, and the slamming of a door. Still shielding my eyes with my hand, I eased around the corner and peered between my fingers. I beheld a yard cluttered with casks, barrels, crates, and an assortment of debris. Clumps of grass and weeds grew here and there. But there were no men, no Auggie Pendleton, and no boy. Puzzled, I let my hand fall to my side.

As I turned to go back around the building, something whistled past my ear, and I heard a *thunk* in the wall behind me. I stopped short and spun around. At first I saw nothing, and thought perhaps I'd heard the strike of a hammer in the distance. Then the shivering of bright feathers caught my eye, and I found myself staring at the flight end of a dart, only inches away from my shoulder, its sharp tip sunk deep into the clapboard.

"And you say you didn't see anyone?"

"Not a soul, Jesse," I said yet again, hanging on to my last shred of patience. When I had hurried back into the Narragansett and told Mrs. Fish what had happened outside, she insisted we go straight to the police. On our way to the carriage, we noticed the young man's bundle of sails was gone.

I had little to tell Jesse about who might have thrown that dart. The three men I had seen playing the game in the tavern had still been there upon my return, and neither Mrs. Fish, Brady, nor the barkeep had noticed any of them leave to go out back.

"It was Auggie. Obviously." Mrs. Fish had made this

claim on the way to the police station. "He left us directly after we asked him what his sister was working on when we saw her earlier."

"Yes, he seems to be hiding something that involves his sister," I said, and added, "Something she wished to hide as well. When Mrs. Fish and I arrived at their home, Miss Pendleton was sitting at a desk going over some papers. When I showed the slightest interest in what they were, she gathered them up and locked them in a drawer. When I asked August about it, he drunkenly said 'the books.' At least, that's what I believe he said."

"The household accounts," Jesse suggested. "The family finances."

"Or bank records." Mrs. Fish's right eyebrow went up sharply.

"The sister, going over bank records?" Jesse sounded skeptical. He stroked a forefinger absently up and down his sideburn as he considered. "But why threaten you over something like that? Especially when you didn't even see what it was."

I sighed. "I don't know."

"Unless he believed you to be onto whatever he and his sister are trying to hide." Mrs. Fish had the look of a formidable society matron about to order an entire house staff to do her bidding. "That dart was a warning for you to leave it alone. But we won't, will we, Emma?"

Jesse's eyes flashed at Mrs. Fish's use of my given name. I could see the familiarity made him uncomfortable, although I didn't know why. He shifted in his chair. "Mrs. Fish, I've sent men over to the Pendletons' house to wait for Mr. Pendleton to come home. They'll talk to him and find out if he had anything to do with the threat against Miss Cross."

The woman raised her palms. "Who else could it have been?"

"I don't know," I said before Jesse could address the question, "but for one thing, Mr. Pendleton was deep in his cups. Whoever threw the dart had full use of his faculties." Though sensible, this fact brought me little comfort. I'd rather the culprit *had* been young Auggie Pendleton playing a drunken prank on me, than a more sinister adversary issuing an overt threat.

Mrs. Fish harrumphed. "If that were true, the thing would have hit you."

"Not if the dart had been meant to convey a message," Jesse said solemnly. "Please, I'd be very grateful if you two ladies would go about your business and allow the police to take care of this. Along with everything else." By everything else, I knew he meant the murders of Prince Otto and the Spouting Rock victim.

"Speaking of which." I paused as a pained expression filled Jesse's face. "Katherine Pendleton recognized the Spouting Rock victim. She said she remembered him from her association with Prince Otto. Said his name was Stern, although . . ." I thought back on our earlier encounter. "She wasn't entirely sure that was it."

"She wasn't entirely sure of anything, but that reminds me." Mrs. Fish dug into her handbag and drew out the photograph I'd given her at the tavern. She handed it to Jesse. "I asked the barkeep and the other men in the tavern."

"You two had no business going there," he grumbled, but without much force behind the words.

"Be that as it may," Mrs. Fish continued haughtily. "Funny thing. The dim lighting in the tavern actually made it easier to identify the man in the picture."

"They identified him?" I slid to the edge of my seat. "Why didn't you say something earlier?"

She gazed at me as if I were missing the obvious. "Because you had essentially been attacked. That's why, my dear."

"Well, what did they say?"

"Who?"

"The men at the tavern." I glanced at Jesse, who appeared bemused by this exchange.

"They said he'd been there. Without bright sunlight, they weren't distracted by the fact that the man in the photograph was much younger than he would be now. The barkeep and two of the fellows at the dartboard were sure he wandered in two nights before my Harvest Festival."

"Drunk?" I asked, remembering what Angus had told me.

"As drunk as the night is long," she sang out, and slapped her thigh.

There seemed to be a plague of that lately.

Chapter 14

After we left Jesse, I insisted Mrs. Fish bring me to the *Messenger*. It took some persuasion on my part, as she more than once suggested going to the Newport Casino for lunch. She also renewed her offer to hire someone to take my place as editor-in-chief. She simply could not understand my preference to fill the role myself and forgo pleasant pastimes. Finally she resorted to asking me how I intended to get home later if I sent her on her way, and I assured her I would be able to arrange a ride.

Nonetheless, she surprised me by climbing down from the carriage and following me inside. Thus I found myself conducting a tour of our offices and introducing her to our staff. Despite our limited resources, space, and scope of subscriptions, she seemed impressed.

"However did you learn all of this?"

"I'm still learning," I told her truthfully, "but I paid very close attention to all aspects of the business while I worked for the *Observer*. And for the *Herald*, too, for that matter."

"And they were willing to share their business secrets with a woman?"

I grinned. "Some were. Others were willing to indulge a silly young girl's curiosity, never thinking I might take it into my pretty head to put what I learned into practice."

She laughed. "Indeed, indeed. You're no one's fool, are you?"

"I try not to be." To my surprise, her approval had me standing taller, and for an instant I felt as I often had when my aunt Sadie was alive—alive and encouraging me to be what I wished to be and live as I saw fit. Oh, but I knew Mamie Fish's endorsement would only go so far, and again I thought of her daughter, Marian. Even as Mrs. Fish inspected our presses and traced the process that brought articles from handwritten notes to typeset print, Marian was being schooled in the skills and responsibilities of a society wife and mother.

Down the corridor and through the closed door of the front office, a telephone rang. Instinct sent me striding in that direction, and I emerged into the sunlit room I shared with Jimmy Hawkins to discover him listening intently and frowning. When he saw me he waved me over.

"She's right here, Detective." He held the receiver out to me and mouthed *Jesse Whyte*.

"What is it, Jesse? Have you learned something new?"

"Can you meet me out at the Pendletons' house?"

"Why, yes, I suppose so. Why?"

"Katherine Pendleton has been murdered."

A policeman admitted Mrs. Fish and me to the Pendletons' house and directed us into the drawing room. I stopped before we reached the doorway. I had told Jesse over the phone that Mamie Fish would probably insist on accompanying me. He hadn't liked the idea, but he hadn't forbidden it either. Now I met her gaze levelly.

"Are you sure you wish to go in? To see this? One is never quite the same once one has viewed a body. And I'm not talking about a deceased loved one who has been respectfully laid out and prepared for burial. I'm talking about someone whose life has been brutally cut short by violent means."

"I understand." She replied with none of her typical hubris, and certainly without humor. I had never seen her in possession of such a serious demeanor. "I did see Otto in the garden, remember."

"That was at a distance. This will be different."

She nodded, and I became aware of low sobs coming from inside the room. There were other voices as well, Jesse's and the uniformed officers', along with the observations of the coroner. I recognized one of the officers, a tall, dark-eyed young man named Scotty Binsford. He had grown up near my home on Easton's Point, and often worked with Jesse. Katherine Pendleton lay somewhere in their midst, but at the moment I could not see her. I searched for the source of the crying and found the housekeeper, Mrs. Jennings, collapsed in the corner of a small sofa opposite the doorway, a damp handkerchief pressed to her face. I went to her.

"Can I get you anything, or do anything for you?" As I sat down beside her, I reached into my handbag for a fresh handkerchief and handed it to her.

"Thank you," she said tremulously. "No. There is nothing. Nothing anyone can do." She fell to sobbing again. I patted her shoulder, assuming it had been she who had found the body. The handkerchief came away from her tear-stained and blotchy face. "And to think, her own brother. God help us all when a young man stabs his own sister."

I pulled away from her. "What? August . . . ?"

"Auggie?" Mrs. Fish hesitated for only an instant before stalking toward the other end of the room, where the police continued their orderly inspection and cataloguing of the crime scene. "Auggie, was it you? Did you do this?" Like a stern schoolmarm, she thrust a finger toward the floor at her feet.

I still couldn't see poor Katherine Pendleton from where I sat, but Jesse's face came into view, his features a mask of impatience. "Mrs. Fish, if you wish to remain, you'll have to go back over there and wait with Miss Cross. But it would be better if you left."

"Why, I never . . ."

I was up and at Mrs. Fish's side in an instant. With a hand wrapped around her upper arm I forcefully drew her away, but not before I took in the scene. Beautiful Katherine Pendleton lay in a pool of blood that originated at a wound to the left side of her rib cage—just as with the other two murders. Her eyes had already been closed, but I could well imagine the death stare the poor housekeeper had come face-to-face with upon finding her mistress. Not far away, Auggie Pendleton huddled in a wing chair, an incongruous sight if ever there was one, for the wing chair was the very symbol of comfort a man could always depend upon in his own home.

Not so today. A policeman stood guard beside him, while Auggie sat hunched over with his elbows on his knees, his head in his hands. He swayed slightly side to side, the result of grief and drink, no doubt. Of guilt? *Had* he murdered his sister?

All this I took in in a matter of seconds, my neck craned even as I walked Mrs. Fish back across the room. On my way I glimpsed another aspect of this hideous development. On a side table, a bloody dagger rested on a man's white linen handkerchief, the contrasting colors driving home the harsh reality of yet another death. Unlike with the other two, however, this murder weapon had been left at the site. Why? It was no ordinary knife, not one to be found in a kitchen, a toolbox, or among a fisherman's tackle. The etching in its gilded hilt declared this an ornamental dagger, and as I instinctively glanced around the room, I discovered a display on the wall not far from where Katherine had been struck down. Two similar, decorative blades graced a gilt-framed square of velvet. A third set of brackets were glaringly empty. Someone—Auggie?—had snatched the dagger from its holder and turned it upon Miss Pendleton.

But why would he kill his own sister, Prince Otto, and the Spouting Rock victim? Why the difference between this and the other two murders? Had today's crime been committed by someone else—an act of anger in the moment, whereas the deaths of Prince Otto and the Spouting Rock victim had been carefully planned and executed with precision?

Mrs. Fish remained on her feet, keenly watching the activity on the other side of the room. I resumed my seat beside the housekeeper. Her sobbing had subsided, and I ventured to ask her a question.

"Did you find her?"

Mrs. Jennings nodded. "And him." She pointed across the room.

"August?"

Another nod. "He was crouched beside her, holding the knife. And the blood—I . . . oh, heavens."

"Mrs. Jennings." I annunciated her name to encourage her to focus. "Did he say anything?"

"He said he didn't do it." Her brow crinkled tightly. "But then why was he there, holding a knife?"

"Sometimes things aren't as they appear." At my observation, Mrs. Fish snorted, before returning her attention to the crime scene. "Then what happened?" I asked Mrs. Jennings.

"I ran. I'd been downstairs in the kitchen, going over the

shopping list with the cook. Neither of us heard a thing. If only I hadn't gone down when I did, maybe . . ."

"You mustn't blame yourself. You couldn't have known what would happen." I gave her a moment to let that sink in. "What did you do after finding Miss Pendleton and her brother?"

"I called the police, of course, and then Cook and I locked ourselves in a pantry until we heard footsteps above our heads. The police got here awfully fast." She said this last as though only now realizing the fact. I hastened to explain.

"They were already on their way. They were looking for August because of something that occurred earlier."

"Yes, you see?" Mrs. Fish came closer and leaned down to speak to us. "He was already in a violent mood. He tried to kill you, didn't he?"

"That's an exaggeration," I said calmly. "No one would use a dart to kill someone. It was a warning."

"All right then." Her chin came up. "A warning of future violence."

"Oh, dear me . . ." Mrs. Jennings clutched her hands together.

"Perhaps," I said, but I still wasn't convinced the dart had been thrown by August. I had little on which to base that opinion, only instinct and the fact that, unless August had done a supreme job of pretending, he'd been too drunk at the time to throw with even a modicum of accuracy.

"I hear what you're saying down there." August jumped up from the wing chair and advanced in our direction, taking several steps before Officer Binsford moved in front of him and took hold of his upper arms. That might have halted August's momentum, but not his protest. "I swear I didn't do it. I didn't kill my sister. I found her like—" He broke off and turned to look down at the body. A sheet lay over her. "Oh,

God. I found her like that. It was already too late. I tried to . . . to . . . But she was already gone."

"Sit down, Mr. Pendleton." Scotty Binsford walked him backward and pressed him down into the wing chair. "Stay put. We'll get to you in a few minutes."

Only when he had stood up facing us did I see the blood smearing the front of his coat and his right sleeve. The fingers of his right hand, too, were stained. Caught crouching over the body, his sister's blood on him—how could the police not believe him guilty? How could I still have doubts? And yet I did.

The other officers had been combing that end of the room for whatever evidence they could find. They had examined the dagger display on the wall, but I feared that would yield few clues as to who had snatched the weapon from its perch. Soon, their activity dwindled, and Jesse murmured orders to two of his men. One of them crossed the room to us.

He spoke to the housekeeper. "Please come with me, ma'am. We'll need to ask the cook to come upstairs. Is there anyone else in the house?"

"No, I already told the detective there's no one else. The girls who clean don't live here. They come in the morning and leave by midday."

"All right, ma'am." The officer gazed through the doorway into the central hall. "We'll go this way, through to the dining room. I just have a few more questions for you. Detective Whyte will have a few of his own, as well."

Mrs. Jennings needed help coming to her feet, so I held her arm and stood up with her. She thanked me, her eyes large and pleading as if to ask me to accompany her into the dining room. She did not do so. The policeman gestured to Mrs. Fish.

"The detective asks that you wait in the receiving parlor, ma'am. Or you may leave, if you wish."

"What? Oh, well, all right. Come along, Emma."

The officer held up his hand. "Miss Cross is asked to stay."

As one might predict, Mrs. Fish expressed her unhappiness with this arrangement in no uncertain terms. Jesse settled the matter by stating unequivocally that she must go and then asked if I would be so kind as to stay and help question Mr. Pendleton. That didn't appease Mrs. Fish a bit, but she turned on her heel and strutted from the room, murmuring about unfairness every step of the way.

"The wound is similar to the others," Jesse said to me once we were alone at that end of the drawing room. "The same kind of precision."

"Like a surgeon's."

"Not quite as clean, but our murderer used a different weapon this time." He nodded grimly toward the dagger. "On the one hand, it makes me doubt Mr. Pendleton could have committed any of these murders. On the other hand, he was caught red-handed, leaning over the body and holding the murder weapon."

"Establishing a motive would help, wouldn't it?" When Jesse conceded that point, I continued, "We need to ask Mr. Pendleton about those papers his sister was working on when Mrs. Fish and I were here earlier. And ask him if he knew the man Katherine identified as Herr Stern."

"In all the activity, I'd forgotten about that. Come with me."

Jesse had Scotty and the other remaining policeman back away as I pulled a footstool closer to August's chair. Before I could sit and ask him anything, the coroner's assistants arrived with a wood-and-canvas stretcher and began the process of lifting Katherine Pendleton's body onto it. August nearly tripped over the footstool in his haste to rise. Scotty Binsford sprang forward and reached for him, but Jesse intervened.

"Give him a moment with his sister before you take her out."

"But, sir . . ." Scotty started to say, but at a look from Jesse he fell silent.

"Wait." All gazes converged on me. "The key," I said to Jesse. "It's probably on her somewhere. Unless there is another."

"What key?" August demanded, and then his demeanor changed. "Now see here, you can't simply . . . It's disrespectful. Don't you dare touch her." He looked affronted, outraged that his sister's body should be searched.

"We need the key to the desk," I gently told him, and pointed into the adjoining study. "At the tavern, I asked you about some papers your sister was perusing when I arrived here this morning. We need to see what they are. Do you have an extra key?"

His forehead knotted with anguish. "No, no I don't. She—" He broke off and stared down at his hand, at the bloodstains on his fingers, as though just noticing them for the first time. His gaze traveled to his sleeve, to the front of his coat. He attempted to brush the stains away, and as his eyes glazed over I feared he might collapse. Somehow, he collected himself and extended the bloodied hand toward his sister's body. "Do it. Make it quick, but be gentle with her."

I could neither watch the search nor listen to August bid his sister good-bye. Instead, I moved into the study where she had been sitting only hours earlier. I went to the desk and brushed my fingers over its surface, marveling at how quickly a life could be erased.

From the drawing room, August's weeping drifted to my ears. Then Jesse softly called me back in. "Ask him about those papers, while I unlock the desk."

"Why ask if you can simply look them over?"

"Because I want to see what he has to say about them. You could also ask him about his vanishing act at the Narragansett. And about that dart."

Nodding my understanding, I sat on the footstool before August. "Mr. Pendleton, why did you leave the Narragansett so abruptly earlier?"

He leaned an elbow on the arm of the chair and let his cheek sink against his fist. "I didn't like your questions."

"Why? I was asking you about those papers your sister locked away in the desk. What is it about those papers you don't wish to talk about?"

"What difference can it make? My sister is dead."

I turned my head just enough to see, out of the corner of my eye, Jesse spreading the sheaf out over the desktop and leaning down low to study them. He shuffled through once, then returned to the topmost page. A ridge formed between his brows. "It might make a good deal of difference. Is there something in those papers you don't want people knowing? Is it about your banking business?"

He started, and I knew I had guessed correctly. My apprehensions for him, and *of* him, grew. Was I sitting before a killer? Standing behind the chair, Scotty Binsford held a pad, his pencil raising a soft scratching across the paper. I was suddenly glad of his presence. "Yes, just some banking business, nothing unusual," August insisted. "But it's . . . it's confidential." He became more animated. "We must protect our clients' privacy, mustn't we?"

"Usually, yes," I agreed. "But these are extenuating circumstances."

He raked a hand through his hair. "I didn't kill her."

I truly hoped not. "Did you throw a dart at me outside the Narragansett?"

"What? No! What a thing to ask. I went outside and I left the vicinity. Walked up to Washington Square and caught the trolley."

"Can you tell me why your sister was going over those

records, then? And why she felt it necessary to hide them from Mrs. Fish and me? We weren't likely to lean over her shoulder. In fact, she made me more curious by rushing to lock them away."

He hesitated before answering, looking like a recalcitrant child. "I can't tell you why. I wasn't here, remember? Who knows what Kay was thinking? Probably checking up on me."

"Why would she do that? Did she mistrust your handling of bank matters? You haven't been . . . cheating in some way, have you?" I avoided the word I was thinking: *embezzling*. Had his sister caught him at it?

"I most certainly was not." His eyes sparked with ire.

"All right," I said gently. "Did she go over the records often?"

He shrugged. "Had I known she did it at all, *I'd* have placed those papers under lock and key." He huffed. "Your questions are growing wearisome. Are you quite finished?"

"No, Mr. Pendleton. I have one more. Did you know a Mr. Stern, in relation to Prince Otto?" I handed him the photograph of my mother and Stuart Gale. "Does his face look familiar, though he'd be almost thirty years older now?"

He studied the image a good long moment. Unlike his sister and Isabel Clemson, he exhibited no sign of recognition— no heightening of his color, no widening of his eyes. "You say his name is Stern? I don't know him. Why do you ask?"

"Because your sister mentioned him."

"The less my sister has to do with any of that bunch, the better." His features tightened in anger. Suddenly, he appeared to realize that he'd spoken of his sister as though she were still alive, and his ire dissolved into grief. His head fell into his hands again. "Oh, my dearest Kay . . ."

"Emma," Jesse called from the study. I patted August's wrist as I rose. When I joined Jesse in the other room, he gestured at the records. "These are loan records, along with applications for new loans. Also, some investment documents. I can't make out anything that she would feel the need to hide from anyone, especially since it's mostly figures the average person would have a devilish time deciphering."

"Yes, but she seemed determined not to give me the chance to try."

His expression turned grim. "I think she discovered something about these records, something she wanted to address without anyone finding out. Such as her brother tampering with the finances."

"I'd had that exact thought. When Mrs. Fish and I arrived this morning, she thought it was her brother coming home, and was most annoyed to discover it wasn't. I expect she wished to confront him about whatever it was she found." I drew in a deep breath, feeling inexplicably sorry for the young man in the next room, whose life of ease and comfort was about to shatter all around him. "He didn't like my referring to these papers earlier, and he likes it no better now, even though his life might depend on his answers."

"I'll give it a try. And I'll have these papers thoroughly examined by someone who knows the banking business inside and out."

"Has anyone been up in Katherine's bedroom yet?" I asked. "There could be more evidence there."

"You and I will go up as soon as I've finished questioning Mr. Pendleton. If you care to wait around that long, that is."

"I'm not going anywhere." Yet I did go as far as the receiving room, where I found Mrs. Fish wearing a path in the carpet with her pacing.

"Well, have they arrested him yet?"

"No," I replied wearily, "but I believe it's imminent."

"Good. When I think of that poor, beautiful child. Her whole life ahead of her." She stopped pacing and gazed out the window. Her long sigh filled the momentary silence before she turned back around. "But for the life of me, I can't fathom why he'd do it."

A matter unrelated to the banking records stirred in my mind. "He was jealous of her."

"Jealous? Of his own sister?"

"Of the attentions paid her by potential suitors."

"Hmm. Brothers can be overprotective."

"Yes, but . . . Did it go beyond that? Could she have forged a new liaison, perhaps secretly, and August found out?"

"Are you saying he might have killed her in a fit of jealous rage?" She looked at me aghast.

"In a way. Or rage over being disobeyed."

"I've never known Auggie Pendleton to be in a rage about anything. To burst out with any strong emotions, for that matter. He's always been even-keeled, calm. Boring, to be truthful."

More than anything, I wanted to get upstairs to Katherine's room and search for clues. August's room, as well. Was there something upstairs that might link him to the other two murders? Despite the aberration of the murder weapon being left behind this time, it didn't take a coroner's report to tell me the cause of death was too similar to the other two crimes to be a coincidence.

Mrs. Fish broke into my thoughts. "Are you ready to leave?"

"Not just yet. Please, you go on without me. Detective Whyte has requested that I stay, but I fear he won't allow you to be privy to our discussions. I don't want you to have to pace in this receiving room indefinitely."

"All right, then. You're to come to Crossways as soon as you're finished here and tell me everything." She gathered up her hat and handbag.

"Mrs. Fish . . ." I had no desire to stretch out an already long day with a detour to Crossways. Besides, if I went anywhere after this, it should be to the *Messenger*, where I might ready an article for the next morning's edition. It wasn't an article I relished writing.

"No arguments, and no excuses. Crossways is on the way to your Gull Manor, after all. I'll see you later."

"We'll see," I murmured after her, but if she heard me, she didn't respond or look back.

Chapter 15

I sat at the edge of a gracefully carved four-poster bed just beyond the rectangle of sunlight pouring through the floor-to-ceiling windows of Katherine Pendleton's bedroom. This might be a leased house, but I judged this room, with its French furnishings and pale blue silk upholsteries, perfect for a beauty like Miss Pendleton. My heart ached that she would never enjoy another moment here, would never gaze at her reflection in the full-length, gold-leafed mirror, or recline in the chaise longue at the foot of the bed, supported by an array of velvet pillows.

I had found a locked diary box on Katherine's writing table. Of sturdy mahogany secured by wide, ornate silver mounts, the casket held five slender books. Their spines gazed out at me, but the greater parts of their embossed, silver-leafed titles were obscured by a hinged, and quite locked, three-inch-wide silver guard. I surmised the books contained information on the household accounts and the like, and perhaps, with luck, Katherine's daily journal.

Did the small ring of keys found in Katherine's pocket

earlier include the one that unlocked this box? And if so, would these journals provide us with any clues into her life—and death?

I set the box aside, for it wasn't all I had found. What seized my fascination now was the small, clear flask that lay in my palm. It was glass, the kind that typically held spirits and could be slipped inside a leather holder. Such a masculine item to be found among a young lady's possessions. I'd uncovered the vessel in Katherine's dressing table, in the top right drawer buried under a plethora of lace mitts and silk scarves. A clear liquid filled it about three quarters of the way. Gin? It didn't appear to have the thickness of a liqueur like anisette.

Jesse was across the gallery in August's bedroom. My instructions were to call him if I found anything interesting, yet before I did, I removed the stopper from the flask and sniffed the contents. A sense of familiarity came over me, and I sniffed again. I felt myself tumbling back in time.

As a child, I'd slipped and fallen on some slick rocks along Narragansett Bay and broke a tooth. The scent in this bottle brought me back to that day, albeit I'd been only six or seven years old. My parents had rushed me, bleeding, first to the office of Dr. Kennison, our family physician, and then to a local dentist. The tooth had been removed, much to my dismay, and this—whatever shimmered inside the tiny bottle I held—had been applied to my gums before the procedure.

I thought about the various types of anesthetics used by dentists to numb the mouth. One especially came to mind.

"Jesse," I called out. "I've found something." My pulse was leaping, for I believed I'd discovered a link to the two previous murders. Jesse's footsteps thudded along the runner in the gallery. He turned into the room slightly out of breath.

"Yes, what is it?"

I held up the flask. "Unless I'm mistaken, I've found more cocaine."

As we learned the next morning, I had not been mistaken about the cocaine. I went first to the *Messenger*, where I personally handed the article I'd written the previous night about Katherine Pendleton's death to the typesetter and bade him be sure it made it into the morning edition. On the way back to the front office I checked in at the newsroom. Ethan was alone. He told me Jacob had gone to the police station to follow up on the details I had given him over the telephone last night.

I attended to a few business matters and signed some papers Jimmy Hawkins had placed on my desk, before continuing on to the police station myself. Although I went with some apprehension that Jesse might wish me to end my involvement in this case, to my relief he seemed happy to see me and waved me over to his desk. Jacob had apparently already left the premises. I must have passed him without seeing him on my way here.

I noticed Katherine's diary box in the corner of Jesse's desk, its silver mounts gleaming under the electric lights. The guard was flipped open on its hinge to allow the journals to slide out, indicating that the key had indeed been on the ring found on Katherine's person. I wondered if Jesse had discovered anything pertinent inside, but before I could ask he revealed the results of the tests on the flask I had also found in Katherine's room.

"You were right. But what remains a mystery is where she came by the drug," Jesse said with a note of frustration.

"Isn't it obvious? I can't think of a single doctor in Newport who would have prescribed it. Not these days." I laid my handbag on the desk along with a basket I'd brought from home. "She knew the Spouting Rock victim. It's the only explanation. She remembered him from among Prince Otto's retainers, and he must have introduced her to the drug then. Unless it was Otto himself."

Jesse let out a breath. "We'll soon know whether that could be possible."

My discovery in Katherine's bedroom had set in motion something Police Chief Rogers had refused to do previously: order an autopsy on Prince Otto. Even now, he did so only begrudgingly. He, and those he answered to, feared an international incident, and their fears were not unjustified. Apparently, the Austro-Hungarian diplomats in Washington, D.C., strongly objected to the procedure and insisted the body be readied for its journey across the ocean to Otto's homeland without further ado. But with a third similar death having occurred, even international pressure couldn't prevent the investigation from running its full course. Jesse's hands were now effectively untied.

August Pendleton, meanwhile, had been placed under arrest on suspicion of murdering Katherine. Even if Jesse had shared my doubts about August's guilt, he had no choice in the matter, not when August had been found crouched beside the body with the knife in his hand. In addition, the police had found no indication of forced entry at the house.

I gestured at the diary box. "Have you discovered anything of interest?"

"I'm still going through them." Jesse ran his fingertip over the spines. "Three are merely records of the household accounting and Miss Pendleton's personal expenses. But the other two journals contain details of visitors and Miss Pendleton's daily activities. So far, though, it all seems straightforward. I've found nothing to indicate any threats to her person, or unusual visitors. Of course, she might not have made a record of everything. Some things she might have wished to fade from memory."

"Would you like me to have a look? Being a woman, I might spot something a man wouldn't deem significant."

He hesitated. "I shouldn't let evidence leave the building."

"Is it evidence if you haven't found anything in them related to her death? And if these journals weren't found at the crime scene?"

A corner of his mouth lifted in a grin and he slid the box toward me. "You make a good point."

"I'll come and get them before I leave."

He nodded. "By the way, your Jacob Stodges was here earlier. Left just a few minutes before you arrived. He's a good reporter, that one. Doesn't miss a detail, no matter how small."

"Yes, I know. He's very good at his job."

"But he seemed put out that you had written the first article about the Pendleton case to go in today's paper, and that anything he subsequently reported will either go in an afternoon extra or tomorrow's edition."

I heard the faint warning note in Jesse's voice. "How put out?"

He met my gaze. "Watch him, Emma. He thinks he could do your job better than you."

This made me chuckle. "As do countless other men in the newspaper business."

After speaking with Jesse, I went to visit August. I had brought with me an assortment of Nanny's baked goods, both sweet and savory, and a few local periodicals to help him pass the time. I did not bring any newspapers. August didn't need to see accusations against him splashed across front pages.

I met with him in a small room away from the cell block to the rear of the police station. He came in scuffing his feet in a show of defiance that melted away as soon as I peeled back the bright gingham covering on the basket.

"Are those for me?" He dropped into the wooden chair facing me, on the other side of the small table between us. He had changed his clothing since I'd last seen him, and though wrinkled, his coat, vest, and trousers showed no signs of his sister's blood. The clothes he had been wearing yesterday had been taken into evidence.

"Yes, Mr. Pendleton, with my housekeeper's compliments."

"Thank her for me. I'm half starved. The food here is horrible."

I could well imagine, especially for a man used to the best. He tucked into an English-style pasty stuffed with chicken and mashed potatoes. He made groans of appreciation and rolled his eyes in pleasure. For the moment, his emotions concerning his sister's death—grief, fear, guilt—were thrust aside.

"Thank you, Miss Cross. I appreciate this. But why are you being kind to me? Don't you think I'm guilty?"

I leaned back in my chair and was silent a moment as I considered how to answer. I simply didn't know, which spoke in August's favor. Something about him, about the circumstances, as incriminating as they appeared to be, kept me from declaring him a murderer.

In the end, I replied to his question with one of my own. "Can you think of anyone who would wish to harm your sister?"

"Of course not. Kay was a popular girl among our set."

I nodded in acknowledgment. "Popular, I would imagine, with young ladies and gentlemen alike." He said nothing to this, so I went on. "At the Harvest Festival, why did you scowl each time your sister danced with a new partner?"

He had been savoring the last bites of the pasty, but now looked up in surprise. "What? The Harvest Festival? What's that got to do with anything?"

"Just this, Mr. Pendleton. The police won't look only at the evidence they collected in your drawing room. They will look into your behavior in recent days and weeks, and into your relationship with your sister. If they discover the two of you had been feuding—"

"We hadn't been."

"But you *were* at odds at Crossways that night."

He flicked crumbs from his fingertips and scowled. "Kay was right that I shouldn't have talked to you at the Harvest Festival. All you want is a story to sell your newspapers."

"That isn't true. I want to see justice for your sister, and for Prince Otto and the other man who was killed. The man named Stern."

"Prince Otto." His pronunciation of the name oozed disdain. He ignored the other name I mentioned.

"You didn't like the prince. Was it because he jilted your sister?"

"He was a bad influence on her."

"How so?"

"He'd have led her astray if I hadn't—"

"Hadn't what?"

His face became shuttered. "Never mind. It doesn't matter now. They're both gone."

I sighed. "What about Mr. Stern?"

He shook his head. "I thought about him after you asked me yesterday. I don't remember anyone named Stern."

I showed him the photograph of Stuart Gale. "Are you quite certain?"

He stared down at it and nodded. "Quite."

Was it possible only his sister had encountered the man during her engagement to Prince Otto? I had one more question for him. I'd saved the most shocking one for last. "How did your sister obtain the cocaine?"

"The what?" He paled. "That's not possible."

"I found a flask nearly full of a liquefied form of it in her bedroom."

Looking believably aghast, he shook his head. "I took pains to see that never happened. It's the reason I came between them."

This revelation startled me. Not so much his actions concerning his sister's engagement, but the reason behind them. "You were responsible for the broken engagement? You knew about the cocaine?"

Then surely Katherine Pendleton must have met with Prince Otto before he died. Perhaps the disdain she exhibited toward Otto at the Harvest Festival had been merely for her brother's sake. I thought, too, of Thea Clemson, who professed to have been in love with Prince Otto. Had he introduced her to the drug as well? Had that been the secret of his power over women? The thought made me shake my head in disgust.

"I knew about it, yes," said August, oblivious to my thoughts. "But I didn't think Kay did. I thought I'd gotten her away in time." He made a fist and struck it against the table. "I got her away from him because I knew he'd never be a good husband, but I never suspected he'd share his ugly habit with her. What kind of man does that?"

"One without a conscience, I'm afraid." To myself, I acknowledged that Prince Otto had been something of a monster, and I hoped Thea Clemson had escaped his snare in time.

"Thank God he's dead, Miss Cross." His voice hissed with loathing. "If he hadn't died, I would have killed him. If he appeared before me this very instant, I'd wrap my hands around his detestable throat and squeeze the very life out of him."

Before August had completed that last sentence, the door opened. I gazed around and saw the astonishment—and the judgment—in the policeman's eyes.

* * *

After leaving the police station I returned to the *Messenger.* The big press stood quiet in the pressroom, and I checked to make certain the morning's run had gone smoothly. I admit I actually crossed my fingers on my way down the corridor, but I needn't have worried. Dan Carter and his assistants met me with assurances that the newsies had picked up their bundled papers on time and were even now making their deliveries.

My next stop brought me to the newsroom. Ethan wasn't in, and I remembered he had an afternoon yacht party to cover. Jacob greeted me with a frown.

"I take it you're just back from the police station. Anything more on the Pendleton case?"

"Nothing Detective Whyte didn't already tell you when you were there."

He looked down at the paper before him. His fingernail scratched back and forth along the grain of the oak desktop. "You might have called me to come out to the Pendletons' yesterday."

"There wasn't time. And I was already there." Even as I spoke, I knew I'd taken a liberty with the truth. Jesse had called me from the police station with the news that Katherine was dead. I might have alerted Jacob to the fact, but Jesse had specifically asked me to join him at the house, because he knew I didn't come merely as reporter, but as his friend, one who had helped him with cases in the past and whose opinions he valued.

Jacob hadn't taken his gaze off me. It sharpened with speculation. "Perhaps you should decide which you truly wish to be, an editor-in-chief, or a reporter."

While his tone struck me as insubordinate, his insight rang with truth. Was my new position as editor-in-chief taking me away from what I truly loved—reporting? Running after the story, no matter the risk, to bring the facts to the reading public?

I couldn't but admit Jacob had a point—but I did so silently. To openly concede the truth would have given this young man an opening to perhaps step in and gradually set me aside. Yes, I had Derrick's sanction when it came to my job, but I certainly didn't want to depend on that. I wished to *deserve* my position, to have *earned* it, and to continue earning it.

"I will bear this in mind in the future, Jacob. In the meantime, we'll have what you're working on now in an afternoon extra, as well as on the first page in tomorrow's edition. The story is yours from now on."

He thanked me rather tersely, but I pretended not to notice. The locked diary box awaited me on my desk in the front office, and it reminded me that while I'd just given Jacob the right to pursue Katherine Pendleton's story, I would not be backing away from it entirely. He might have the bylines in the *Messenger*, but I wouldn't rest until I'd pieced together these three murders and the reasons for them. The cocaine? No, I didn't think that was it. That had merely linked the three victims as having known one another, having had recent interactions with one another, and having shared a secret. I also wouldn't rest until I'd discovered whether the Spouting Rock victim was Stuart Gale. Would Katherine's journals provide the clues I needed? I took out the key Jesse had given me and inserted it into the lock.

Chapter 16

Jimmy Hawkins, sitting at the desk across from mine, inquired whether I needed any help with what I was doing, indicating the diary box. I assured him I didn't, that I was probably on a fool's errand anyway, and encouraged him to continue with his own tasks. With that, he bent over his work and I began poring over the diaries.

If August Pendleton hadn't murdered his sister, then someone else had to have been at the house yesterday. With no signs of forced entry, the assumption could be made that Katherine had known her killer, had admitted the individual voluntarily, and had done so without the housekeeper's knowledge. This suggested Katherine had expected her visitor, and had been ready to open the door when he or she arrived.

With that in mind, I slid two of the volumes from the diary box: Katherine's daily journal and the visitors and addresses book. I opened both side by side on my desk and flipped to the days before she died, searching for anything unusual. She had recorded going to several luncheons and listed the names of those who had accompanied her. She had also attended the pre-opera soiree at Bailey's Beach, which put her in the same vicinity as the Spouting Rock victim the night he died. Had she met him somewhere on the sand to obtain the cocaine? Had the prince been there as well? What about her brother? The journals gave no hint.

On the day she died, yesterday, I saw nothing recorded—no activities and no visitors. With a sigh, I sat back and stared out the window facing Spring Street. Pedestrians hurried by, along with the usual buggies, wagons, and carts, all raising clouds of dust. A ringing bell heralded the approach of a trolley, and a moment later it rumbled by. I turned my attention back to the journal labeled "Visitors and Addresses." The pages in the visitors' section were divided into sections corresponding to the days of the week. Yesterday's section was empty. . . .

No, it wasn't; something, a single letter, perhaps, had been rendered in pencil in the upper left corner. I bent lower over the page, then whipped open my top drawer and seized the magnifying glass I kept there for deciphering small print. I held it over the mark and pushed the journal closer to the window to benefit from the sunlight.

C. It was faint; Katherine had barely pressed her pencil onto the paper. I stared harder. Was I only conjuring something I wished to see? Was it merely a stray mark where perhaps her pencil had slipped from her grasp? The other entries were all in ink. Why pencil? Why so faint? And what did the letter signify?

C . . . for club . . . carriage . . . Clemson. The name leaped to my thoughts. Had Eugene or Isabel Clemson paid Katherine a visit yesterday? If so, who had contacted whom? And why? Had Katherine discovered something about one of them? Had there been a confrontation?

A sudden sharp rapping startled me from my speculations, and I looked up to see Mrs. Fish staring at me through the window. She didn't look pleased. She pointed at me, then dropped her hand to her side and marched to the door.

"And where were you yesterday?" she demanded upon entering the office. "You said you'd come by Crossways on your way home."

I'd never said any such thing; she had. But I didn't remind her of this. Across the office, Jimmy also glanced up, disconcerted by Mrs. Fish's dramatic entrance. I gave him an infinitesimal shrug and turned back to my visitor. "Mrs. Fish, it was a hectic afternoon, and I needed to write up the details of the crime in order to get them into the morning's edition."

"*Humph.*" She sidled up to my desk. "What've you got there?"

"These are Katherine's personal journals. I'd hoped to find some indication of who might have visited her yesterday."

"You still believe in Auggie's innocence, I see."

"Generally speaking, yes, although I admit to harboring a doubt or two. Either way, the police would like to rule out any other possibilities, and Detective Whyte asked me to take a peek at these."

"More like you twisted his arm into letting you have them." She grinned, letting me know she didn't disapprove of such tactics. It appeared she had forgiven me. "So, have you found anything?"

We had Jimmy's full attention now. I couldn't blame him. The death of a beautiful young woman made a compelling story, a mystery begging to be solved. His interest reflected that of the general populace, who would be scrambling to buy newspapers today.

"Look at this." I pointed to the C and handed her the magnifier. "What do you think? Is it a letter, or just a stray mark?"

"Looks like a C to me."

I lowered my voice. "Clemson?"

"Hmm . . ." She looked about her, and I realized I hadn't offered her a chair. Quickly I rose and brought the spare side chair we kept for visitors. She made herself comfortable while still studying the page in the journal. "It could also stand for Charles."

Puzzled, I shook my head.

"Charles Eldridge," she clarified.

"Oh, yes. Aunt Alva's houseguest. He danced with Katherine at the Harvest Festival, and her brother seemed none too happy about it."

Mrs. Fish nodded sagely. "Which could be why she penciled in this reminder of his pending visit so cryptically, in case her brother happened to see."

I shook my head and showed her the guard on the diary box. "These journals are kept under lock and key. And they were found in Katherine's room."

"That may be so, but perhaps Auggie keeps a spare key. They're locked, yes, but that's probably to keep nosy servants from prying into affairs that are none of their business. Look at the other books." Her fingertips danced over the silver-gilt, leather spines. "One is marked household expenses. Another, cash accounts. My guess is Auggie had access to these books."

"That does make sense, I suppose."

"My dear, I always make sense."

"But why would Charles Eldridge have murdered Katherine Pendleton? He seemed enamored of her. You even encouraged him not to waste time in making his feelings clear to her."

"Exactly." Her enthusiasm made me jump. With a glance over her shoulder at Jimmy, she lowered her voice. "And perhaps he did just that, yesterday, and she rejected him."

"And he murdered her in a fit of disappointment?" I shook my head. While crimes of passion were not infrequent, they usually entailed more than a broken heart. "And what reason would he have had for murdering Prince Otto and the Spouting Rock victim?" Yet, even as I asked, several reasons came to mind.

"Just because the answer to that isn't immediately evident, my dear, is no reason to believe one doesn't exist."

I knew she was right. The office telephone rang, startling us both. Jimmy answered it and held out the receiver to me. "Detective Whyte." He sighed. "It's never anything good when that man calls."

I couldn't argue with him about that. Nonetheless, I jumped up from my seat and hurried over. "Yes, Jesse?"

Mrs. Fish followed me, and bent her head close to mine to listen in.

Without any precursor, Jesse said, "We've found two links between the prince and the Spouting Rock victim. Traces of cocaine were found in his nasal cavity during the autopsy. And the desk clerk who's been away these past couple of days is back. He's able to describe a man who visited the prince in his suite, and he sounds like our man from Spouting Rock. I'm there now. I hate to ask this of you—I know how busy you are—but can you come to the Ocean House and bring that photograph of yours?"

"I'll be right there."

"As will I," Mrs. Fish said before I had hung up.

"Yes, I'd say that could be him." The clerk absently scratched at his receding hairline. "He was older, as you say, but the likeness is strong."

"Are you sure?" Jesse prodded.

"Pretty sure." The man stared down at the image for several more seconds.

I didn't know whether to be encouraged or thwarted. True, the likelihood of the prince and the Spouting Rock victim having known each other was stronger than ever, but I felt no closer to proving—to myself at least—that Stuart Gale had been the man accompanying him.

"Can you tell us anything about him?" I asked, and ignored the censorious look from Jesse. "Or about what he said to you when he came into the hotel?"

"Well, now, let me see . . . He asked which room the prince was staying in, and rather than tell him right off I used the in-house telephone to ring the prince's suite. Had to make sure the prince wanted visitors, you understand. The man went up, and some quarter hour later, give or take, the pair of them came down to the lobby." A ridge formed above his nose. "They were speaking in German, come to think of it. I could hear them because they came down the main stairs." He pointed to the wide staircase only feet away from the front desk.

Jesse looked disappointed. "Then you don't know what they were saying."

"No, not until the older one, the one in the photograph, switched to English."

Mrs. Fish let out a gasp. "And what did he say?"

Once again, Jesse expressed his disapproval at Mrs. Fish's and my attempts to question the clerk. Apparently, he'd wished me to bring the photograph and then step aside, but he should have known better than that. I was not a reporter for nothing. And as for Mrs. Fish, well, there wasn't much that deterred that woman.

The clerk had paused, thinking, and then raised his eyebrows and said, " 'Don't worry, I'll take care of it.' That's what the older gentleman said. To which the prince responded, 'Make matters clear. I never bluff.' At least, I think that's what he said. His English . . . it wasn't as good as the older gentleman's. The accent was much heavier."

Mrs. Fish leaned over the counter toward the clerk. "You heard that and didn't think to alert anyone?"

He pulled back. "Alert whom, madam? About what?"

"About an obvious threat." Mrs. Fish thrust her finger toward his chest, once, twice, as though to poke him, though she stopped several inches short of making contact.

Beads of perspiration broke out across the man's brow. "They might have been discussing anything. Business dealings. A polo match. And none of it is any of my business."

I agreed with Mrs. Fish in general. Those statements did sound like threats, but I also sympathized with the desk clerk. Like those who served in the cottages, his job was to ensure order and see to the comfort of his guests. Beyond that, he was to remain invisible as well as deaf to private conversations. A hotel that didn't meticulously guard the privacy of its guests would not remain in business for long.

"Mrs. Fish, our part here is done. Why don't we leave and allow Detective Whyte to finish up with this gentleman."

She harrumphed, a sound that had grown familiar in recent days. "Are you attempting to manage me, young lady?"

"Of course not. I simply—"

"All righty, come along." She linked her arm through mine and nodded her good-byes to Jesse and the clerk. For now, I left my photograph with Jesse, who looked exceedingly relieved to see us go.

Mrs. Fish's victoria carriage, once again manned by a driver and footman, had waited for us in Washington Square. Rather than climb in beside her, I convinced her to go about her business and allow me to make my own way back to the *Messenger*. She protested, but I assured her the walk would do me good, and that the work waiting on my desk could not be ignored.

She shuddered. "Are you quite sure you wouldn't rather I hired someone to take care of all that nonsense for you?"

"Positive. I'm quite happy with my position, thank you."

She shook her head in mystification and waved as the carriage pulled away. With a little sigh, I started down Spring Street, blending in with afternoon shoppers. I did a bit of window shopping myself. When I came to Molly's Dress Shop, I couldn't help ducking inside.

"Emma, how lovely to see you today. It's been an age." Molly Tucker had always been Mother's favorite modiste in town. I couldn't afford her dressmaking services, but I often bought fabrics and trim with which Nanny turned out old dresses and made them look new and fashionable again. While most women of the Four Hundred bought their apparel from House of Worth, Rouff, Redfern, and other preeminent designers, Molly always stocked little treasures that were out of reach for most local Newport women—fine lace, silks, and velvets—which brought the summer set into the shop.

Molly herself was dressed as I often did, in a plain, crisp shirtwaist and a dark, slim skirt that flared as it swept the floor. With her hair loosely piled high, she looked the very image of one of Charles Dana Gibson's illustrations of the modern young woman, despite her forty-odd years. Molly came around her work counter and lightly hugged me. "Are you looking for something in particular?"

"Oh, I don't know. I was walking back to the *Messenger* from the Square, and couldn't resist popping in."

"Well, I'm glad you did. It's quiet now. Have tea with me." She led me into a small back room that contained a table and two chairs. A doorway led farther back, into a storeroom lined with floor-to-ceiling shelves packed with assorted fabrics. She filled an iron kettle at the sink and set it on the coal-burning stove in the corner. "I always take my lunch in here, where I can hear the bell if anyone comes in."

She inquired after my parents, and then we caught up on the many weeks we hadn't seen each other, including my explaining how I'd come to be the editor-in-chief of the Newport *Messenger.*

Her eyes sparkled at my successes. "I see that paper all over town now, whereas before it barely circulated."

"The credit for that goes to the owner, Derrick Andrews," I admitted. "I'm only running things while he's tied up in Providence."

She asked me all sorts of questions about Derrick, including whether there might be a wedding in my future. Molly had never been one to mince words. I assured her she'd be among the first to know whenever I happened to marry; after all, I would certainly need her services then.

Eventually, we came to the subject of the recent murders. There wasn't much I could tell her that she hadn't already read in the newspapers—at least not without betraying Jesse's trust.

Finally, a canny look came over her. "You're obviously not going to tell me, Emma, so I'll have to ask. Was he or wasn't he?"

I drew an utter blank. "Was who what?"

She leaned forward and propped both hands on her hips. "Was the Spouting Rock victim your half brother's father or not?"

"You've heard about that."

"Of course I have. I'm no gossip, but you don't work in a shop in this town without hearing things."

Her first claim might be rather dubious, but I couldn't deny the second. "I suppose most of Newport has heard by now." I sighed and sipped my tea. "But the truth is, I don't know, and neither does Brady."

"Wouldn't it be something if he was? Can you imagine, showing up after all these years. Why, I was still a young girl when he supposedly went down on that yacht." She shook her head in apparent wonderment. "Like a ghost rising from the dead, only to end up dead again."

The conversation had taken a morbid turn, in my opinion, and I wished to steer us into more congenial waters. The bell above the shop door tinkled before I could speak.

Molly jumped to her feet. "If you'll excuse me, I'll go see who that is and what they need."

I drained my cup. "I should be getting along anyway. Thank you for the tea, Molly."

"Do come back soon," she said over her shoulder as she disappeared into the shop.

Before I exited, a display of flowered cambric and matching flocked ribbon caught my eye. I fingered the light fabric and thought what a lovely shirtwaist Nanny could make with it. "I believe I will be back soon, Molly."

A cry of distaste followed immediately upon my declaration, and I turned about to see Isabel and Thea Clemson standing with Molly at the counter. Mrs. Clemson held a length of frilly white broderie anglaise in her hands. She dropped it to the counter as though it singed her palms.

"What are you doing here?" she challenged me. "Have you been following us?"

Taken aback, I pressed a hand to my breastbone. "I've been here since before you came in."

Poor Molly looked baffled, and Thea Clemson turned scarlet. And yet, I perceived a silent appeal in Thea's eyes, a message I couldn't decipher, delivered with an urgency that impressed upon me the need to speak with her alone. There could be no opportunity at present, however; her mother's presence made that impossible.

Mrs. Clemson drew herself up and linked her arm through her daughter's. "Come, Thea. We shan't give our business to a shop that lowers itself to the level of such a patron."

Thea's eyes flashed in shock, along with an emotion that might have been outrage. "Mama, really . . ."

Mrs. Clemson heeded her daughter not at all, but forcefully walked her to the door. It slammed behind them, leaving Molly and me stupefied.

"Molly, I'm so sorry. I didn't mean to chase away business."

"What on earth was that about?" She came to stand beside me and gazed out the wide front window. The Clemson women hurriedly crossed the street and scrambled into a waiting carriage.

The unpleasantness and its regrettable result—the loss of a sale for Molly—raised a gnawing in my stomach. "I'm afraid I've given them cause to resent me." I briefly explained about some—though not all—of the questions I'd asked the Clemson family concerning Prince Otto's death. "They certainly had no reason to take it out on you. I'm terribly sorry."

"Don't worry, Emma. They aren't my only customers." She smiled and turned to the cambric I'd been admiring. "Would you like me to save you a few yards of this? And the matching ribbon?"

I thanked her, not only for yard goods, but for not holding me responsible for her lost income.

When I arrived home later that same afternoon, a telegram awaited me on the post tray. It had been sent from the town of Annecy in France.

Emma
In answer to your questions: Two Americans, five
Europeans, heavy wagers laid on race. Stuart hoped to

*pay off substantial debts. Three men died including other
American. Search launched, bodies never recovered.
Yacht's owner, one Albert Goldschmidt.*
   Your loving mother.

For some minutes, I stared down at that short and wholly
inadequate reply to the telegram I'd sent after the Spouting
Rock victim's death. I don't know why I had expected or
hoped for more. Too much time had passed since the yachting accident, and I certainly couldn't blame Mother for her
cryptic answers. Not for the first time, I speculated on
whether Stuart Gale might have faked his death to escape his
debts. The accident itself could not have been planned,
surely, nor the deaths of the other men. But perhaps Stuart
had seized the opportunity to trade places with one of the
dead men, or somehow lead his rescuers to believe him to be
other than who he was.

Had one of those other crewmembers been named Stern?
Again, the records that might have proved my theory no
longer existed, if they ever had.

The one name my mother had remembered tumbled
through my brain: Goldschmidt. A German name, possibly
Austrian. The notion sent me hurrying to the telephone beneath the stairs, and I asked the evening operator to connect
me to Crossways. *Please be at home, please be at home . . .*

But of course, Mamie Fish was not at home that evening.
It wouldn't be until the next morning, after I'd spent yet another restless night, that I would have my answer.

"Goldschmidt, you say?" Like many people, Mrs. Fish
had the habit of yelling into the telephone, and I held the ear
trumpet several inches away from my ear. "Yes, I've heard of
the family. There were members of the Goldschmidt family
in Paris last spring, and again in Venice. Lovely people,

very refined, although the old gentleman is quite a hoot, I can tell you . . ."

"Mrs. Fish, can you tell me anything about their background?"

"Why, of course, my dear. They're cousins of the Rothschilds."

Chapter 17

After disconnecting with Mrs. Fish, I went into the parlor and perched in the corner of my increasingly threadbare sofa. The owner of the yacht Stuart Gale had supposedly died on was a Rothschild. Prince Otto had ties to that family as well.

Something else prodded at the back of my mind, preventing me from relaxing enough to lean back against the cushions. The cocaine. It had been in the possession of all three victims. In my mind that connected Katherine Pendleton to the Spouting Rock victim and Prince Otto, and not merely in the past. Now the hotel clerk had established a sure link between the Spouting Rock victim and Prince Otto.

Something else, something more important still, continued to evade me, a thread hanging just beyond my reach. I heard footsteps, and Nanny entered the room with Katie behind her. Katie carried a tray with a teapot and cups and set them on the table before the sofa.

"Thought you could use more tea this morning." Nanny lowered herself into the armchair opposite me with a soft groan. She rarely sat on the sofa anymore; she said dislodging herself from its down cushions had become too difficult in recent days. I regarded her pale, velvety skin and her faded blue eyes behind her half-moon spectacles, and not for the first time felt a pang of worry.

Even so, I was about to say I didn't want any more tea—I'd drank enough at breakfast—but Katie had already begun pouring and handed a cup and saucer first to Nanny, and then to me. I thanked her and sipped dutifully.

And then it struck me.

"I'd told him I didn't want any tea," I said aloud.

"Told who, dearie?" Nanny asked me absently. Katie, on the other hand, regarded me with concern. She waited for me to continue.

"Harry Forge," I said. "When I visited him to question him about Otto and the Spouting Rock victim, he plied me with tea."

"And cakes, too, I should hope." Nanny chuckled, but Katie remained solemn.

"Why do you think he did that, Miss Emma?"

I met Katie's gaze. "I considered it merely hospitality, at first."

Katie frowned. "At first?"

Nodding, I continued. "And then I thought he was trying to entice me to stay longer. He became . . . flirtatious. And not in a pleasant way. He made me uncomfortable, and I found myself pushing past him and hurrying to the front door."

Nanny had stopped smiling and set her teacup aside. "Why, that brute. That disrespectful beast. Wouldn't I like to say a thing or two to him."

"When I got outside," I went on, concentrating on the memory, "I didn't feel myself. Not myself at all."

"What do you mean, Miss Emma?"

"I had the jitters, like there were wasps loose inside me." I almost felt that way now, but this time it was anger setting the hornets loose.

"How very strange." Katie stared down into her cup. "Was it very strong tea?"

"No, it wasn't the tea." Outrage sent me to my feet. "It was what he put *into* the tea, or had his man put in the tea before bringing it out to us. I'd wager anything it was cocaine."

Nanny, too, came to her feet, faster than I'd seen in quite a while. "You must call Jesse immediately and tell him about this. Have that man arrested for trying to poison you."

"I certainly will tell Jesse at the first opportunity, but I can't prove a thing, can I?" I began to pace. "But he wasn't trying to poison me. He was trying to throw me off balance, perhaps make me feel disoriented enough for him to—" I broke off as indignant fury sent my pulse pounding in my temples. "Well, if nothing else, his little deception certainly links him to three murdered people."

"Good heavens, Emma." Nanny stepped in my path and seized my hands. "Do you think he's the murderer?"

Behind her, Katie gasped and whisked a hand to her mouth.

"I don't know. But I believe he knows more than he was willing to tell me. Though he tried to deny it, surely he must know the identity of the Spouting Rock victim."

Nanny's gaze bore into me. "What are you going to do?"

Before I could answer, a fierce barking went up outside, in front of the house. I slipped my hands free of Nanny's and ran to the front window, where I saw Patch jumping in circles around a newly arrived carriage. A by-now familiar one.

Mrs. Fish had returned.

*   *   *

Our search for Harry Forge brought us to the Casino. Despite the most recent murder, and the fact that this one involved a popular member of the Four Hundred, today's tennis tournament had not been canceled.

Matches were held on the lawn within the long, enveloping arms of the horseshoe pavilion that comprised a restaurant, covered walkways and porches, the bowling alleys, and the main casino building, whose wide entrance we had just walked through.

Mr. Forge was no mere spectator, but a player, teamed with another Harry—Harry Lehr—against Oliver Belmont and my cousin, Alfred Vanderbilt. The match appeared to have been going on for some while when Mrs. Fish and I arrived. The players were perspiring heavily in the morning sun, their white tennis togs clinging to them in a way that would have been entirely inappropriate under any other circumstances. A fine crowd encircled the court, with many more ranged along the covered porches, both the ground floor and above, where they could view the match while escaping the sun.

We weren't there five minutes before Jesse joined us. As we had planned, we met him in front of the tower, beneath the Tiffany clock. Like many of the men present, he had dressed in a suit of lightweight seersucker and wore a straw boater to shield his head from the sun. We didn't speak to each other, but instead moved off into the crowd, Jesse keeping Mrs. Fish and me in his sights. I had telephoned the police station before leaving Gull Manor and explained to him what I needed. I'd also conveyed what had happened at Harry Forge's house—the tea, its odd effect on me, and his attempt to detain me there.

When the match ended, Mrs. Fish and I wasted no time in moving in to congratulate the winning team, consisting of the two Harrys. The excitement began to die down, and

Mrs. Fish engaged Harry Forge in a conversation about a charity event she wished him to help her organize when they all returned to New York in the fall. She did virtually all of the talking, allowing him little more than grunts of agreement. She claimed his arm and led him slowly away from the crowd. No one seemed to notice, for another match would soon begin. Mr. Forge seemed a bit bemused by Mrs. Fish and her rapid-fire talking, until he noticed me standing off to the side.

"Will you also be in New York this fall, Miss Cross?" A salacious smile accompanied his question, arousing only my anger.

"I'm afraid not," I replied with false sweetness. "I'm not a summer visitor to Newport. I live here." Mrs. Fish had not relinquished his arm, and after a glance at me, she continued walking, compelling him to come along or publicly behave in an ungentlemanly way. I knew Harry Forge was no gentleman, and with an inner shudder I contemplated what might have happened if I hadn't had the presence of mind to leave his house when I did, not to mention not drinking any more of his tainted tea than I had.

We moved beyond the pavilion toward the Casino's theater. With everyone's attention on the tennis court, this area was empty. Good. Mrs. Fish brought Mr. Forge to a halt, and I moved in closer.

I once again showed him the photograph of my mother and Stuart Gale. "You said he was familiar. I believe you know exactly who he is."

Though the photograph held his gaze, his thoughts were obviously elsewhere—probably on whether or not to admit the truth. The distant *thwap-thwap* of the tennis ball counted off the seconds. Mr. Forge's nose flared as his good humor turned to anger. "This amounts to calling me a liar, Miss Cross. And you, Mrs. Fish. I wouldn't expect this sort of behavior from a woman of your standing. But then, you seem to be keeping rather low company these days." He shifted his gaze to me.

Behavior, indeed; he was one to talk. Despite the insult, Mrs. Fish's eyes twinkled. She was enjoying this, I could tell, and obviously looked forward to seeing it through to its outcome.

"Well?" Harry Forge demanded. "Nothing to say for yourselves? Why should I stand here and endure rudeness from either of you?"

"Because you've little choice, Mr. Forge." Jesse, who had approached us unobserved—at least by Mr. Forge—joined our little circle. Mrs. Fish and I had been expecting him. He held up his badge before replacing it in his inner coat pocket. "You can answer Miss Cross's questions here and now, or you can do so at the police station. It's entirely up to you, sir."

Mr. Forge took his time in sizing Jesse up. Applause broke out within the pavilion, followed by cheers. An insolent smirk curled Mr. Forge's lip. "Do you always take your orders from women half your size?"

I started to protest but Jesse held up a hand to silence me. "You know, Mr. Forge, you have a point. This is my investigation, after all, and Katherine Pendleton is dead. You know about that, don't you?"

"Of course I know. What's that got to do with—"

Jesse held out the same hand again, this time to silence the man before him. "Who gave her the cocaine, Mr. Forge?"

"What?" The man's face turned ruddy. "I . . . I don't know what you're talking about."

This time I wouldn't be silenced, by either man. "Yes, you do, Mr. Forge. I'll wager if a thorough search of your house was made right now, an elixir containing a good amount of cocaine would be found there. I wonder if a search need even be made. It's probably right on your kitchen work counter, where it's handy for your butler to mix into your tea." I spoke that last word with emphasis. Mr. Forge's lips thinned.

"Answer my question, Mr. Forge." Jesse made a show of taking a pad and pencil from his coat pocket.

"I gave Katherine nothing," the other man said, his jaws clenched. "Besides, there are no laws against it. It's nothing more than what's found in countless patent medicines."

Jesse nodded as if in agreement, but a vein thrashed in his temple. "You're right. But should it become known that you supplied a beautiful young debutante with a drug that has been acknowledged to be potentially harmful, I think it would be safe to say your social calendar will become a gaping chasm for the next several years at least."

"I told you I didn't give it to her." He swallowed hard, making his Adam's apple bob sharply. "That's the truth."

"Then where did you get yours from, Mr. Forge?" I raised my eyebrows at him.

He scowled back. Then he nodded at the photograph still in my hand. "From him. If that *is* him."

"The man who was murdered at Spouting Rock," I said without surprise.

He nodded.

"Tell us his name." Jesse once more set pencil to paper.

Harry Forge expelled a breath. "Sturm. Gabriel Sturm."

"Not Stern," I said. "Miss Pendleton told us his last name was Stern."

"Close," Mrs. Fish observed. "Likely she didn't want us to know his real name, or that she knew him well at all. Not if she wished to keep us from learning her little secret."

"Why did you lie about recognizing him when I asked you the first time?" I tapped my foot in impatience to hear the truth.

Mr. Forge turned a little away from me, as if he found speaking to blank air easier. "Because I didn't like admitting to knowing the likes of him. Gabriel Sturm was a shyster and gambler, and a deplorable influence on Otto. He used the prince's money to pay for his own excesses, and in return the prince used *him* to strong-arm those in his debt. That's why he brought Sturm to America. Had Sturm not been murdered, he'd have twisted more than a few arms among the Four Hundred. Many of whom were your guests at Crossways that night, Mrs. Fish."

Mrs. Fish narrowed her eyes in speculation. "That still doesn't explain why you lied to Emma—that is, Miss Cross here—about recognizing the man."

Mr. Forge hesitated. The steady beat of the rackets against the ball was beginning to wear on my nerves, and I noticed Jesse pressing his pencil against his notepad until a sliver of the tip broke off.

Finally, Harry Forge spoke. "The ... the age difference put me off at first."

Jesse let out a laugh. "Hardly. Come now, Mr. Forge. Why did you deny knowing this Gabriel Sturm? Let's hear something approaching the truth for once." His notetaking forgotten, he let his hands fall to his sides. "Where did you spend the spring, Mr. Forge? Were you in Prince Otto's company, and perhaps this Gabriel Sturm's? Did something happen between the two of you?"

"It would be easy enough to find out the truth." Mrs. Fish turned to Jesse. "We can't do a thing without a few dozen other people knowing about it, and that's not counting the press." She placed a hand on Mr. Forge's shoulder. "Go on, Harry. Tell the man what he wants to know. It'll all come out anyway."

Harry Forge nodded with a show of resignation. "All right, yes. There were enough witnesses to tell you that I crossed the Atlantic with the prince and Gabriel Sturm. Two weeks ago. And during the voyage I had it out with Sturm.

I'd grown sick and tired of how he was using Otto and leading him to self-destruction."

"'Had it out with Sturm,'" I repeated. "As in, you argued?"

"Yes, we argued. But that's all we did."

"There were witnesses?" I asked.

He shrugged. "I suppose our voices were overheard. But I tell you, that's all it was. An argument."

"You're something of a hypocrite, aren't you, Mr. Forge?" I couldn't help pointing out the obvious, while another burst of applause from the court seemed to emphasize the point. "You say Mr. Sturm was leading the prince down a self-destructive path, but what about your own habits? What about you . . ." My voice rose in anger. "Leading me astray with your cocaine-tainted tea? Where were your noble intentions then?"

"I didn't mean any harm." He wiped the sweat off his brow with his sleeve.

"No harm?" That was all I could manage; I was near choking on my indignation.

"Look—" Whatever Harry Forge would have said dissolved into an *oomph,* forced out of him by Jesse's elbow jabbing him in the ribs. I let out a gasp; I'd never before seen Jesse manhandle anyone. Not a suspect, not a hostile witness, no one. I wondered, if Jesse's hands hadn't been occupied with his pencil and notepad, would he have used his fist?

His features impassive, Jesse straightened his coat with a twitch of his shoulders. "I'm terribly sorry, Mr. Forge. I didn't mean any harm. Are you all right?"

Mrs. Fish stifled a giggle. Mr. Forge raised his gaze to Jesse slowly, as if he feared making eye contact would bring on another jab. "I'm fine. Now see here, am I under arrest or not?"

"Not," Jesse said succinctly. "At least not yet. We'll see. If I were you, Mr. Forge, I'd give up my dangerous habits.

They're bad for one's health, in more ways than one." He turned to Mrs. Fish and me. "Ladies, if you wouldn't mind, I have a word or two I'd like to exchange with Mr. Forge in private."

"You're sending us on our way?" Mrs. Fish's hands went to her waist. "After we—"

"Mrs. Fish, Detective Whyte obviously has some official police business to finish up with Mr. Forge." I linked my arm through hers and drew her away. "Why don't we watch some of the match."

"Oh, very well. But I don't like being dismissed. I surely don't. And another thing . . ."

The Four Hundred had come out for the match in large numbers, and familiar faces surrounded me as Mrs. Fish and I rejoined the crowd. I half hoped to find Brady here, and left Mrs. Fish's side to stroll along the sidelines and the covered walkways. My hopes might have been in vain, but my efforts did not go unrewarded. On the patio of the restaurant, I spied Thea Clemson sitting by herself at a corner table. A second cup of tea and a place setting sat before an empty chair, signifying that she had been accompanied. Her mother? Probably. I glanced around but saw no sign of the woman. Of course, that didn't mean she wouldn't descend upon me with the swiftness of a dragonfly on evening gnats if she saw me anywhere near her daughter.

The thought didn't deter me, and I climbed the steps to the patio and approached the table. Most of the other tables were occupied, as customers enjoyed a meal while watching the match. Thea, however, showed no interest in the tennis match. Instead, she sat with her head bent over an item cradled in her hands.

"Miss Clemson."

Her hands closed around the object and whisked it to her

lap as she looked up, clearly startled. Then she relaxed. "Oh, it's you. Whatever do you want?"

"I wished to apologize for upsetting you on the previous occasions we've met."

She pursed her lips in a way that let me know she wasn't in a forgiving mood. But then she did something that astonished me. She burst into tears.

Not a sound escaped her, but her shoulders shook fiercely with her effort to silence her sobs while the tears streaked down her cheeks. She retreated under her hat brim, and her knuckles whitened around the object she held.

I quickly looked around at the other diners. So far, no one seemed to have noticed Miss Clemson's emotional distress. Thank goodness for the match. I chose a seat that would further help shield her from scrutiny, and leaned over the table toward her. "Miss Clemson, what is it? Can I be of assistance in any way?"

She shook her head while her lips remained tightly pressed together. And yet, I didn't have the impression she wished me to leave her, or that I had caused her tears. No, I believed they had been gathering long before I arrived on the patio. I reached across and gave her shoulder a squeeze, then folded my hands on the table before me and waited, all the while serving as a wall between her and the others on the patio. Finally, she lifted the back of her hand to dab at her eyes.

"I'm terribly sorry," she said with a hiccup. "That's not something I typically do."

"There's certainly no need to apologize to me."

"I don't suppose there is. Except . . . thank you for sitting there." She darted glances over my shoulders. I looked around as well. The attention of everyone around us had remained on the match, their meals, and one another. "I don't know what I would have done if all these people had seen my moment of weakness. It would have been too, too shameful."

"I'm glad I could be of service. Well, I suppose I should leave you alone now." I slowly gathered myself to stand.

Her features crumpled with the further threat of tears, and she raised the object she held to eye level. Nestled in her palm was a gold locket with a faceted ruby mounted on the cover. She opened it. "It's Otto," she explained without prompting. "He gave it to me the night he died, when he came to see me. It was his mother's, and he'd put a portrait of himself inside. How handsome he was. Don't you agree, Miss Cross?"

She held out the locket for me to see. The image of the dark-haired, dark-eyed young man immediately seized my attention. The miniature portrait, rendered in oils, was small by any standards, yet I could make out enough detail to shock me to my very bones. I raised my gaze to Thea's face, and suddenly understood more than I wished to.

"If Mother knew I had this," she said, "she'd take it away from me. Probably destroy it, at least the picture." She tucked the locket into her bodice and pressed a reverent hand over her heart. "I don't know why she hated Otto. I never knew she did until that day you and Mrs. Fish came to talk to us, and I admitted that Otto and I had planned to marry. The way she reacted, and the things she said after you left. Terrible things about Otto and his family. I suppose Mother believed he took advantage of me. But, Miss Cross, he never did. He was always a gentleman. But now I'm so afraid it was Mother who . . ."

I went utterly still. Thea didn't have to continue; she obviously feared her mother had murdered Otto in a desperate attempt to keep the pair apart. I admit I'd had the same notion, and even now I didn't rule it out. As I groped for something comforting to say without making myself a liar, Thea gave herself a shake and drew up straighter.

"It's silly of me, isn't it, Miss Cross, to think my mother could do something so unthinkable. Of course she couldn't have. And . . . she was surrounded by so many people at the Harvest Festival. She couldn't have slipped away without a few dozen people noticing. Isn't that right?"

I half nodded. There had been so many guests at Cross-ways, in so many parts of the house and grounds, that any one of them could have slipped away without the others noticing. But if Thea took my silence as affirmation, I wasn't of a mind to contradict her.

"This . . ." She again pressed her palm over the locket. "This was meant as a promise. Otto said there would be a ring soon, and a wedding. But now that will never happen, and I don't know what to do, Miss Cross. I don't know how to go on."

This extraordinary speech left me without words of my own. My mind wheeled like gulls searching for a meal.

"Miss Cross? Have you nothing to say?"

I reached across to lay my hand over her wrist. "I'm de-termined to help find the prince's killer and bring him to jus-tice. And I hope that when that happens, it will bring some small comfort to you, Miss Clemson."

She leaned back and nodded. "Yes, there's nothing more to be said, is there? No one and nothing can bring Otto back. I shall live out my life alone, and I must grieve pri-vately, mustn't I?"

I wished to tell her that she would not remain alone, that in time, she would find someone else to love and grow old with. I wished I could have told her that her mother had been right, that she and Otto could not have married. But I could not say any of those things to someone so heartbroken and inconsolable, or so young. She would not have believed me, and such words would not have helped. Not then.

"Is there anything else I can do for you, Miss Clemson?"

She nodded. "Yes, if you see either of my parents, do not mention my distress to them, and certainly don't tell Mother what I'd been suspecting of her. Will you keep this a secret, Miss Cross? I know you're a reporter and that you work for the *Messenger*, but I've also heard that you can be discreet."

"Indeed I can, Miss Clemson. There is no story here, nothing to tell anyone. You have my word on it." I remained another few moments while Thea took a handkerchief from her bag and finished drying her eyes. Then, after assuring her she no longer appeared as if she'd been crying, I left her.

Chapter 18

My next request left Jesse befuddled, but he saw the urgency in my expression and agreed. After leaving the Casino, Mrs. Fish and I went in separate directions—her turning south on Bellevue to return home, and me heading north, across town. Jesse accompanied me, and at Friendship Street he helped me down from his carriage and led the way into the hospital.

With a flash of his badge he gained access to the basement morgue, and there Prince Otto's body was brought out and the drape covering him lowered to reveal his face. I had mentally prepared myself for the smell and the sight of a several-days-old body. Even so, my stomach churned and I resolved to complete my errand as soon as possible. It didn't take very long, actually, to confirm what Thea's miniature portrait had suggested to me. I nodded to Jesse, who in turn nodded to the physician who had come down with us. The man drew up the sheet and wheeled the body away. Jesse and I made our way back outside to his carriage.

"I'll need to speak with Isabel Clemson as soon as possible," I said along the way.

"She was at the Casino, wasn't she?"

"Yes, the whole family was there."

"Later, then. This isn't something you can bring up in a public place." Jesse helped me up into the carriage and took up the reins.

"Indeed not. Or where her husband or Thea might overhear. This isn't going to be easy." I mulled over my choices and sighed. "An afternoon tea would be ideal, somewhere she won't expect to be confronted." An idea came to me. "Aunt Alva. She'll hold a tea if I ask her, I'm sure of it. Assuming her social calendar isn't already full."

"But will Mrs. Clemson attend without her daughter?" Jesse turned the carriage onto Broadway.

"If she does bring Thea, I'll find a way to speak with her alone." A look came over his face, and I hastened to speak before he did. "You needn't worry. Belcourt will be perfectly safe. There will be plenty of people about, between the guests and the servants. If Isabel did have reason to murder Prince Otto, she won't have the opportunity to do likewise to me."

"I could call on her and ask her the same questions, or have her brought down to the station."

"That's a bad idea," I told him bluntly. "For one, she might not be guilty of anything more than an indiscretion, and an open accusation could ruin her life."

"Then you don't intend to ask her outright?"

"Of course I do. Just away from prying eyes and ears."

I telephoned Aunt Alva that evening. It took some doing to persuade her to agree. Not that her calendar precluded her having the time, or that she didn't like the idea of holding an afternoon tea for her female friends. On the contrary, the idea appealed to her. No, what caused the problem was her inability to understand why the suggestion came from me, usually the last person to care about such things.

"What do you have up your sleeve, Emma?" she pressed. If I knew anything about Alva Vanderbilt Belmont, it was that one could not get past her stubborn resolve without satisfying her curiosity.

"It has to do with the recent murders, but in a roundabout way," I told her, and before she could question me further, I added, "I am expressly forbidden by Detective Whyte to say anything more. Will you help me, Aunt Alva?" I ended on a note of finality that brooked no further debate and crossed my fingers it would work. One never knew with Aunt Alva.

I heard a sigh over the wire. "Of course I will. I owe you my daughter's happiness, don't I?" I resisted replying to that, especially since I didn't believe Consuelo Vanderbilt to be particularly happy in her new life. The letters I'd received from her sometimes led me to regret the part I'd played in leading her to her current circumstances. Before I could ruminate further on the matter, Alva's voice again leaped from the receiver. "Who's to be on the guest list?"

I felt a little twinge of triumph. "Whomever you like. Make it an assortment of ladies, but do include Isabel Clemson."

"Isabel, eh? Interesting. What about her daughter?"

"I suppose you should invite her, too, or it will appear odd."

"And what are you planning once everyone is here?"

"Leave that to me. Just let me know when, and I'll be there."

An invitation arrived that very next afternoon. Aunt Alva must have threatened the local printer with taking her future business elsewhere, or she had paid an exorbitant fee for such speedy work and delivery. At any rate, I found myself back at Belcourt two days later. I went as a guest and dressed accordingly, in a light brown silk with ecru lace at the cuffs, collar, and waistline. The dress had been Aunt Sadie's, but Nanny had removed the bustle with its out-of-date draping, loosened the contour around my shoulders to give a slight leg-o'-mutton flair to the sleeves, and added the lace trim, rendering the garment perfectly acceptable, if not quite the latest from the Paris fashion houses. My purpose in my attire was to blend in with the others, so that when the opportunity arose to follow Mrs. Clemson and steal a private moment with her, she would not notice me until I stood right before her.

Upon arrival, I was led upstairs, not to the dining room as I had expected, but farther down the hallway to the ballroom. Indeed, Aunt Alva had invited too many guests to fit them in her dining room. A buzz of feminine voices greeted me as I stepped into the Gothic-inspired room, with its arched, carved ceiling and spectacular wall of stained glass windows, each one depicting a medieval scene. There were even suits of armor standing sentinel at either end of the long room.

Some fifty women occupied round tables festooned in pastel linens and graced with crystal vases bursting with fresh flowers. I couldn't help chuckling as I searched out Aunt Alva. I'd asked for a simple tea party, and I'd gotten a spectacle of summer pageantry. A good thing, then, that I'd slipped my notepad into my handbag at the last minute, a longtime habit not easily broken. I would want to pass these details on to Ethan for his society column in the morning.

"Well, what do you think?" Aunt Alva's deep-set eyes twinkled and her full cheeks rounded yet more with a self-satisfied grin.

"I hope you didn't go to too much trouble."

She gave my hand a squeeze. "Have you ever known me to do anything by half?"

"Certainly not," I quipped in return, speaking nothing more than the truth. She indicated where I should sit. Mrs. Fish, Mrs. Oelrichs, and several others I knew fairly well occupied my table. Isabel Clemson did not. She and her daughter sat at a neighboring table with their backs to me, while being within my view. Silently I thanked Aunt Alva for her perception. It wouldn't do to put Mrs. Clemson off by seating me with her; she would immediately become wary and go to lengths to avoid me. I doubted she even knew I was there.

But she would.

As the footmen served the soup course, Tessie Oelrichs led the conversation, speaking in great detail about the new cottage she and her husband were planning to have built on the ocean-facing side of Bellevue Avenue. Rosecliff, they would call it, and the house would be modeled after the Grand Trianon at Versailles. Briefly I wondered how Aunt Alva had taken that news; her own Marble House had been modeled after Versailles' Petit Trianon. Did she believe her friend was trying to outdo her, as her former sister-in-law Alice Vanderbilt had done when she'd had Richard Morris Hunt design The Breakers? The competition among the women of the Four Hundred never ended.

"White, inside and out," Mrs. Oelrichs was saying, "large and open and airy. No closed-in spaces for Hermann and me, thank you very much. The ballroom will give onto both the front and back gardens, and with all the French doors open, the sea breezes will simply pour over us like an incoming tide."

"Sounds positively drenching," Mrs. Fish murmured, though loud enough for all to hear. Mrs. Oelrichs pouted at the resulting titters of laughter; a moment later she joined in.

"Well, the house will take full advantage of its location. That's all I can say." She reached for her tea, but on second thought abandoned her teacup in favor of the champagne flute beside it.

My amusement dissipated when Mrs. Clemson came to her feet. Her daughter glanced up at her and spoke some words, which her mother answered with a smile and a shake of her head. Good; wherever Mrs. Clemson was going, she would go alone. I waited for her to move about three quarters of the way to the doorway before rising and following, careful to walk behind her daughter's seat and not in her line of vision.

In the hallway, I watched Mrs. Clemson's retreating back. She made her way to the far end, where she entered Aunt Alva's bedroom, and from there, I assumed, the bathroom. The bedroom would not be private enough for my needs, for another guest might wander in. But then I remembered that, like the hall in which I stood, the bedroom opened onto the upper veranda. Perfect. I hurried down the hall.

A female attendant sat in a chair in the far corner, on hand to help adjust a bodice or fix a button. We exchanged a smile and a nod, and she returned to the piece of sewing in her lap. I took up position beside the French door leading outside and I hoped no other guests happened by. When the bathroom door opened to my right, I stepped in Mrs. Clemson's path.

She drew back and scowled at me from her greater height of several inches. But, flicking a quick glance at the attendant, she spoke in a whisper. "What do you want? Had I known you would be attending this function—"

"Yes, I know, you wouldn't have come. I have a question for you, Mrs. Clemson." I spoke quietly and politely, but directly.

"Haven't you asked enough questions? Done enough harm?"

No, I thought, I hadn't begun to do harm to this woman's life. I didn't like to do it now, but how could I ignore what I had learned two days ago, from her own daughter, no less, and which might have a bearing on not only one, but all three of the murders. Prince Otto, for daring to love Thea; Gabriel Sturm—perhaps for knowing and threatening to tell everyone the truth; and Katherine, who also might have stumbled upon Isabel Clemson's secret. If I had grown suspicious based only on a miniature portrait, then surely the woman who had once been engaged to Otto would see the evidence before her as clear as day.

"Well?" The woman before me seethed, and I knew if I didn't speak she would brush past me and hurry away, probably as far away from Belcourt as she could get.

"Come outside with me, ma'am." I reached for the latch and opened the door.

"What *is* this about?"

"It is nothing you'll want overheard."

For a moment I thought she would pull away and stalk off. But then, with a venomous look, she stepped outside. I followed, and when she turned around to challenge me once more with her scowls, I spoke.

"Who is Thea's father, Mrs. Clemson? Because I am positive it is not your husband."

Mrs. Clemson stood immobile for the span of a single breath. Then her knees gave away and she collapsed. I reached with both arms to catch her and pulled her against me to prevent her from falling to the deck. Lounge chairs lined the wall behind us, and I half carried, half dragged her to one and lowered her into it. Not a moment too soon, either. Despite her slim, angular figure, the tall woman challenged my stores of strength. She flopped against the back of the lounge, her head drooping and her eyes closing.

Quickly I peered at the French door into the bedroom. The curtains over the glass panes obscured us from the attendant's view, so I needn't worry about her coming out to check on us.

"Ma'am?" I seized Mrs. Clemson's hand and patted it firmly several times, raising a slapping sound. Her breathing increased to rapid panting, and her eyelids fluttered. She blinked and opened them, and when her gaze found me I saw sheer terror in their depths.

"How do you know? How *can* you know?" Despite the anguish in her tone, she spoke barely above a whisper.

I kept my voice low as well. "I know because of her resemblance to Prince Otto. He greatly resembled your daughter. Didn't he, Mrs. Clemson?"

"I . . ." She turned her face away from me. "Dear God."

"They were siblings, weren't they?"

Mute, she shook her head over and over, more like a nervous twitching than a gesture of denial.

"They were siblings, yet, unknowing, they formed an understanding," I persisted. "Why did you never tell your daughter the truth?"

The lines etched in her face aged her a decade. "How could I? That would have amounted to telling her she was illegitimate. How could I do that to my daughter? And my husband . . . he would have left me. Left us both to fend for ourselves. Why would he have raised a daughter who isn't his?"

"So instead you created an impossible situation."

"I had little choice. Do you think I intended for Otto and Thea to know each other? No, I wished never to lay eyes on him—or his father—again. But it's not so easy, Miss Cross.

Those of our class are not so great in number, nor is the world so large that we can avoid knowing one another. What excuse could I have given my husband not to follow our friends to Paris, Italy, and Vienna each year? How could I avoid accepting invitations to balls and other occasions, time after time, year after year?" Her explanations hissed like darts against my ears. "It became inevitable that they would come to know each other. But there were always so many people surrounding us, so many other children and, later, young men. Why should she notice Otto over anyone else? *Why*, Miss Cross?"

It struck me that she was not asking a rhetorical question, but that in her desperation she groped for answers. I had none to give her, while at the same time her admission of the truth gave her more than ample motivation for murdering the prince. What about Gabriel Sturm? Katherine Pendleton?

"Who else knows about this?" I asked.

"No one. Not even Otto's father knows Thea is his daughter. Our . . . liaison was short, quickly over. My husband had been detained in London on business, and . . ." She turned away again, tucking her chin low. "At first, they didn't look much alike, Thea and Otto. Even now, most people couldn't see it." She whisked back around, her eyebrows knotting in anger. "How could you have seen it? You didn't know Otto."

"I saw him in death. And . . . I've seen a portrait of him." I wasn't about to disclose Thea's secret of the locket.

"And from *that* you drew your conclusions?" Her head fell back against the lounge. A long breath escaped her.

"Perhaps most people wouldn't have seen it. But I'm trained to notice such details. And with the recent deaths, I've been even more attuned to subtleties than usual."

"I suppose I'm now a solid suspect, aren't I? Killed off the prince to protect my daughter, eh? Is that it?"

"Did you kill Otto?"

Another breath poured out of her. "No. I did not. But I might have, if someone else hadn't. Especially once I'd learned of his and my daughter's plans. Could you have blamed me, Miss Cross?"

"No," I said truthfully. "I don't believe in anyone taking the law into their own hands, and I could never condone such a thing. But understanding the reasons for it . . . yes, I believe I could."

As if the past several minutes hadn't occurred, she sat up straighter and met my gaze soberly. "Now what? Do you go to the police with this? Tear my marriage apart? Destroy my daughter's life?"

"Are you sure your husband doesn't know the truth?"

"Eugene?" She blinked in surprise. Then her brows gathered shrewdly. "You think *he* might have killed Otto."

"You and your husband have the strongest motives of anyone for having committed murder, Mrs. Clemson." I spoke matter-of-factly, not necessarily accusing, but using simple reason.

"Well, I know I didn't do it, and my husband would never risk—" She broke off.

"Risk what, Mrs. Clemson?"

The anger returned to her features. She looked down over the veranda railing, to the courtyard below. "Eugene would never risk returning to prison. There, now you know everything, Miss Cross, and the real reason we didn't want Thea at Crossways that night. Oh, Prince Otto was only one reason I didn't want her there. You see, Mamie Fish knows about my husband's past, and we always fear she'll blurt out things no one has any business knowing. Her husband somehow uncovered the facts."

I found myself riveted to her disclosures. "And what are those facts?"

"My husband spent time in prison as a young man. He had worked his way up to clerking for the steel company that employed him at the time—an operation no longer in business. A few of his coworkers devised a plan to embezzle funds from the company, and they arranged for Eugene to be their scapegoat. They walked away with untold thousands, while he spent two years in penitentiary. But he could never prove their guilt. All he could do was start over."

"And Thea has no idea."

"Of course Thea has no idea. No one does. My husband changed his name and built a new life for himself. I have no idea how Stuyvesant Fish learned of his past, but I do know that so far, neither he nor Mamie have told anyone." She let out a mirthless laugh. "Someday, I've no doubt, the ax will fall, and it will be by Mamie's hand." A few seconds of silence ticked by, and then she sighed. "Eugene would never risk going back to prison, not even to protect Thea."

I wasn't so sure of that.

"And now you know the entire, sordid truth, Miss Cross. Tell me, will society read about us in your *Messenger* tomorrow? And will the police barge into our home to drag us off to jail?"

Again, I had no good answer for her. If either she or her husband proved guilty, then yes, all of this would be reported in the *Messenger*, and the police would indeed take either or both of the Clemsons to jail. I could assure her of only one thing. "If I can protect your daughter's innocence and her reputation, I will, Mrs. Clemson. And now you'd better get back to the ballroom, or Thea will come looking for you."

"Miss Cross, wait." She unfolded herself from the lounge chair and pushed to her feet. "Thea has a chance to start over. Charles Eldridge has shown an interest in her. He'd make a good husband for her, but if the slightest breath of scandal should touch her . . ."

My eyes narrowed in speculation. It seemed odd that Charles Eldridge, until so recently interested in Katherine Pendleton, had so swiftly found someone to replace her. Then again, for an eligible bachelor on the hunt for a wife, one young debutante was often as good as the next. I nodded to Mrs. Clemson, but I made her no further promises.

Chapter 19

Nanny had a surprise for me when I arrived home that afternoon. I found her in the kitchen, preparing supper. Through the window above the sink I saw Katie in the laundry yard, hanging up the wash. Patch ran back and forth between her basket and the clotheslines, as if directing her activities while narrowly missing tripping her at every turn. They seemed to have a rhythm, though, and Katie never lost her footing or appeared cross with our pup.

Setting the potatoes aside, Nanny filled the kettle and set it to boil. "Sit. I have some interesting news for you." She wouldn't tell me until our tea had brewed properly and a few of her maple biscuits sat on a plate between us. "Were you able to speak with Isabel Clemson today?"

"I was. She admitted to having had an affair with Otto's father, and that Otto and Thea were half siblings." For an instant I thought of my own half sibling, struggling to come to terms with a father who had abandoned him, whether figuratively or literally, before Brady had grown old enough to remember him.

Nanny nodded as she took this in. "How horrible if those two children had gone any further in their regard for each other. Or did they?"

It was unlike Nanny to voice such conjectures out loud. I set her mind at ease. "Thea is an innocent. I believe her that nothing untoward occurred between them. Now . . ." I took a sip of tea, savoring the rejuvenating effects of the strong, dark brew. "What do you have to tell me?"

She, too, sipped her tea before replying. "I've been doing some checking for you, as I usually do." She referred to Newport's network of servants who enjoyed trading news and anecdotes with one another. They would meet at the market, on the trolleys, in the delivery hallways of the cottages, with their heads together, their voices low, their eyes alight with shared secrets. Barely a thing happened among the Four Hundred that their servants didn't witness, and soon those details made the rounds of the servants' network. "Did you know that Isabel Clemson's mother volunteered as a nurse during our Civil War?"

I stared at Nanny blankly.

"Emma, don't you understand? The woman had medical knowledge, which she might have passed on to her daughter."

Slowly I raised my teacup to my lips and sipped, then cradled the cup between my palms. "Do you know where, and how long, she served?"

"According to Susan Hicks, who is Tessie Oelrichs's lady's maid and who heard this from Mrs. Clews's housekeeper, who had it from the very woman who used to cook for Mrs. Clemson's parents, she—Mrs. Sturgis, that is— moved around to the various field hospitals and . . ." She leaned forward to stress her point. "She assisted in surgery."

I frowned. "Would a nurse have enough knowledge of anatomy to be able to pass the information on to her daughter, who would then be able to put it into practice in the act of murder?"

Nanny's silver eyebrows peaked above the rims of her half-moon spectacles. "You've been looking for someone able to pierce the ribs in just the right place to strike the heart. Do you know of anyone else with a medical background who also happened to have a motive to kill Prince Otto and the others?"

"No, but that doesn't mean another such a person doesn't exist." I blew out a breath. "I suppose this should be brought to Jesse's attention."

"You suppose? I may have just solved this case for you."

I plucked another maple biscuit from the plate. "You may have at that."

"Then what's wrong?"

"I can't help feeling sorry for Thea. She's already suffering a great deal, and I can only imagine what it will do to her if her mother is guilty. I had hoped it might be one of our other suspects. Not August Pendleton, though." I shook my head. "I believe he's another innocent, caught up in something, but not murder. Then there's Harry Forge—now he's a man whose morals aren't what they should be. He'll stoop low to get what he wants."

"Low enough to commit murder?" Nanny placed her fingers beneath my chin, lifting it slightly. "A parent will go to great lengths for the good of their child, with little thought as to the consequences to themselves. Don't forget that."

"Back to Mrs. Clemson."

"Or Mr. Clemson."

"I feel sorry for him, as well," I admitted. "He's had to overcome quite a lot in his lifetime to be where he is today." Would he risk everything to protect his daughter's reputation?

"His criminal past," Nanny said with a sage nod.

"You know about that?"

"Of course." Her eyes twinkled behind her spectacles. "The servants always know."

A telephone call at the *Messenger* the next day sent me over to the police station. Jesse had a request for me.

"I'd like you to talk to August Pendleton," he said when I arrived. "We have a theory that might actually help prove his innocence." He sat me down beside his desk and explained. "We've had a financial secretary from the Bank of Newport examining the documents found in Katherine's desk. There doesn't seem to be anything illegal going on, no reason for Katherine to have suspected her brother of any wrongdoing, nor he of her."

"Then why all the locking of drawers, and why did August refuse to talk to us?"

Jesse explained his hypothesis, and then escorted me to the small interviewing room where I'd first spoken with August Pendleton. A few minutes later a uniformed officer brought that young gentleman in.

August looked weary and frightened, in some disarray, but otherwise none the worse for wear, which assured me he was being well treated. Jesse and the officer went to stand outside the closed door.

Mr. Pendleton gazed at me from beneath a shock of hair that draped his forehead. "What is this all about?"

"That is what I'd like to ask you," I said as amicably as I could. I had no reason to challenge him or put him on his guard. Jesse wished me to question him because August would not respond to police inquiries, stating only that they were trying to trick him or trap him or otherwise establish his guilt—which was not the case at all. "Why won't you speak with Detective Whyte? He's a good man; I can vouch for that. And if the truth be told, sir, he has come round to believing in your innocence."

"Is that why he sent you in here? He thought a female, and a pleasant-looking one at that, will loosen my tongue?"

Rather than reply, I took a new tack. "Don't you wish to walk free, Mr. Pendleton? And prove to society that you didn't murder your sister? Surely you loved her very much. What reason could you possibly have had to harm her?"

Turning pale, he slumped inward, his face hovering above the table as though he might be ill. "I didn't. I could never."

"Then what have you been hiding from the police? What was Katherine trying to hide when Mrs. Fish and I visited her? The police have found nothing incriminating in the documents." A possibility came to me with such sudden clarity, I nearly gasped. I took a moment to compose myself. "Mr. Pendleton . . . Auggie . . ." I reached across to him to place my hand over his wrist. "It was Katherine, wasn't it, overseeing your banking business. She kept track of the figures and the investments, didn't she?"

Still refusing to look at me, he was shaking his head. His arm slid out from under my palm. In a voice that barely carried across the table, he said, "I'll be ruined if people find out. I'll lose everything, especially now that she's gone. Our customers, our investors, will lose all faith in me and the bank will close. Or it will remain in business, but I'll be voted out by the board members. What am I going to do?"

"Then I'm right." That I had guessed correctly startled me, as did the conclusion that followed. "This is why you didn't like the idea of her marrying. If Katherine had a husband, he might have stepped in and taken over at the bank."

He nodded grimly. "I couldn't manage it. I never could. Katherine was far more clever than I. But no one could ever know that. I'm Father's heir, and I'm supposed to be in charge. What would people think if they knew my sister has been covering for me?"

"They'll never need to know. You'll hire someone to help you, Auggie."

"Father never did. Oh, he had accountants and financial assistants aplenty, but he oversaw everything." He glanced up at me briefly. "He insisted upon it. Just as Katherine did." His head fell into his hands. "I'm a complete failure."

"Mr. Pendleton, please look at me." I reverted to his surname to help boost his confidence. When he looked up warily, I continued. "You will not be a failure. You will hire discreet people to help you and you will *learn* how to oversee your business."

"I don't know . . ."

"The alternative is hanging for a crime you didn't commit. Now, I see no reason why anyone other than the police must know what you've just told me. But you *must* tell them, Mr. Pendleton. Don't you see, this gives you a reason for having needed your sister alive. It makes no sense that you would have murdered her when you needed her so badly."

His hands came away from his face and he sat up straighter. "That's true. But you're a reporter, aren't you? That's why Katherine didn't want me talking to you at the Harvest Festival. She was afraid you'd ask too many questions and I'd end up telling you something I shouldn't." How like a child he sounded, how desperate and naïve.

"I am a reporter, true, but not an unprincipled one. I assure you, I have no desire to see your bank close and all your employees put out of work." I noticed Jesse peeking in through the small window in the door. "Now, you think about what we've discussed, Mr. Pendleton, and when Detective Whyte speaks with you again, you're to tell him the truth. Think of Katherine. She would want you to go free, wouldn't she?"

I left him nodding at my question and looking a good deal less frightened than when I'd arrived. Jesse and I returned to the main section of the police station. Along the way, he pointed out to me that while I might have prevented August from being formally charged in the death of his sister, he might still be implicated in the deaths of Otto and Gabriel Sturm.

"I suppose I'll have to have a few words with Mrs. Clemson and see if she has a verifiable alibi for when Katherine Pendleton was murdered," Jesse said when I'd explained everything I'd learned the day before, including what Nanny had told me. "I agree with you that her mother having volunteered as a nurse doesn't make Isabel Clemson guilty by default. Then again, this is our only lead that might explain the killer's finesse with a knife. So far, there is no other evidence of a medical nature. Not to mention that Mrs. Clemson has a pretty strong motive for wanting the prince out of the way."

"The strongest we've come across so far," I agreed, looking up at him where he perched at the corner of his desk. "Even stronger than August Pendleton wanting revenge for the way Otto treated his sister."

"And unless Eugene Clemson knew of his wife's infidelity, I can't see a good reason for him to have dispatched the prince." He tapped the back of his foot against a leg of the desk. "As for Mrs. Clemson, one might suppose this Gabriel Sturm, and perhaps even Katherine Pendleton, knew the truth and had to be gotten rid of as well."

"At one time, they were all part of the same circle," I added. "Katherine, Sturm, the prince, and the Clemsons. Anyone spending enough time with Thea Clemson would likely see the resemblance between Otto and her."

Jesse slid to his feet. "Which makes me highly uncomfortable. Who else might have realized the truth?"

My eyes widening at his intimation, I came to my feet as well. "Who might be next, you mean."

He nodded, his features tightening.

An impending dread spread through me at the thought the killer might not be finished. "What about August Pendleton? What are you going to do about him?"

"I'd still like to hold on to him, but in light of what you've told me, I should probably release him—for now. I just hope we can trust him not to flee Newport."

"He won't. Where would he go? He's too recognizable and would be apprehended before he made it out of Rhode Island."

"You can be sure I'll alert the wharves and the train depot to watch for him."

"Jesse, I said this to Nanny, and I'm going to repeat it now. I don't know what the motive might be, but don't discount Harry Forge in all of this. I don't trust him. He's not a good man."

"No, he isn't." A dangerous glint entered Jesse's eye. Reluctantly he said, "But would Forge know how to knife someone in the heart the way our killer did? Somehow, I don't believe so. He doesn't strike me as the sort who's proficient in anything besides womanizing and enjoying himself."

"Yet he argued with Sturm, and he was part of Otto's circle of close acquaintances." Did I *want* Harry Forge to be the guilty party? Yes, part of me did. I would certainly shed no tears for him if he were. "*And* he shares their penchant for cocaine. A motive might well have stemmed from that."

"It feels as though this case will never be solved."

I placed a hand on his shoulder. "But it will be. One way or another."

* * *

From the police station I returned to the *Messenger*, where I once again tried to focus on business. While I hadn't ignored my responsibilities these past several days, I feared I hadn't attended to details with as much attention as I should. With good reason, true, but Derrick had put his faith in me. I'd be a fool to squander his trust, while at the same time proving the skeptics correct that neither I nor any woman could fill such a role. So yes, my self-respect and my determination to vindicate myself spurred me on.

Within the pile of paperwork cluttering my desk, I came across a requisition for printing supplies, including newsprint. This surprised me, as we had accepted several deliveries not long ago. And while extra runs, such as our afternoon editions, could potentially deplete our resources, there hadn't been enough of them lately to have done so. Jimmy had initialed the purchase order in a hurried script, as he'd apparently taken Dan Carter's word that the pressroom would be stilled without the new supplies. I couldn't fault Jimmy for that; Dan had been with the *Messenger* for years under its previous owner, and had worked in the printing trade a decade before that. We all presumed he knew what he was doing.

Jimmy had left the office on errands, so I vacated my desk to make my way back to the supply rooms and to find Dan. The presses were quiet this afternoon, as all the imperative news had made it into our regular morning edition. I walked through the pressroom, where Dan's assistants were cleaning the plates and the lines that ran from the steam-powered engine to the machinery. Good; we didn't need another dead press on our hands. I didn't bother asking them about the requisition. They'd only shrug and refer me to Dan. Nodding my approval of their activities, I passed through into the main, and largest, supply room, where the rolls of newsprint were kept.

A frown formed on my brow as I surveyed the deep shelves and the gaping spaces where rolls of paper should have been. How could we have gone through so much newsprint in so short a time? We were on a monthly delivery schedule, and I remembered the last one well enough. Over my shoulder, I called into the pressroom.

"Do either of you know where Dan is?" I heard a reply that he would be found directly. In the meantime, I noticed that on the top row of wooden shelving, some rolls had been turned differently than usual. Typically, they were placed end out, but these were turned with the paper facing out, the long way. Were there more rolls behind that front row, making it seem as though we were low on paper?

I reached up, but not to attempt to remove a roll. They were much too large and heavy for me to manage. Even the men teamed up to heft the paper into the next room and slide it onto the spindle on the press. Rather, I merely meant to nudge a roll aside and peek behind it to see if there were more. I couldn't quite reach, and set my foot on the edge of the bottom shelf to boost myself higher.

I heard a creak and then a splintering. Before I could identify the source, the entire shelving apparatus sagged to one side. Quickly I stepped down, but as I did the newsprint began rolling. Those on the top shelf, facing outward, came at me like boulders rolling down a steep incline. I didn't even have time to cry out. I bounded backward, out of the way of the collapsing shelves, but the rolls gained momentum on their downward journey and flew out toward me. I ducked my head, turned aside, and held up my arms to ward off the blows. My right arm, shoulder, and then my hip took one, two, three great wallops in rapid succession that left me staggering in both pain and fear of broken bones.

The pain radiating through me wrung tears from my eyes and stole the breath from my lungs. How I remained standing, I'll never know. I found myself up against the wall opposite the shelves, half leaning, half sagging, cradling my throbbing arm with my other hand, terrified to move at all lest I worsen my injuries.

Slowly I became aware of voices and activity around me. Dan Carter's voice rang out, shouting commands to his assistants to restore order. There were other voices as well: those of the printer and his assistant, then Ethan's and Jacob's, and finally Jimmy's. Someone kept repeating my name . . .

Blinking away my bewilderment and forcing myself to focus through the pain, I raised my chin and made eye contact with Dan, who stood over me with a frightened expression. I had rarely ever seen anyone look so alarmed, and as I took in the scene of fallen shelves and scattered rolls, I realized I was lucky to be standing; possibly lucky to be alive. Had I not moved far enough out of the way, who knows? A broken back? A broken neck?

Death?

Despite my fierce protestations, I soon found myself riding beside Ethan on his pony cart to Newport Hospital. A good portion of my aches had begun to subside, as had my trembling as the shock of the incident wore off. Only my arm continued to concern me, and with each jolt of the wagon over the road, my fears of a broken arm grew.

"Who would have stacked the newsprint like that, Ethan?" I mused aloud. "Everyone at the *Messenger* knows better." As we left Spring Street and headed onto Broadway, I cradled my arm in my good hand and held my breath.

"Maybe it wasn't one of us."

I squeezed my eyes shut against the pain radiating from my shoulder to my fingertips. If it hadn't been one of the *Messenger*'s employees, the alternative was equally unsettling, for it meant whoever murdered the three victims, and perhaps tried to warn me off with a dart, was now coming after me.

Yet, as unpalatable as that might be, I would not be put off until the individual had been brought to justice.

"What about the deliverymen, Miss Cross? Might they have stacked the newsprint the wrong way?"

"If so, Dan and his assistants would have seen it and made it right."

"Perhaps they did see it but didn't take the time to re-arrange, and don't like admitting to it." He shifted the reins to one hand and made an adjustment to his derby.

I squinted as sunlight hit me full in the face. At the same time, I took in what Ethan had suggested. If Dan and his assistants knew the newsprint had been stacked incorrectly, but had said nothing, had they also known about the spilled ink that shut down our main press for hours, but hadn't wished to admit to it? Were my employees taking advantage of me?

I shook my head. "The incorrect stacking wasn't the only cause of the accident. All I did was attempt to nudge one of the rolls aside. Those shelves should have held up, but it was as if someone had loosened the brackets."

Surely no one at the *Messenger* would have done that. But then, who? And how did they gain entrance to that part of the building?

Would they invade my home as well? And what about Mrs. Fish? Was she in danger? If so, the blame lay solely with me. I might have put my foot down and refused to involve her, but her connections and influence had been convenient for me, and so I had held my tongue. I regretted that now, and resolved to have an earnest discussion with Mrs. Fish at the first opportunity—such as the next time she appeared on my front drive, eager to track down a murderer.

In front of our tiny hospital, Ethan helped me down from the cart and walked me inside. I was immediately taken into an examination room on the first floor. Ethan put up a bit of a fuss when I suggested he return to work, but I assured him

I would be in good hands and would check in at the office as soon as I knew the extent of my injuries. Even without a doctor's expertise, I could attest to being of sound limb, except for my arm. That appendage continued to throb, and I treated it tenderly as I waited to be seen.

Hannah Hanson was the first to come hurrying into the room. "Emma, what happened? I was told you were brought in with a possible broken arm?"

I tried to smile in a cavalier fashion, but a twinge caused me to reveal the truth with a grimace. "It hurts a bit," I told her, and proceeded to explain what happened.

"You poor dear." Slowly and carefully, she helped me out of my carriage jacket with a minimum of discomfort. Hannah was not only a skilled nurse, she had had practice in the past tending my injuries. She knew my pain threshold as well as my tendency to downplay such matters.

The doctor arrived and spent a good quarter of an hour moving my arm, bending it at the elbow, and prodding with his fingertips. Despite the resultant shooting pains, he declared my arm badly sprained, with stress to the tendons in my shoulder, and a bruised collarbone. After hearing about my accident, he pronounced me lucky.

"You really must be more careful, Emma," Hannah chastised me after the doctor had left us alone. She helped me on with my jacket, and then slipped a sling over my arm and around my neck.

I chuckled. "And how do you propose I do that?"

She showed me a rueful expression, and then joined me in chuckling. "I haven't the faintest idea. You and I are not ones to sit quietly at home, are we? No, we're professional women, and that means enduring a few bumps here and there. Literally and figuratively."

Now that I'd calmed down, been assured I hadn't suffered a break, and was experiencing less pain since my arm had been immobilized, I used the opportunity to raise another matter. "Hannah, have you seen Brady lately?"

"You mean you haven't?"

"He doesn't wish to speak to me." The reality of that sent a wave of sadness through me. Brady and I had always been close, even during his years of recklessness and irresponsibility. That he had effectively shut me out of his life hurt more than my injuries. "So, how is he?"

She hesitated before admitting, "I haven't seen much of him either, and when I have . . ." She let out a sigh. "I don't relish telling you this, but each time I've seen him he'd been drinking. I'm worried about him, Emma. And . . ." She looked away.

"Yes?"

When she looked back, there were tears gathering in her eyes. "I understand the possibility that his father has been hiding all these years is eating away at him—at his soul. But I cannot be a witness to his self-destruction. I'm sorry, Emma, but I can't."

I gripped her hand. "You have no need to be sorry. Brady alone is responsible for his actions. Not me, not you, not even his father." I spoke brave words, but my heart was breaking for my brother.

"Do you think, perhaps, if you and I were to speak with him together," she said softly, "that he might listen?"

She sounded so forlorn, I wished nothing more than to encourage the notion. But in truth, I didn't know how to reach Brady without being able to answer his questions about his father. Thus far, no firm answers about Gabriel Sturm had been forthcoming. I knew only that he had been part of Prince Otto's retinue, and that, according to Harry Forge, he had been a grasping and negligent influence on the prince.

"I never know where he is anymore," I replied honestly.

"I might. He'd asked me to join him today at the Casino. There is more tennis, and afterward a musicale at the theater. Please, Emma, come with me. It might be worth a try."

"When is your shift over?"

"In about an hour. And I always keep extra clothing in the nurses' dormitory, so I needn't stop at home first. We can take the trolley." She smiled gratefully. "Oh, I hope we find him there."

"So do I, Hannah." I smiled back, but privately I feared what we might find at the Casino. Would Brady be drunk? Angry? Deaf to all reason? For Hannah's sake, for Brady's, as well as for my own, I said a silent prayer.

Chapter 20

Although late afternoon shadows draped the Casino, bright electric lights lit the lawns inside. The throng ranged around the tennis court seemed but a mirror image of Mrs. Fish's Harvest Festival, with so many of the same people in attendance. I saw Mr. and Mrs. Fish, Aunt Alva and Oliver Belmont, the Oelrichses, the Astors, and countless others. Up on the restaurant's patio, Mr. and Mrs. Clemson were having dinner, but Thea was not with them. I spied her a few minutes later, strolling with her hand firmly ensconced in the crook of Charles Eldridge's arm. As he had partnered Katherine at Crossways that night, he seemed to effortlessly guide Miss Clemson along the walkways. In her tiered silk gown, she appeared to float at his side.

At first I thought it strange that she would agree to walk with him; then I realized she must have wished to escape her parents, even for a short time, and perhaps allow them to believe she had moved on from her infatuation with Prince Otto. I did not believe she yet understood the reason for her mother's vehement objections.

Hannah and I made a circuit of the pavilion. I heard Brady's voice before I laid eyes on him. Though he hadn't been there when we'd first passed by, he now stood in front of the clock tower; or rather, he wavered unsteadily and shouted partially incoherent encouragement to the tennis players.

Hannah grimaced at one particularly ribald shout. "Oh, dear. Perhaps we shouldn't have come," she murmured to me.

I strode resolutely toward my brother. A pair of matrons nearby turned their mouths down in distaste at his antics and sidestepped away from him. Brady seemed oblivious and went on shouting and waving his arms about as though signaling directions to the players. My heart ached that my brother had fallen so low in so short a time. He had made such strides in his life, only to come to this.

But he was not beyond hope. When I reached him I attempted to slip my good arm through his. "Brady, I think you've had enough tennis for today."

"Em!" he cried out with undue enthusiasm. "What a surprise to see you here. And Hannah! Well, this is jolly, isn't it?" His eyebrows converged in a frown as he noticed the sling holding my arm. "What the holy hell happened to you?"

"A small accident. Would you please lower your voice?" I glanced around us. "You're creating a scene. People are staring." Indeed, a number of people had turned around to convey their disapproval. I was glad Mrs. Fish hadn't seen me and decided to leave her friends to join me.

"Let 'em stare." Brady's voice rose. "Go ahead and gawk, all of you."

"Brady, please come with us." Hannah flanked his other side and tried to latch on as I had. "We can have a nice quiet dinner together."

"And miss the tennis? Don't be silly." He pulled his arms free, only to slip one around Hannah's shoulders in a manner that made her blush violently and attempt to pull away.

He held her fast and leaned in closer. "Emma thinks you and I should wed. What do you think, old girl? Is she right?"

"Brady, please," Hannah pleaded in a fierce whisper. Tears threatened.

"Let the young lady go, Brady." Startled, we all three glanced up at Charles Eldridge. Thea Clemson stood off to one side, her back to us as she scanned the crowd, or pretended to. I guessed she merely wished to avoid being part of an unpleasant scene. Mr. Eldridge took Hannah's hand in his slender, sinuous one, and gently extricated her from Brady's hold. "Are you quite all right, miss?"

Hannah gazed up at him as if entranced. His eyes narrowed in return as he took in her features, and I thought I saw a hint of speculation in his gaze. Before I could be sure, Hannah nodded and thanked him, and he released her hand. I introduced them, but their greetings were summarily drowned out as Brady voiced a protest about Hannah leaving his side.

Another man came up behind him. He was tall like Mr. Eldridge, but without his elegance. No, a slight cragginess in Harry Forge's face spoke of past brawls, resulting in a former break in the bridge of his nose. Had I once thought him handsome? I cringed at the memory of my last encounter with him. As welcome as Mr. Eldridge's intervention was, I felt no gratitude toward Mr. Forge and only wished him to go away.

"Harry, there you are." My brother, on the other hand, seemed genuinely pleased to see him. "I thought you'd gone."

"Not yet, old man. I was waiting for you." Harry's gaze skipped from face to face, lingering a moment longer than necessary on mine. A shiver traveled my back. Then he regarded Brady with a wide grin. "I detect your sister putting a damper on your evening. Shall we go?"

"You don't know the half of it." Despite Brady's words,

his pleased look continued, and it appeared he would happily go with Mr. Forge.

I stepped between them. "My brother doesn't need to go anywhere with you, Mr. Forge."

"He's not himself, obviously." Harry Forge spoke quietly, for my ears only. "I merely mean to convey him home and fill him with strong coffee."

"No, thank you." I turned away from him in dismissal. "Brady, let's go."

My brother dug in his heels. "I don't need you playing nursemaid, Em. Or any of you. If Harry and I have other plans, it's none of your business."

"That's the spirit, old man." Mr. Forge's high humor restored, he slapped Brady on the back, a gesture that threatened my brother's balance. At a cheer from the crowd, Brady's attention swerved back to the tennis match. In that instant, Harry Forge again spoke quietly to me. "Let me bring him home. I promise no harm will come to your precious brother. Would you rather he remain and continue to make a fool of himself? Not all reporters will be as charitable as you with his good name."

I gritted my teeth and sized the man up. I didn't trust him; I had no reason to. Could he possess a modicum of decency? He hadn't shown me any, certainly. He seemed steady enough on his feet, but still I wondered if he had imbibed a cocaine-laced elixir tonight. I decided to speak the truth. "I don't trust you, Mr. Forge. Not after what you did to me when I visited you in your home."

"No harm came to you, did it?" An eyebrow went up in question.

Before I answered him, I caught sight of Hannah's wretched expression. My determination to resist Mr. Forge's offer of assistance began to dwindle. It was Charles Eldridge who presented a solution.

"Miss Cross, if I may." Mr. Eldridge bent his head to accommodate my shorter stature. "If your brother is willing to go quietly with Harry, I suggest you let them."

"But—"

"My carriage is larger than Harry's. You and your delightful friend here may ride with me. We'll follow to make sure your brother arrives home safely."

Relieved, I quickly agreed, then felt a twinge of misgiving. I gestured toward Thea Clemson, who had thoroughly ignored us these many minutes. Mr. Eldridge stepped to her side.

"Miss Clemson, will you excuse me temporarily? I promise I'll return before too long, but I always say if one can render a good deed, then one must. Don't you agree?"

To my astonishment, Thea shrugged. "You needn't hesitate for my sake, Mr. Eldridge."

"I shall return you to your parents, then." He reached for her hand and raised it to his lips. "Are you quite sure you won't mind, my dearest Miss Clemson? I wouldn't wish you to feel neglected."

I frowned. Unless I was greatly mistaken, Charles Eldridge had entirely switched his affections from the unfortunate Katherine Pendleton to the very much alive Thea Clemson. In so short a time? Had he only been humoring Mrs. Fish the other day at Belcourt when she had teased him about setting his cap for Katherine? Had he only danced with Katherine while he waited to partner Thea at the next opportunity? Perhaps so. It seemed to me, and I guessed anyone else watching, that Charles Eldridge's cap was firmly set for Miss Clemson.

But as for the young lady herself? I felt a surge of sympathy for Mr. Eldridge, as I believed it would be a long while before she allowed herself to fall in love again.

*   *   *

The two carriages were brought up to the Casino entrance. Hannah and I watched as Brady climbed precariously into Harry Forge's curricle. I studied Mr. Forge for signs of inebriation. Then again, I had driven my gig under the influence of cocaine and done well enough. The memory of that day once again filled me with outrage, and I loathed trusting the man with my brother's welfare. I half wished Brady had refused to go along with Mr. Forge. My only solace was that Hannah and I would be following closely in Mr. Eldridge's larger phaeton.

He offered his hand to help me up, taking extra care to steady me as my incapacitated arm set me off balance. Once I'd settled on the leather and velvet seat, he offered Hannah assistance.

"I suddenly remember where we've met previously, Mr. Eldridge," she said.

The gentleman hesitated before asking, "Have we met? Forgive me, I can't seem to recall. . . ."

"In Providence. At the hospital." Hannah accepted his hand and slid in beside me. A moment later Mr. Eldridge came around the carriage and stepped up. With only an inch or two to spare between the three of us, we set out a few carriage lengths behind Brady and Harry Forge. Dusk had descended over the island, the last rays of the setting sun streaking fire across the western sky.

"I'm afraid you must be mistaken, Miss Hanson."

"Could I be?" She leaned forward to see around me and studied Mr. Eldridge's aquiline profile. He faced forward, yet I sensed his keen awareness of her scrutiny. A wariness came over me, though I could not have explained it. Hannah continued. "No, I don't think I am mistaken, sir. Were you not a medical student a few years back? Is it not *Doctor* Eldridge now?"

"No, indeed." He sounded stern, almost angry. "I am not a doctor."

Hannah sat back. "It's uncanny, then, the resemblance." Her features tightened in concentration. "But . . . Eldridge . . . the name is as familiar as your face. Yes, I'm certain it was you. You see, I was training to be a nurse at the time. This would have been four years ago."

"No, Miss Hanson, I am afraid you are mistaken. My interests lie in my family's coal mines in Pennsylvania."

"Why, yes, I remember hearing about your family's mines," Hannah persisted.

Their conversation puzzled me, but I'd become aware of something else as my hand drifted to the seat at my side. Between the rows of tufting, velvet-covered buttons held the upholstery in place. Blue velvet.

A sense of dread crept over me as I thought back to the morning in the morgue when Brady, Hannah, Jesse, and I had viewed Gabriel Sturm's body. There had been blue thread tangled in his fingers, as if he'd latched on to something for dear life. In his panic, had he blindly attempted to climb into this carriage, only to be dragged down off it? If I searched thoroughly, would I find a missing button somewhere on this seat?

Hannah continued to insist that she had met Charles Eldridge at Providence Hospital; he continued to deny it, his irritation evident. The carriage sped up, and I glanced down at his hands. They held the reins effortlessly, the long fingers conveying signals to the horse with the finesse of . . .

Of a physician. Only a physician, or one who had trained to be one, had such mastery of his hands.

Was Charles Eldridge so in love with Thea that he had considered Otto a rival who must be eliminated? But no, it couldn't be that simple. At the Ocean House Hotel, the desk clerk had heard Gabriel Sturm say, "Don't worry, I'll take care of it." And Prince Otto had responded, "Make matters clear. I never bluff." What was Sturm supposed to take care of? How did Charles Eldridge fit into their plans?

However much I burned to ask, to confront him, I had Hannah's safety to consider, as well as my own. The streets were dark now, and Mr. Forge's carriage no longer occupied the road ahead of us. That was because, I realized, we hadn't headed west into the Point when Mr. Forge did. We had stayed on a northerly course, and now the tall iron fences of the cemeteries on Farewell Street loomed on either side of us. I wished Hannah would cease questioning Mr. Eldridge, but to my frustration, she persisted.

"I remember hearing you'd had to withdraw from your courses," she was saying. "There's no shame in that, Mr. Eldridge."

"Do shut up, Miss Hanson."

Hannah gasped. "What?"

"I said shut up."

The carriage jolted as Mr. Eldridge veered off Farewell Street. The motion jarred my shoulder and I barely kept from yelping. In my rising trepidation, it took me a moment to gain my bearings. He'd turned in at the gates of the Common Burying Ground. The vehicle pitched and lurched over the rocky, uneven ground. My spine pressed against the back of the seat as we climbed the hill to higher terrain. A forest of stone arches and the occasional turret-shaped obelisk rose up around us.

"Mr. Eldridge," I calmly began. A sharp point at my side silenced me.

"Not a word out of you. Either of you." He jerked his chin in Hannah's direction. "Convince her."

I half turned to Hannah. "He's got a knife at my side, Hannah. Please, do as he says."

Her gasp reached my ears, but if I'd expected hysterics, she proved me wrong. I should have known a nurse of her experience would be well versed in keeping her fears in check. If only she hadn't recognized him. Or had it been Mr. Eldridge's intent all along to kidnap us?

To kill us?

After several minutes of a teeth-clattering ride, he brought the carriage to a stop beneath some trees. Low headstones and simple markers dotted the sloping ground. Not far away, the fences converged in the far northeast corner of the cemetery: God's Little Acre, where a century and more ago, African residents of Newport had interred their dead. To Newport's shame, many of them had been slaves.

"Get out, Miss Hanson, but do so slowly. *Very* slowly." He jabbed the knife point clear through the layers of my clothing, including my corset. I uttered the beginnings of a cry before I swallowed back the sound. "If you don't cooperate," he said, still addressing Hannah, "your friend will suffer."

Without taking her eyes off us, Hannah slowly slid to the end of the seat and backed her way down from the carriage. Once she stood on solid ground, Mr. Eldridge pricked me again to set me moving. "Slowly, now," he repeated.

He slid along the seat with me, never relinquishing the knife's claim on my side. As I stepped down, Hannah reached up to help me. I had a fleeting urge to shove Charles Eldridge and start running, taking Hannah with me. But in the dark, and this far from the Burying Grounds' entrance, it would not be difficult for Mr. Eldridge to catch either or both of us. There were headstones everywhere, some so small as to be virtually invisible until one tripped over them. Besides, with one arm in a sling, I wouldn't have the balance to outrun him. No, I would stay alert for the first opportunity to oppose our captor, but I'd do nothing rash.

"We don't understand what's happening, Mr. Eldridge," I said in a pleading tone. "Why are you doing this?"

He laughed, a low, deep sound. With the knife, he gestured for us to step away from the carriage. Doing so threw us deeper into shadow, for the branches above our heads blocked out the moonlight.

"How long have you been in love with Thea?" I asked him bluntly, seeing no reason to go on pretending ignorance.

"Forever," he said. "Misguided girl, throwing herself at Otto. He was deceiving her, you know. He never loved her, not a bit."

"Then why . . . ?"

He stepped closer and pointed the knife at me. "Because he'd been blackmailing her mother for years. He and Sturm. They knew the truth about Thea's parentage. Good God, any fool with eyes could see it. They also knew her mother would go to any lengths to protect her daughter. I'm surprised she didn't kill the pair of scoundrels herself."

The truth of the prince's perfidy threatened to make me ill. Despite the sort of men with whom the prince had spent his time, I had believed Thea's claims of mutual young love. Of something earnest and not driven by lust or greed. But I'd been terribly wrong.

"You wanted to protect Thea," I murmured, yet I couldn't bring myself to believe Mr. Eldridge's motives had been the least bit honorable.

"Of course I did. Do you think I'd let them continue to take advantage of her? They'd have ended up destroying her innocence. I'd seen their handiwork before. Ruined women, bereaved families."

While I distracted Mr. Eldridge, I noticed Hannah peering about at the ground. Did she have an idea, a plan? These particular headstones dated back well over a century; some as much as two. Many were chipped, broken. Could we defend ourselves with a stone fragment? I kept talking. "You met Sturm at Spouting Rock, didn't you?"

He nodded once. "He thought he was going to threaten

me, intimidate me into keeping silent. I'd found out about the blackmail from Sturm himself months ago. Idiot got drunk one night in Vienna and hinted at the whole thing. It didn't take much for me to figure out who and what he was talking about. So that night at Spouting Rock, I gave him the surprise of his life. Too bad he wasn't surprised for long."

That explained the conversation overheard by the clerk at the Ocean House. "And then you took care of Otto at Crossways."

"I couldn't let him take things any further with Thea. Her future was at stake. *Our* future."

Judging by Thea's reactions to him at the Casino, there would be no future between them. But I wanted to keep him talking as long as possible. Not that I had any hopes of someone coming along and intervening; not here, in God's Little Acre. But I remained attentive for any avenue I might turn to my advantage. "How did you get the prince to meet you in the garden?"

"That was easy. I forged a note from Sturm himself. That idiot Otto hadn't missed his minion yet."

Gabriel Sturm and Prince Otto had been playing a dangerous game, and they had both lost. But there had been a third victim. "And Katherine Pendleton? What did she do to deserve her fate?"

Here he shook his head and sneered. "Katherine, alas, decided to be a busybody. She saw that I had feelings for Thea. She told me my lovesick eyes gave me away. And of course she knew what Sturm and Otto were up to. I'd forgotten all about her predilection for their *tonics*. And damn it all if she didn't sneak out herself to meet Otto in the garden at Crossways."

"She saw you murder the prince?"

"No, but apparently she saw me out there. It was only the next day when his body was found that she put it together."

"What were you doing at the Pendletons' house?" I demanded. "Did you go there specifically to murder Katherine?"

"I had no such intention." He sounded indignant. "I thought she had invited me to tea, to discuss banking matters with her brother. I'm a customer of their bank, you know. But when I arrived she made her accusations, threatened to go to both the police and Thea, and actually tried blackmailing *me*. Can you imagine? I suppose it was something else she learned from Otto and Sturm."

"So you took the dagger from the display." Beautiful, intelligent Katherine Pendleton had gotten in over her head. What a tangle, what a tragic waste of a young life. For Otto and especially for Sturm, I couldn't work up much sympathy. Another thought occurred to me. "That wasn't the first time you'd found a weapon at your disposal."

"What do you mean?"

"You'd done so earlier that same day, on the docks. It was you who threw the dart at me outside the Narragansett. You must have followed us after we left Miss Pendleton's house."

"That's enough talking. You've made the same mistake Miss Pendleton did. You and your friend here." He waved the knife back and forth at us, and a dollop of moonlight slid along its length. It was long and slender, like Mr. Eldridge's hands, and as sharp as a surgeon's blade. "You—over there." He motioned for Hannah to move several more feet away from me. "Now kneel there, and wait your turn."

Hannah hesitated, a stubborn desire to refuse thrusting out her jaw. I caught her gaze and nodded. Several gravestones surrounded us, and one in particular arched upward almost waist high.

Mr. Eldridge stepped closer to me, until we stood face-to-face. He leered. With a flick of his knife he rent a small tear in the sling around my neck. He pulled back to thrust again, and I instinctively lurched backward, lost my footing over rocks or roots, I didn't know which, and fell hard on my backside. My spine struck something solid behind me, and pain shivered up my back.

What happened next was a dark blur, but Hannah managed to lever her feet beneath her and dived at Mr. Eldridge's legs. He tumbled backward. There came a thud and a crack, and as Hannah and I watched, frozen in place, Mr. Eldridge hung motionless, propped up by the headstone he'd fallen against. A second later he slid limply down the front of the stone and collapsed in a heap on the ground. The only sound came from the breeze and the frantic pounding of my heart. Then Hannah spoke.

"Gracious, did I . . ." A hand pressed to her mouth, she struggled to her feet. "Did I kill him? Oh, Emma, is he dead?"

With one arm, I used the headstone behind me, the one I'd struck when I fell, to raise myself to standing. Grasping Hannah's hand, I leaned toward the fallen man and strained my eyes to see into the shadows. Something wet and oozing marred the top and front of the headstone. Mr. Eldridge's blood. I saw no obvious wound in the face staring up at us—past us—but he had hit the stone with the back of his head. The body lay utterly still.

"It's all right, Hannah. You did what you had to. You saved us both."

"I'm a nurse. . . ." Her knees began to give way. I put my arm around her and supported her against my side.

"Come. We must get back into town. Marlborough Street isn't far." And on Marlborough Street, the police station. Hannah knew as well as I how close it lay, but I discerned her bewilderment, her lack of bearings. "Come with me, Hannah. We'll go and get help."

Obediently, like a small child, she moved her feet and matched my stride. "Will they arrest me, do you think?"

"No, Hannah. They will not arrest you. You acted in self-defense."

"I wish . . ." She never told me what she wished, her voice dying like a soft wisp of night air. But I knew. We hurried along, hand in hand, stumbling as we went, almost as if we were being pursued. We *were* pursued, and always would be, by dreadful events over which we had had no control; by the sightless stare of a man forever burned into our memories. It was something I had learned to live with these past several years. But would Hannah? Only time would tell.

Chapter 21

"They had been blackmailing me for years." Mrs. Clemson tugged nervously at the cords of her handbag, which occupied her lap. "What happens now? Must my daughter and my husband learn the truth?"

Jesse and I faced Mrs. Clemson in my front parlor, he and I in the armchairs, Mrs. Clemson across from us on the sofa. We had arranged this meeting here, away from prying eyes in town as well as to ensure her husband and daughter did not overhear our conversation.

My arm throbbed in the sling, more a result of the jarring ride and the tumble I'd taken in the graveyard than the actual accident at the *Messenger.* I still had questions about the collapse of the shelves, and my suspicions. There had been too many mishaps at the newspaper to be coincidental. My first instinct was to blame Charles Eldridge. The first setback, that of the clogged line that powered the main press, had occurred the day Gabriel Sturm had been found at Spouting Rock. By now, many of the Four Hundred were familiar with my investigative activities. Had Mr. Eldridge sought to keep me so busy with overseeing the repairs that I wouldn't have time to help the police with that first murder?

As for the collapse of the shelves, true, he couldn't have been sure I would be the victim, yet any victim would have served to halt another day's activities, as had happened yesterday. Once again we fell behind on production, and today's morning edition would go out late. It would be another blot on our performance, and make both our subscribers and our advertisers doubt whether they could depend on the *Messenger.*

Subduing a sigh, I turned my attention back to Mrs. Clemson. She was still explaining.

"My husband, Eugene, didn't wish to attend the Harvest Festival, and he couldn't understand why I insisted we do so. But you see, I wanted to confront Otto in person and beg him to leave us alone. I had no idea at the time that he and Thea had any sort of understanding. Had I known, I might have killed him myself."

"I'm glad you didn't have the opportunity," Jesse said.

Mrs. Clemson nodded her agreement, her eyes falling closed for a moment. "You haven't answered my question, Detective. Must my husband and daughter know of my involvement with the prince and Gabriel Sturm?" Her hands tightened into fists around the cords of her bag.

"Mrs. Clemson, as far as I'm concerned, and I believe I can speak for Miss Cross as well, what you tell your family is entirely up to you. You are in no legal trouble, and are not guilty of anything that I'm aware of. We merely asked you to speak with us today so we could gain a full understanding of the circumstances that led Charles Eldridge to murder three individuals." As Jesse finished speaking, I nodded my agreement.

A look of bewilderment claimed Mrs. Clemson's features. "I'd had no idea Charles was so smitten with Thea. Oh, we knew he'd taken an interest, as have other young men. She's an heiress, after all. But to go to such lengths . . ." She shuddered. "Thank goodness she didn't end up married to him. What would we have done then?"

As neither Jesse nor I had an answer for her, we ended our meeting and wished Mrs. Clemson well. Jesse and I drove into town together in his gig, since I would be unable to drive until my arm healed. Outside the police station, I thanked him and prepared to continue on my way.

"Thank God you're all right," he said. "You and Miss Hanson. I can't begin to think . . ."

"I know, Jesse." I touched his wrist. He and I had come to terms recently after several years of wondering if perhaps he and I might have a life together. It was not to be, but I would always, always value his friendship. "I'm quite all right. I'm strong, Jesse. But I'm worried about Hannah. I'm afraid of how this will affect the rest of her life."

"I hope she'll be all right."

"I'm going to go meet her now. And you'd best get to work."

He hesitated to leave me there on the sidewalk. "Are you sure you don't want me to bring you the rest of the way?"

"No, I'd like to walk," I told him, and set out to Farewell Street. Several minutes later, I found myself once again surrounded by the headstones of God's Little Acre. Hannah had already arrived, and I went to where she knelt in front of one of the largest headstones. She was digging in the dirt with a spade; beside her sat a pot of bright purple asters with yellow centers. There was also a bucket of water with a damp rag hanging over its side. Blood no longer smeared the headstone, but the water in the bucket bore a pink tinge.

"I couldn't read it last night," she said in lieu of a greeting. She sat back on her heels and looked up at me. "Our rescuer's name is Mingo Malbone." She turned back to the stone and gently grazed her fingertips across the etched writing. "Mingo is an African name, I would think. I can't help but wonder if he had been a slave or a free man. Many of the people buried here were either slaves or servants. The Malbones were a wealthy and influential family in Colonial times. I don't doubt they owned slaves. I hope Mingo lived a good life," she concluded, and leaned forward to continue digging.

"The stone is large," I pointed out, "larger than most of the others nearby. I think that shows that his place in the Malbone household was a valued one."

Hannah nodded. I crouched beside her and, as well as I could with the use of only one arm, helped her set the asters into the freshly turned soil. Hannah had telephoned me earlier and asked me to meet her here. This seemed to be her way of thanking our rescuer, as she had termed him, for our deliverance from Charles Eldridge's knife.

We had just gotten the flowers into the ground and were patting the soil back into place when I heard footsteps thudding up the hill toward us. I ignored them. We had nothing to fear now, after all. "They're beautiful," I told her, and gave the soil a final, firm pat.

"Em! Hannah!"

I shaded my eyes from the sun as I turned toward the voice. Hannah rose to her feet. "It's Brady," she said with a note of wonderment, and helped me up.

When Brady reached us, he looked sheepish. He removed his straw boater and nipped at his bottom lip. "Jesse came by last night, late, after . . ." He shuffled his feet. "Well, he slapped me around a bit until he had my attention, and then he told me what happened out here, with Eldridge. Good God, both of you—" He broke off, sprang forward, and caught us both in his arms. He was hurting me, but I let him until he eased away of his own accord. Hannah blushed furiously.

"How did you know you'd find us here now?" she asked him, pretending to adjust the brim of her hat while in actuality shielding her face until the redness faded.

"Jesse, again. He thought I might want to know. And I did. But what are you doing back here? I would have thought this is the last place you'd want to be."

We pointed out the asters and explained about thanking Mingo Malbone. If Brady found the idea a dotty one, he didn't let on.

"It's good to see you looking so well," Hannah said to him.

"By 'well,' I assume you mean not drunk."

Hannah blushed again, lightly this time, and nodded.

"I'm through with that. That's a promise. I've been a fool lately, and that's a fact. And there's something in particular I need to say to you, Em. And it's this: I don't need to know whether this Sturm character was my father or not, and I'm not going to fall apart over it again. Because after Jesse knocked me about last night—"

"I thought you said he *slapped* you a bit," I interrupted.

Brady chuckled. "Well, let's just say he thumped some sense into me, and I realized that, whether or not my father survived the yachting accident years ago, he had already abandoned our mother and me—by living recklessly and irresponsibly. I have no desire to be like him, and I'm content to leave him in the past."

"Oh, Brady, I'm so happy to hear that." I threw my good arm around his neck and squeezed.

While Brady and Hannah wished to bring me home to rest, I insisted on going only as far as the *Messenger*. They protested, but I assured them I would stay well away from shelves and other dangers that might be lurking. But I wished to oversee an inspection of the entire office, as well as call in a locksmith to change the locks to the outside doors. Someone indeed wished the *Messenger* to fail, but I refused to let that happen under my watch.

I walked into an empty front office, but I thought little of it since I didn't keep Jimmy Hawkins chained to his desk. I was about to sit at my own desk when voices from somewhere down the hallway brought me up sharp. Distinct tones of anger drew me down the corridor to the typesetting room. The sight that greeted me halted me in my tracks.

Dan Carter, his two assistants, along with my head typesetter, John Davies, and my two reporters surrounded another man who occupied a wooden chair—Jimmy. They'd apparently tied him to it, his hands secured behind his back. Their shouts blended into an uproar of indignation. Around their feet lay scattered an untold number of tiny metal squares. John Davies's assistants were on their haunches, gathering up the type and replacing them in their cases.

"What on earth is going on here?" Immediate silence fell as they all turned to regard me. All except Jimmy, who stared at his feet.

John Davies thrust a hand toward the floor in an almost violent gesture. "Do you see what he did?"

My gaze shifted from the mess on the floor back to Jimmy, huddling in his chair. He refused to meet my eye. My mouth opened and my heart dropped. "No."

Dan Carter stepped away from the others and approached me. "We caught him red-handed, Miss Cross. He came in early, thought he was here before anyone else, and did this." He, too, gestured at the floor behind him.

"I was already here, but Jimmy didn't know it." Jacob Stodges, the man I had come close to accusing of the recent sabotage, came forward to stand beside Dan. "I heard a clatter fit to raise the dead and came running in to investigate, and there he was. And there the type was."

I moved past them. The circle of the other men opened and made way for me, allowing me to come toe-to-toe with Jimmy. "Look at me."

It seemed to take an age before he blinked and raised his chin to look up at me. His lips formed a pinched line; his cheeks stood out with heightened color. He said nothing.

"Why, Jimmy? I trusted you. *Derrick* trusted you. I could perhaps understand your resenting taking orders from a woman. Perhaps you wanted the position. But why would you betray Derrick this way?"

When his silence continued, John Davies cuffed him on the shoulder. "Answer Miss Cross." He raised his hand to strike again.

"Don't." I held up my good hand. "And untie him."

Dan Carter hurried over. "But Miss Cross, he's responsible for what happened to you yesterday. He's dangerous. We should call the police."

"We don't tie people up here," I said simply. My head was beginning to throb, and my injured arm ached anew. Once Jimmy had been freed of his restraints, he massaged his wrists and came to his feet. I was about to repeat my questions, but he spoke before I could.

"I was paid by Mr. Andrews to do these things."

Dan gave a groan of outrage. "Mr. Andrews would never—"

"Not *Derrick* Andrews. His father, Lionel."

This news felt akin to being struck by those rolls of newsprint all over again. "Why would he do this?"

Jimmy drew a deep breath and sighed. "Because he wants his son to stay in Providence. Because he doesn't want him to have any reason to come back to Newport. Because . . ."

When he trailed off, I finished the thought. "He doesn't want his son anywhere near me, and he thought having me fail at this business would set me in a bad light. An *unworthy* light." It appeared I now had two individuals attempting to steer Derrick away from me, his mother *and* his father.

"I didn't want to do it, Miss Cross." Jimmy held out a placating hand as he spoke, but Jacob Hodges slapped it to his side. Jimmy ignored him and continued pleading. "Lionel Andrews is a powerful man. He can make sure a fellow never works another day in his given profession. He didn't ask me, he ordered me. I had no choice, Miss Cross. Honestly."

"Don't listen to him, Miss Cross." This came from Ethan, and I realized that Jimmy had most likely also damaged Ethan's pony cart, forcing Ethan to spend his hard-earned money on repairs.

A sudden weariness came over me. "Go, Jimmy. Get out and don't come back. And don't expect a reference."

"But . . . I tell you this wasn't my fault. You can't just throw me out like this."

"You heard Miss Cross." Dan Carter's booming voice filled the room. "Out with you. Now."

I turned away from them all. To my back, Jimmy called out a final appeal. "Don't tell Derrick. You won't, will you?"

I left the room without answering and slowly made my way back to the front office. There, I sat at my desk and stared out the window. What would I do? Derrick had brought Jimmy Hawkins down from Providence to help run his newspaper. Jimmy had betrayed us both. Yet if I told Derrick the truth, I must tell *all* of the truth, and that story involved his father. Lionel Andrews was apparently willing to hurt his son's investments rather than see him living in Newport and associating with me.

Father and son had already had one falling-out, over a disagreement two years ago. It had resulted in Derrick being disowned and spending the next year in Italy. Now they were making amends. If I went to Derrick with this news of

Jimmy's treachery and his father's role in it, I would be driving a wedge further into their relationship, perhaps permanently. Did I wish to be responsible for that?

The answer was no. Therefore, I would say nothing of any of this to Derrick. Perhaps Jimmy would return to Providence and his former position at the *Sun*, and possibly give the excuse that he found me an unsatisfactory employer. The notion didn't unsettle me. I knew Derrick wouldn't simply take his word for it; he'd never have allowed me this opportunity if he hadn't trusted me.

Oddly, my decision, once made, sent a feeling of calm through me, along with a sense of optimism. Our saboteur had been identified and ousted, which meant nothing now stood in the way of the *Messenger*'s success. Starting today we would begin anew and surge forward, and without my having to involve Derrick or anyone else outside of our small and loyal staff. We had persevered.

I had persevered. At Crossways, at God's Little Acre, and at the *Messenger.* With a sense of elation, I decided there was nothing I couldn't do.

Author's Note

Marion "Mamie" Fish was born in Staten Island and grew up in New York City, and was of Dutch, German, and French ancestry. As conveyed in the story, she received minimal education and was functionally illiterate. Her husband, Stuyvesant, or Stuyvie as Mamie called him, was also of Dutch origin and a descendent of Peter Stuyvesant, a prominent founder of the New York colony, then New Amsterdam. The Stuyvesant family made their fortune in New York real estate, and Stuyvesant was president of the Illinois Central Railroad at the time of the story.

Mamie, Alva Belmont, and Tessie Oelrichs, who would later preside over the beautiful Rosecliff on Bellevue Avenue, formed society's "Triumvirate." In short, the trio became society's leaders as Mrs. Astor began to slow down with age. Their style, however, was markedly different from Mrs. Astor's. Staid and dignified took a back seat to assertiveness and ostentation, and Mamie Fish certainly was both. The tongue-in-cheek welcome she shouts to her arriving guests at the Harvest Festival was taken from history. The chimpanzee guest of honor in the story was an adaptation of two incidents. The first occurred when Mrs. Fish told her two hundred guests that the Czar of Russia was expected, but it turned out to be practical joker Harry Lehr, who appeared that night dressed in regal robes, wearing a crown, and carrying a scepter. The other incident involved Harry Lehr and his wife, Elizabeth, hosting a party for

Prince del Drago of Corsica. However, it was a monkey in formal attire who graced the dinner table that night.

It's true that Mamie didn't always do as her peers did, and this was never more evident than when she insisted on a very American, Neo-Colonial design for Crossways. In keeping with American traditions, her Harvest Festival became a yearly occasion, although I moved up its first occurrence to the year the house opened. I took creative license with the inclusion of the scarecrows, but the twelve-foot jack-o'-lanterns by the front door, Mamie's chair made of farm implements, many of the decorations, and the peasant-style garb sported by her guests are all true-to-life details. Also true is that at the time of the story, Crossways had no dedicated ballroom, which was added some years later as entertainments became even more lavish. Until then, as in the story, the drawing room and front hall were utilized for large parties.

Spouting Rock was a geological phenomenon in a rocky precipice at the junction of Bailey's Beach and the Cliff Walk. The house called The Rocks, a timber and granite Queen Anne villa owned by Henry and Lucy Clews, looked down over the beach and Spouting Rock. At some point in the early twentieth century, Henry Clews became tired of people crossing his property to view the geyser and had it destroyed. I allude to this in Mrs. Vanderbilt's joke that she wouldn't blame Mr. Clews for taking a stick of dynamite and doing just that.

Bailey's Beach remains a private, membership-only beach club. Local Newporters and most tourists today, as then, instead enjoy the waves and sand at Easton's (First) Beach and Sachuest (Second) Beach (in Middletown).

No trip to Newport is complete for me without a jaunt through the Common Burying Ground on Farewell Street. I'm a firm believer that cemeteries offer invaluable insight into the history and social development of a place. The Malbone family's presence in Newport dates back to the mid-eighteenth century; the original Captain Malbone made his fortune as a shipping merchant and, sadly, a slave trader. Newport was, at the time, part of the trade triangle that involved slaves, molasses, and rum. Mingo Malbone was one of that family's servants. His headstone stood out to me particularly due to its size, which was substantially larger than those around it. Does this indicate that his place in the Malbone household was a valued one? I would like to think so.

A word about Belcourt. From 1956 until 2012, the house was owned by the Tinney Family, who changed the name to Belcourt Castle, filled the house with their collection of antiques, and offered "haunted tours" to tourists. During this time, changes were made to the interior of the house that were not historically accurate. Today, Belcourt is owned by Carolyn Rafaelian, CEO of Alex and Ani Jewelry, who has undertaken the colossal task of having the original architectural and design details of Belcourt fully restored. My husband and I were privileged to take a partial tour during one of our recent Newport trips, and before we left we wandered into the main workroom, where a master craftsman explained the meticulous process of re-creating doors and moldings in the original Gilded Age style.

Seeing these mansions restored in such a way is thrilling, but it isn't always the case. Crossways has since been divided into condominiums, and there have been some period-inaccurate changes made to it. Still, the house continues to occupy its rise overlooking the Atlantic Ocean, a regal testament to Mamie Fish's indomitable spirit and determination to do things her way. Crossways is not open for tours.